"Arnold Falls has the feel of an instant classic, with shades of Richard Russo and T.C. Boyle but a sweetness and optimism that sets it apart. Charming, delightful, and endless fun, the novel is a considerable achievement from a noteworthy new talent." — BlueInk Reviews

"Incredibly funny." — Kirkus Reviews

"An all welcoming sanctuary filled with food, wine, music, merriment, and love." — Chanticleer Book Reviews

"By turns hilarious and poignant...Suisman's comedic novel will charm readers with its endearingly eccentric characters and its slice-of-life portrait of a disreputable corner of New York State...A charming, funny novel." — Book Life

"An endless supply of belly laughs." — The Wishing Shelf Book Awards

HOT AIR

CHARLIE SUISMAN

Copyright © 2021 by Charlie Suisman

All right reserved.

No part of this book may be reproduced in any form or by any electronic or mechanical means, including information storage and retrieval systems, without written permission from the author, except for the use of brief quotations in a book review.

This is a work of fiction. Names, characters, businesses, places, events, locales, and incidents are either the product of the author's imagination or used in a fictitious manner. Any resemblance to actual persons, living or dead, or actual events is purely coincidental.

Prologue

T he fact of the matter is, somebody stole the statue of Hezekiah Hesper, and for months nobody noticed. Leader of the gang that settled Arnold Falls, Hesper was a man with few virtues, fewer admirers, and no memorial until 1903, the town's centenary, when it was reluctantly agreed that a statue of the man should be commissioned, if not generously funded. The result was a shabby affair — sheets of tin crudely assembled, promptly rusted, with a plaque describing Hesper as a "foundering" father.

The old rogue had then languished in a corner of Benjamin Arnold Park, ignored by all except the dogs, fine judges of character, unwavering about the sort of tribute Hesper deserved. When the statue was removed from its stand one moonless night in March 2018, Hesper was in people's thoughts the same as he ever was, which is to say, not at all.

Chapter One

G ick-gick-gick.
"That's —"
"Shhh. Jeebie. Listen."
Gick-gick-gick-gick.

"It's the mating call of the northern cricket frog," Will says.

"Not exactly a sonnet."

"It is if you're a frog," Will points out.

"How can you tell it's a northern cricket frog?"

"What does the gick-gick sound like to you?" he asks.

"Like two pebbles tapped together."

"Exactly. That's how you know it's a northern cricket," Will says.

It's a mild Friday afternoon at the beginning of June and Will and I are sitting on a large rock by the small, marshy pond at the eastern end of what will be Van Dalen Park. Looking west, you can see the Hudson River; to the north is the spot where the historic Dutch House stood until it was destroyed one morning last year by a developer.

"I love summertime because nothing ever happens in summer, except some frogs hook up," I say.

"But —

"Summer encourages living in the present tense, that's why people like it."

"Except —"

"Not so much thought. Just the moment."

"Jeebie, this is...something big," Will says, looking at me.

"What is? Us?"

"No. Well, sure. Obviously."

He gives me a kiss.

"But the northern cricket frog? It's endangered. This habitat needs to be protected."

If you haven't been following along, Will and I have been together since last fall. I'm not entirely sure how it all came to pass — seems there were a lot of cooks involved in that broth. I'll probably never know because Will refuses to name names. One thing I do know: I'm extremely glad it happened. Anyway, after a series of events unfortunate and fortunate, the town is getting a new park, Van Dalen Park, right where we are.

Ointment, meet fly. When Will says the northern cricket frog is endangered, I'm sure he's right. He's starting his masters program at Cornell in Conservation Biology in a few months and he knows this kind of stuff.

"People want a ball field," I say.

"I get it. But they can't infill at this pond."

When he says that, Will's green eyes are fiery.

"Your eyes are fiery," I say.

"If they're so fiery, call the fire department."

He's only saying that because he's a volunteer fireman and he thinks, because of a certain incident, that I like to call in — in his words — no-alarm fires.

"You're thinking about no-alarm fires," he says.

"No."

"No?"

"Yes," I say. "But also...I love your passion about stuff. Like frogs. And going for your masters in Conservation Biology. And the hinky monkeys book."

"We're doing that together," he says.

Will's also a talented illustrator. And he got a book offer out of the blue — something that just doesn't happen — for his hinky monkeys series.

"Yes, and I love working on it with you," I say. "But it's your project, Will. You created the whole thing. I'm there to support you. Nelle's planning her album. Jenny's got the town to run and Wilky to care for."

"Jeebs, you helped stop that idiotic tire factory. You helped save Chaplin. Jenny wouldn't have gotten elected mayor if it weren't for you," he says.

"All past tense."

"You're Wilky's godparent."

"Sinecure," I say.

"You're a successful voiceover artist."

"Old news."

"What happened to loving summer because you live in the present tense?" Will asks.

"That was then."

"Then, meaning two minutes ago?"

"Yes."

"Before this sudden midlife crisis," Will says.

"I'm not having — midlife? Midlife!"

Will squeezes my hand. "Aging gay-man crisis?"

"Preposterous," I say. "Nothing to do with aging. Everyone wants to feel useful."

He puts his arm around me, and I lean my head into his shoulder. We stay like this for a while.

"We should call Jenny about your discovery," I say. "They're going to have to rethink this part of the park."

"We'll see her tonight at Doozy's birthday."

"True."

We look out over the marsh, considering frogs and life. Everything seems warm and peaceful and possible. I know how lucky I am. It's just...

"Gick-gick-gick," Will says.

"In iambic pentameter, please. Looking into my eyes."

"Gick-*gick* gick-*gick* gick-*gick* gick-*gick* gick-*gick*."

It has the desired effect. Yes, reader, I swoon.

Chapter Two

The crowd lounging in front of the courthouse is loudly enjoying the inarguably Friday-at-fiveness of the moment, loudly enough that the sound has had the temerity to travel into the courthouse, down the long corridor, and then, unwisely, to disturb the peace of Judge Lionel Harschly's inner sanctum.

Heaving a slow, primordial sigh, Judge Harschly walks toward his secretary, who hands him the document he needs without his having to ask for it.

"Thank you, Vera. Go home. Enjoy the weekend."

"Thank you, Judge. You, too."

"What are you making?" the Judge asks.

"Cacio e pepe."

"Spaghetti?"

"Bucatini. Homemade."

"Your husband is a lucky man to have you," Judge Harschly says.

"Stating the obvious," Vera says.

Judge Harschly chuckles as he strides out into the hallway, still in his robes, the wiry seventy-two-year-old making short work of the corridor to the lobby. The judge swings open the front door of the courthouse and sees the source of the noise problem: at least a dozen layabouts laying about on the steps, including the former mayor, Rufus Meierhoffer, and his invariable sidekick, Dubsack Polatino. He also spots the newly installed, bushy-bearded town hermit, hired by Rufus in one of his last acts before leaving political life.

The judge, who is also president of the town council, had sat through the arguments for hiring an Arnold Falls hermit, airy assertions by then-Mayor Meierhoffer's crew that having a resident hermit would be good for business, catnip for travel writers in need of a punchy hook, another notch in Arnold Falls' tourist-attraction belt. As a practical matter, the hermit would be a caretaker for the shambolic, little lightning-splitter house referred to as 'the hermitage' because, in the 1890s, an ornery fellow called "The Old Hermit" inhabited the place without showing the slightest interest in either his fellow man, or more damningly, the goings-on of his Arnold Falls neighbors. Wisest possible strategy, the judge thinks approvingly.

Apparently, several towns in European countries had hired hermits in recent years, and that was seen as sufficient proof of concept for the council. Judge Harschly had snorted at the idea then and snorts again now, this time inhaling an unmistakable waft of Clagger, the local hooch, which he figures is fueling the elevated noise level.

"*Bupbupbup!*" Judge Harschly says vigorously. He has their attention. Looking down at the document in his hands, he reads in an assertive voice:

"Our Constitution, and various lesser documents therefrom derived, chargeth and *commandeth* all persons, being assembled, *immediately* to disperse themselves, and peaceably to depart to their habitations, or to their lawful business —

although I doubt many of you have a lawful business if I know how to read a crowd — upon the pains contained in the act for preventing *tumults* and *riotous assemblies*. God Bless this land!"

"Not the Riot Act, Judge!" Dubsack says.

"Yes, the Riot Act! I've read it, now disperse ye."

There is grumbling along the lines of 'Oh, well, he's read us the Riot Act', 'no arguing that', 'we better go home', and the crowd does in fact disperse in all directions. Before returning inside, Judge Harschly looks back to survey his jurisdiction, noting that the hermit has yet to summon enough get-up-and-go spirit to actually get up and go.

"Say, you're not much of a hermit, are you?"

"Why's that?" parries the hermit.

"Well, you seem pretty sociable to me."

"Takes all kinds to be a hermit," the hermit says.

"I wouldn't have thought so. That strikes me as counterintuitive. Seems like it would take a *particular* kind of person. But I don't have a great deal of experience with hermits, so I'll take your word for it."

The hermit stands and stretches, picking up his bindle.

"What's your name, anyway?" Judge Harschly asks.

Over the years, Judge Harschly's ears had become highly reliable tuning forks, sensitive to the merest wisp of a tendril of off-note prevarication. A Rolls Royce of b.s. detectors, as his wife says.

When the man doesn't answer in the exact meter expected, there is a flutter in the air and his tuning fork hums before the man answers, "Marvin. I'm known as Marvin the Hobo."

"Little bit of an accent of some kind?"

"I've been around," says Marvin.

"I'd say that a hobo and a hermit, strictly speaking now, aren't the same thing at all," the Judge says.

"You're right about that...I'm sorry I didn't catch your name."

"Judge Harschly."

"Judge Harschly? Seems unlikely, but I'll take your word for it. I *was* a hobo who had been riding the rails since I was eleven. After seeing so much of the country, I've now transitioned into hermitude."

"Strangely enough, that makes a great deal of sense to me."

"Do you happen to know where I can find whale blubber?"

"Sure I do. Just go down to the harbor. But you'll have to bring your time machine with you because Arnold Falls hasn't processed whale blubber in over a hundred years. Mind me asking why?"

"To lay in for a long winter."

"It's June," Judge Harschly says.

"Gotta walk a mile in my shoes."

"Possibly germane, without answering the whale blubber question. I'll let it stand. Well, I have a wife who will read *me* the Riot Act if I'm late. Welcome to Arnold Falls. I hope you find what you're seeking here, Marvin."

They shake hands and Judge Harschly watches Marvin walk away, before the Judge returns to his now Vera-less chambers. He's looking forward to the weekly Friday date night with his wife, Elena, a tradition of nearly forty years. He hangs up his robe, grabs his crumbling briefcase, and turns out the lights.

Waving goodnight to Hamster, who is mopping the floors, Judge Harschly exits back onto the courthouse steps, from which he sees several things happen in quick succession.

First, he observes a woman being chased by a turkey across the park, and hears her shout, "No, Keaton! It cannot be!"

Something is familiar about this and Judge Harschly does one of his squint-and-peers to try to make sense of what is taking place. Is that Bridget Roberts? Gave her a warning for Clagger intoxication a while back. Officiated her wedding to that lovely gal last Thanksgiving. What the devil is she up to now?

He then watches the turkey make a beeline for Bridget's posterior. Bridget yelps loudly. It feels like a déjà vu.

Suddenly, there is a sharp clap of thunder and it starts to hail from the cloudless sky. This thunderhail, as it's being called, is a new twist on Arnold Falls' longtime, unexplained hail affliction.

And after that he hears someone say through a bullhorn, "Cut!"

Ah, yes. The television series *Merryvale* has just started filming. Not Bridget. That must be an actress *playing* Bridget. Or a character like her. Gadzooks, the last thing Arnold Falls needs is more characters.

FAYETTE DE LA NOUILLE, THE STAR OF *MERRYVALE*, THE forthcoming series for Campfire, is back in her trailer, having sought refuge from the hail along with the assistant director, Trevor Aitken.

"I could do without the hail, but I'm falling in love with this little town," she says, sitting at her makeup table. "So ADORABLE I could squeeze it to DEATH in my ample BOSOM!"

Trevor is standing behind Fayette's chair, looking at her

through the mirror. Given his British-bred preference for understatement, Fayette's rhetorical flourishes, the all-caps overemphasizing, strike him as not entirely authentic. Perhaps they're a defense against shyness or insecurity. They make Fayette seem open and direct, but he has the feeling they're a kind of *mis*direction.

"Everyone falls in love with Arnold Falls at first sight, Fayette. Give it some time."

He tries to identify her perfume, which she has applied liberally. As she types on her iPad, he scans her face. Fayette de la Nouille. He doesn't have a read on her yet. When Christine Baranski had bowed out of the production a few months before shooting began, they considered dozens of people to take over the role of Luba. Fayette is an offbeat choice, without a long resume for someone her age (which he puts somewhere around the fifty mark), and he's just caught up with the handful of indie films she's done. She certainly has presence.

Trevor wasn't in on the casting, in any case. Arnold Falls' wunderkind director, Giles Morris, had only asked him in April to dust off his directing chops as assistant director of *Merryvale*. The show is based on the series of portraits in *The New Yorker* by Alec Barnsdorf about a hapless little town in the Hudson Valley that bears some resemblance to Arnold Falls. It was a break from Trevor's usual work for the Nyqvists (of Hullaballoo Circus fame) and they had been their usual, gracious selves in letting him take the opportunity.

"Give it some time? Time marches ON! I want a house here," Fayette says. "I already have a real estate agent."

The thunderhail turns fierce. Fayette glances upward and says, "Oh, what a CHEAP portent!"

"You've only been here a few days."

"What's your point, love?"

"Which realtor did you go with?" Trevor asks.

"He has a long name. I picked up his card somewhere." She rummages through a pile of papers next to her makeup tray. "Rufus..." She hands the card to Trevor.

"Rufus Meierhoffer? He's in real estate now? He used to be the mayor."

"Wonderful," she says. "He'll know all there is to know!"

"That, Fayette, is unlikely."

"Well, I want to learn EVERYTHING I can about this town and everyone in it."

"Inadvisable," Trevor says.

Ignoring him, she says, "I'd love to meet the person that my character is based on, too."

"Alec says there aren't any exact parallels," Trevor says.

"But I was told that my character, Luba, was similar to someone called Bridget."

"Honestly, Fayette, I don't think that's a good idea. Best to make her your own."

"No harm can come of it, surely," Fayette says.

A large chunk of hail thumps the trailer window.

"HA!" Fayette shouts to the window. "You don't scare me!"

BRIDGET ROBERTS AND TRUDY BETTENAUER HAD DECIDED, after their wedding last Thanksgiving, to keep their own last names and skip all the hyphenating. But they'd merged nicely in other ways, alternating their time between Bridget's home in Arnold Falls and Trudy's in Blue Birch Corners, six country miles between them, also known as a fifteen-minute drive through twisty roads.

Trudy is out on Bridget's back porch, finishing the Friday

crossword puzzle, having a gin and tonic to celebrate the end of the week. Gussie, Bridget's dog, is lying on his back, legs splayed, while Delphy, Trudy's dog, rests her head on her paw, close to him.

Bridget sees both dogs wag their tails when she returns from a walk in the woods to forage the last of the ramps this season.

"Oo will boy moy ramps? Fancy a bunch, guvnor?" Bridget says.

Trudy smiles. "Sustainably harvested?" she asks, putting down her book.

"Only the leaves, not the bulbs! I am an evolved human being! Had to wait out the hail storm. I brought in the mail," she says, leaving it on the wicker table next to Trudy. She turns to the seated figure in the corner. "Sorry, Martha, no fan mail today."

Bridget remembers first seeing Martha in the car on that freezing, late fall morning, thinking a lovely old lady had frozen to death. She had turned out to be a realistic-looking mannequin, the Martha Washington model, made for use in first-responder training. After Bridget dropped countless hints, Trudy had given her her own Martha as a wedding gift.

"There's a package for you on the hall table," Trudy says.

Bridget goes to put the ramps in the kitchen and comes back out with the package and a Clagger and tonic, sitting in the chair next to Trudy.

"We've had a lot of squirrels visiting today." Trudy says.

"I left Corn Nuts for them over there by the azaleas. They go like hotcakes," Bridgets says as she opens her package.

"*Merryvale* was shooting around town," Trudy says. "I'm glad Jenny was able to get them to film here instead of Blue Birch. That never made sense to me."

"I think they tried to get permission when Rufus was mayor but...Oh, look! It's here!"

Bridget pulls a white cloth object out of the parcel. "I love it! Martha's actual mobcap. A piece of American history!"

"It would be if the provenance were clear."

"'May have belonged to Martha Washington' is good enough for me," Bridget says, placing the mobcap on Martha's head. "Much, much better. A lot of money, but she's worth it. Oh, and I borrowed a book for her from the library."

"When you say borrowed..." Trudy asks.

"I did not lift it from the library, if that's what you're implying. That would be taking candy from a baby. Where's the fun in that?"

"What did you get for her?"

"*U.S. History for Dummies*," Bridget says. "I thought she might want to catch up."

"Thoughtful of you."

"I wonder what Martha was really like, don't you?" Bridget says as she sips her cocktail.

"I read a biography of her ages ago. Capable, I think. Good at managing things."

"That sounds right. Though there can be a big difference between who we are and who people think we are."

"I suppose that's true," Trudy says. "What's on your mind, sweetheart?"

"Watching Wilky come into his own so quickly with Jenny is lovely. It's just —"

Bridget feels Trudy's eyes on her.

"Go on," Trudy says.

"It can be so confusing for an adopted child. Oh, well, you know what I mean."

Trudy raises her eyebrows.

"I sent in for a DNA test," Bridget says.

"Did you really?"

"I did. For the second time. There was a problem in the lab with the first test. I should get the results sometime in the next few weeks."

"Then I think we should drink in honor of your adoptive and your biological parents, whoever they may be."

They clink glasses.

"And to the pride of Ashtabula," Trudy says.

"Oh, I don't know about pride. Queen of Ashtabula, maybe. Or First Lady."

"How about Empress?"

"Yes, that works, too," Bridget says. "I like Empress of Ashtabula. Sounds like a tarot card."

JENNY HAS A FEW MINUTES TO CHILL ON HER BarcaLounger, footrest extended, before she and Wilky head over to Nelle's for Doozy's birthday celebration.

It's been a good week: they've finally got the plan for the new baseball field in Van Dalen Park and *Merryvale* has started shooting in town with no complaints, at least not yet. But it's Wilky who's made this week, as he does every week, indeed every day.

She takes off her glasses and looks down at him: he's lying on the floor, wearing her Red Sox cap, reading *The Goblet of Fire*. Tishy, Jenny's assistant at City Hall, had loaned Wilky her treasured Harry Potter books and had gotten him hooked on the series.

"Wilks, do you want to go to Boston next month?"

"Okay," he says.

"To Fenway Park? Red Sox play the Blue Jays?"

He lets out a yelp, jumps up, and does a little dance. "Thank you, Mayormama!"

His recent nickname for her, Mayormama, has stuck because people (herself included) think it's funny and that's enough for Wilky. He has a knack for getting people to laugh. She doesn't know if it's his nature or if he's trying to combat a lifetime's worth of sadness already meted out to a nine-year-old boy. Maybe it's both.

"It's a long drive to get there," Jenny says.

"I will be perfect. I promise!"

Jenny smiles at him, thinking you *are* perfect, my sweet child, but not daring to say it out loud. It had taken over a year and four trips down to Haiti before she could bring Wilky home and she's reluctant to do or say anything to tempt fate. It had gone smoothly, as these things go, though she had found out that Wilky was actually two years older than the orphanage had claimed. They had fudged the number because they thought he would be more likely to get adopted if he were younger. She didn't care either way.

Her restless nights before bringing him home were driven by worry that she was taking on too much, especially as a single, working mom. Yet from the moment they had left the orphanage together to go to the airport, it was a different and vivid apprehension that insinuated itself: that Wilky would be left alone again. Jenny's dad was gone, her mom was not in good health, and she had no siblings. During the flight home, she had started a mental list of potential godparents.

"Wilky?"

He looks up at her and smiles with that little gap between his two front teeth and with those big, brown, almond-shaped eyes.

"Come on, we've got to get ready for Aunt Doozy's birthday party."

Chapter Three

✤

"I had an idea in the shower."

"Best place for ideas," Nelle says.

Will and I are at Nelle's, having cleaned ourselves up after our romp around the marsh, where all that gick-gick-gicking led to Will's discovery about the northern cricket frog. Will squeezes the growler of ale he's brought into the fridge. I leave two bottles of Chianti on the counter.

"Help yourself to whatever you're drinking," Nelle says, eyeing the Chianti. "So?"

"Little libraries."

"Little libraries?"

"You know, the outdoor cabinets that towns put up with books in them for people to borrow?"

"I know what they are. You want me to reverse engineer why you had an idea about little libraries? I'm cooking."

"Smells amazing!" Will says. "What are you making?"

"Paella," Nelle answers.

"What can I do to help, Nelle?" Will asks.

"How are you at shucking oysters?"

"Aces."

Nelle hands the bowl to Will. "Everything you need is on that counter. Meanwhile, I'll try to pry open whatever your boyfriend has on his mind."

"I was saying to Will that I feel at loose ends."

"What kind of loose ends?"

"Loose loose ends. Useless."

"Okay. And how do little libraries help?" she asks, pouring broth into the skillet.

"I think it would be nice for the community."

"Do it," Nelle says. "It's solid. Do it. Ask Theo Nyqvist to build them."

"Good idea. I love paella," I say.

"So does Aunt Doozy," Nelle says.

Aunt Doozy, ninety-four years old as of today, has worked for decades at The Chicken Shack, where the fried chicken is almost as beloved as Doozy herself. She's the daughter of Arnold Falls' highly successful (and only) black madam and might have gone into her mother's business but for Doozy's lifelong difficulties with flatulence. Nelle has spent a lot of time with her recently since Doozy's childhood pal, Emma Rose, died last November. They've grown close.

Nelle says, "Doozy told me that her mother would make it once in a while — one of the girls had shown her how to do it. I asked if she had the recipe but she said that the only thing like that she'd gotten from her mama was for the Shack's fried chicken."

"She's kept that recipe secret all these years," I say.

"I think Aunt Doozy has a lot of secrets," Will says without looking up.

"What makes you say that?" Nelle asks, knocking back half a flute of Champagne.

"I don't know. I just think so."

Handing me a corkscrew (which means she's ready for red

wine), Nelle says, "You're right, Will. She doesn't like to talk about herself and she definitely doesn't spill the tea about anyone else."

"I'm looking forward to the exhibition," Will says.

"Me, too," says Nelle. "Maybe we'll learn some of those secrets."

The Red Light Museum (Where People Come to Honor the Past®) is opening their big summer show in August about Aunt Doozy's mother, Miss Georgia, and her life as a madam, one also renowned as a great beauty.

The doorbell rings and I let in a different sort of madam, Madam Mayor, with her newly adopted son, Wilky.

"Wilky! Jenny!" says Nelle, running over to greet them.

Wilky gives hugs to each of us.

"What are you doing, Uncle Will?" he asks.

"Shucking oysters," Will says. "Have you ever had oysters?"

Wilky nods and says in his Haitian accent, "Me and Mother Jenny" (which sounds like Muhduh Gggeny) — "went to Mystic in Contenticut and after we go for fish. I tried them. Good. What's shucking?"

"Opening," Will says. "Opening the oysters."

"Say that right away, Uncle Will. Save time."

Will grins as he inserts the knife near the hinge.

"What are you drinking, Jenny?" Nelle asks. "I don't have Jim Beam. How about Jack Daniels?"

"Thanks, Nelle. Too many balls in the air these days for the hard stuff. Beer?"

"You're in luck, Jenny," I say. "Brewmaster Will has brought some of his summer ale. It's really good."

"Try it," Will says.

I pour for Jenny and hand her the glass.

"Will, that's crazy good!" Jenny says.

"Cheers, Mayor," he says.

"Jeebie, can you switch the TV to ESPN?" Nelle asks.

"Put it on mute for now."

"You just want to tease me because you know I have no idea what channel ESPN is. What do you want to watch?"

"The channel is 512. The Red Sox are playing the Astros and Doozy will want to have it on," Nelle says.

"That's baseball, Uncle Jeebie," Wilky says.

The others find this funny.

"Jeebie?"

"Yes, Jen?"

"How would you like to take care of Wilky in a couple of weeks? For two nights."

"Love to," I say, looking at Will, who gives a thumbs up.

"Okay with you, Wilky?"

Wilky nods his head vigorously.

"Where are you going?"

"There's a New York mayors conference in the city on June thirteenth and fourteenth. Tishy can't sit because she'll be on vacation in Anaheim at a Power Rangers event."

"She promised to bring me something back," Wilky says.

"First time Wilky and I won't be together," she says.

"I won't cry all night, I promise, Mayormama."

We chat and nosh for twenty minutes or so before the guest of honor arrives — Doozy in a pink, 1950s swing dress and chunky, Hoka sneakers — along with her old friend Ruby Winter, striking and ageless as always, in a sunflower-yellow sundress, who's up visiting from the city.

"Good, you got the game on," Doozy says. "Oh, they're playing the Astros. Skip it. Astros cheat."

"Happy birthday!" we say, and Doozy waves off the fuss. "Sorry we late. We had to stop at Argos. They wanted to do a birthday toast."

"Several," Ruby says.

Wilky walks up shyly to Doozy.

"Hello, Aunt Doozy, happy birthday," he says and puts his arms out. I watch Doozy as she hugs Wilky, two skinny bodies folding into each other, her face crinkling into a smile, a sepia image in real time.

Ruby says, "I'm Ruby, Wilky. I hear you're a fine, young man."

"Nice to meet you, auntie," he says.

"Aunt Doozy, can I ask you a question?"

"Go on, Jeebie," Doozy says.

"Why are you holding rosary beads?"

"Emma Rose gave them to me, a few days before she passed. Feels good to touch." She looks toward the television.

"Do you have a bet on the game?" Jenny asks.

"Naw, that was something Emma Rose and I did together. And just the ponies, not baseball."

I take Doozy and Ruby's drink orders as they sit on the couch.

Wilky asks, "Who's your favorite player, Aunt Doozy? I like the Red Sox, too. Mayormama takes me to a game this month, playing the Mariners!"

"You'll have a good time. Well, favorite players? Let's see. Loved when Pedro Martinez pitched. I like that Xander fellow."

"The X Man! I also love Devers because he's from the D.R.," says Wilky.

"Speaking of baseball," I say, "Will made a discovery today."

"At the marsh in Van Dalen Park," Will says.

"What did you find?" Jenny asks.

"Well, you're not going to like this, Jen."

He explains the northern cricket frog problem of in-filling the marsh for a baseball diamond.

"Hmmm. That's not good," Jenny says. "We had over three acres with the marsh gone, which would have given us room for bleachers and a dugout. With the marsh, under two acres. I don't know where else a diamond could go. We just got plans finalized!"

"You mean you can't have baseball there?" Doozy asks, sipping her beer.

"The northern cricket frog is endangered," Will says.

"Ruby," Doozy says. "What did they play, long time ago? Like baseball but smaller everything?"

"What was that called? I remember it. Wasn't it gumball?"

"That's it! Gumball!"

"What the heck is gumball?" Nelle asks. "We can start with the oysters."

We settle in at the table.

"Ruby, they play gumball on a smaller field?" Doozy asks.

"I don't remember at all. You know who would know? Alfie Trowbridge. He still with us?"

Doozy says, "Mm-hm. A hundred-four now."

"He's at AHA," Jenny adds, referring to the Arnold Home for the Aged.

"That's right, Ruby. He was one of them came up with the game," Doozy says, slurping an oyster.

"How do you play?" Wilky asks.

Doozy looks to Ruby.

"I think it *was* a small field. The bat and ball were smaller. Or maybe the ball was bigger like a softball. I don't remember it catching on too well."

"How do you like the beer?" Will asks Doozy.

"This beer's good. Very good," finishing the mug.

"Will brewed it," I say.

"You brewed this?" Doozy asks. "It's good. I forgive you for messin' up my park with your frogs."

Doozy suddenly has an odd expression on her face and she starts twirling her rosary beads. Ruby and Jenny look down at their drinks. Will looks at me. I look at Nelle. There is a long moment of silence.

"What happen?" Wilky asks.

"Nothing," Jenny says. "Gumball is a great idea! Let's find out more."

"Tss-tss-tss-tss," Doozy laughs.

"How many drinks did you have at Argos?" Jenny asks.

Ruby says, "They kept toasting Doozy."

"Don't matter, Ruby."

"Okay, I'll bite," I say. "Aunt Doozy. Is there something you want to tell us? For instance, how you have a park? Most people don't. Have a park."

Doozy looks at Jenny.

"You knew about this!" I say to Jenny.

"Course she did," Doozy says.

Then Doozy proceeds to tell us the story of how she came to bankroll a new park for Arnold Falls.

It's almost midnight when Will and I leave Nelle's to walk home. It's quiet, except for the crickets.

"The crickets are fortissississimo."

"You're making up words," Will says.

"I'm not. It means super loud. The musical notation is ffff."

"The crickets produce sound through stridulation. Not made up either," Will says.

"It's been a crickety day. Your northern cricket frog produced unexpected revelations."

"Doozy's story about the Patty O'Patties stock is crazy."

Doozy had explained that Miss Georgia was given 100 shares of Patty O'Patties stock by a former client, Pat McClement, when his burger chain went public in 1965. Untouched by her mother or by Doozy, she's now got a fortune stashed away. I couldn't believe it, but I couldn't be happier it happened to Doozy.

A little later, when we're getting ready for bed, I say, "Too bad about the baseball diamond. The only other land that's big enough is Midden Park. Can you play baseball on a Super-fund site?" I ask.

"I don't think so."

"Looks like we may have gumball in our future."

"If anyone can remember how to play it," Will says, turning off the light. "Market day tomorrow, early start."

After a few moments, I ask, "How much do you think Doozy's stock is worth now?"

"Eleventy zillion," Will says, yawning.

"Sounds about right," I say.

Chapter Four

❦

It's just past opening time at the farmer's market, and Will is still setting up Eiderdown's booth. This season's apples haven't come in yet, but the farm's crimson-red strawberries have and they're up there with the best he's ever tasted.

He looks across the lot to see Marybeth arriving. She waves to him and he grabs a quart of strawberries. Walking over to her, he says, "You finally did it!"

"Heritage veggies for the people," Marybeth says.

"Here," Will says, handing her the strawberries. "These are amazing."

"Thanks, Will."

He's happy that Marybeth and Duncan are, as of today, vendors at the farmer's market. Duncan is Jeebie's oldest friend — they go back to first grade — and he likes them both a lot, which isn't a heavy lift.

"How did you persuade him?" Will asks.

"You mean selling at the market?"

"Yeah."

"Duncan listens when the bank account speaks."

"Gotcha."

"These are delicious, Will! Wow!"

"Where's Sadie?"

"With my mom," Marybeth says.

"Crap, the face lotion people!" Will says, looking several booths down.

"Who's that?"

"They just started last week. If they offer you a sample, say no."

"Really?"

"Trust me."

Duncan comes back from the truck carrying several boxes of produce. "Hey, Will."

"Try one of Will's strawberries," Marybeth says, handing him the berry basket.

"Great!" Duncan says.

"*Witness Protection! Witness Protection!*"

"Here they go," Will says.

"What the hell?" Duncan says.

"*Face serum that beats wrinkles into submission! Witness Protection! Even your worst enemies won't recognize you.*"

"Seriously?" Duncan asks.

"Have fun, newbies," Will says and walks back to his stall. The first hour passes quickly with hardly a break. He likes it when it's busy because he can let his mind wander, even if it rarely wanders far from Jeebie.

"That'll be $9.50," he says to his customer. He puts the ten into the cigar box.

He understands Jeebie wanting to feel useful. Will knows how lucky he is to be able to do all the things he does. Tyler's story stopped at high school. Football shoulder injury, fentanyl, gone. Just fucking gone. Miss you, little brother.

"Can I get my change?"

"Oh, sorry," Will says.

There's no one at the stall, so he swigs some water and sits down on a crate. He watches Bridget Roberts, wearing her prized, new mobcap, take the bait from the Witness Protection woman. Bridget rubs lotion all over face.

He wants to go somewhere. Travel. With Jeebie. Stay at the Auberge of the Flowering Hearth if it still existed. He grins and thinks of Jeebie and how flummoxed he'd been that time at the library. That was the tell, the first time a relationship with Jeebie seemed possible. The six months together have passed so quickly and it's been great. But now he's got a bad case of wanderlust. He and Jeebie haven't traveled together yet and he's longing for new horizons. First, Paris. Then, maybe a trip to Japan, or Cape Town or Iceland, or a long weekend at Fawlty Towers — if only. Or travel the world with him, no itinerary at all.

Bridget walks to The Pepper People, the stall next to his, and begins gathering up the coveted Jimmy Nardellos. She gives him a quick wave and a smile.

"How's the Witness Protection feel?" Will asks.

"Tingly," Bridget replies.

"Are those spicy?" a voice says.

Bridget turns to see the hermit.

"No, just very flavorful. One of my favorites peppers and you don't find them a lot."

She's forgotten to bring a bag with her, so she's cradling the Jimmy Nardellos in the crook of her arm.

"I'll have to try some. I'm Marvin. Marvin the Hobo."

"I'm Bridget. I thought —"

"I'm the hermit. Former hobo. Why don't you put those peppers in your cap? Excellent hobo tip, no charge."

"Oh, no! This is a very valuable cap. It probably belonged to Martha Washington! First time I've worn it myself. It adds a festive note of 18th-century elegance to this shorts-and-sandals crowd, don't you think?"

"I guess so," Marvin says. "Museum piece, huh?"

"Could be, but it belongs to my Martha, who does neighborhood watch from mmm mor. It's hmmmhh mmmh hm mmmhy. Muh-moh. Mmmuh hahhhuh? Moohh!"

"It's the Witness Protection, Bridget," Will says. "Your face will be frozen for a while."

"I tried it just after she did," Marvin says. "The beard is very drying. Moh moh! Mow maw mih moo may mih mahs?"

"About an hour," Will says.

"Mow mah moo muhmermah mim?" Bridget asks.

"I don't know, I guess I speak cryonics. Don't worry about it, you'll be fine. And your skin will be radiant," Will says, suppressing a smile.

"Muh ih maw," Marvin says, and walks off.

"Muh mih ee may?" Bridget asks.

"He said 'fuck it all.'"

"Hi, Uncle Will!" Wilky says, running up to him for a hug. "Wilky!"

"Hi, Will," Jenny says, lugging two full bags of produce. "Bridget, I need to talk with you about something."

"Migh mah maw mih mow."

"She can't talk right now," Will says. "Witness Protection."

"Even better," Jenny says.

"Migh maw meeh."

"She's all ears," Will says.

"Can you come with me tomorrow to AHA to talk with Alfie Trowbridge? You two go way back, right? I need to find out how you play gumball. We can't fit a baseball field into the new park, thanks to a discovery by a certain party."

Will smiles.

"Moh ah ma a muhme mah."

"Hmm. Not sure what she said. Is that a yes?"

"Moh ah ma a muhme mah!"

"Just nod if you'll come with me tomorrow, 10 a.m."

"Might be tricky to nod," Will points out.

"Okay, blink your eyes fast if you'll come."

Bridget blinks.

"Great, see you tomorrow, Bridget. Come on, Wilks."

Jenny takes Wilky's hand and walks off.

"*Moo-Mee!*"

"Excuse me!" Will says.

Bridget holds out a cellphone to Jenny.

"Is that mine? Of course it's mine."

"Mahmee! Mah Mahmee!"

"Sorry! Not sorry!"

"What is going on?" Wilky asks.

"It's a good question," Jenny says. "Come on, I'll explain."

"Mah moo, Mih."

"You're welcome, Bridget. Any time," Will says.

He sits down and eats a strawberry, thinking: even a standard-issue, long, sandy beach at sunset. All to themselves.

"Alfie! Oooh-oooh, Alfie!" There's no response. "Let's just go in," Bridget says to Jenny.

Bridget looks at Alfie Trowbridge lying atop his bed, on his back, in this small, lilac-colored room at the Arnold Home for the Aged. His skin is sallow, his thatched hair haywire, his eyes shut.

"It's close in here," Bridget says under her breath to Jenny. "Could use some fresh air. He could use some Witness Protection, too, to be honest. Good morning, Alfie. How are you today? It's Bridget Roberts and I'm here with the mayor of Arnold Falls, Jenny Jagoda."

Alfie opens his eyes.

"I was one of your best customers, Alfie," Bridget continues. "Your Clagger was always primo. But Alfie the Fourth is doing a fine job with the family business."

Alfie grunts.

"Do you have any Clagger with you?" he asks hoarsely. "Just a sip before I go."

"I don't think that's a good idea," Jenny says.

"You a doctor?" Alfie asks.

"Alfie, we're here because we need to know the rules for gumball," Bridget says.

"For *what?*" he wheezes.

"Gumball, the game you invented, like baseball, that you could play on a smaller field."

"Oh, gumball. Didn't catch on," he says.

"But it's going to have its moment!" Bridget says. "Think what a legacy you'll leave to Arnold Falls!"

"Fuck Arnold Falls," he says before segueing into a hacking cough.

Bridget pulls out a flask and looks at Jenny. Jenny shakes her head.

"Do you remember the rules, Alfie?" Jenny asks.

"I invented them. I'll tell you if you give me a nip."

"Well, I guess a little won't hurt," Bridget says. "Jenny, give me one of those plastic cups." She splashes a bit of Clagger into it and hands it to Archie.

"Small pour," Archie says, drinking it down. "Hits the spot."

"Gumball, Archie," Bridget says.

"Top me up," he says.

Bridget does.

"Right-ee-o. Baseball for pussies."

"I'm sorry?" Jenny says.

"That's what we called it. Rules aren't too much trouble. But the point of it is..." His eyes close.

"Archie?"

"Hm?"

"The point of it is?"

"Archie?"

He whispers, "Point is..."

Jenny leans in close to hear him.

"What's the point, Archie?"

Archie mumbles.

"Say it again?"

"Something with a D," Jenny says. "I think he said dugout. 'Think dugout'? Did you say 'you think'? You think in the dugout? Go on. You think in the dugout. Then what?"

"Archie?" Bridget says, leaning in. "Drink in the dugout? He said *drink* in the dugout. That sounds right. Archie? Archie?"

"Archie? No!" Jenny says.

"He's fine. Aren't you fine? All liquored up."

Archie is motionless. Jenny and Bridget look at each other.

Bridget urgently jabs her thumb toward the door and they scurry down the hall to the lobby.

Once they're outside, Bridget says, "Well, I thought that went well."

~

"MORNING, TISHY," JENNY CALLS FROM HER OFFICE.

"You're in early, Mayormama," Tishy says. "Know what day it is?"

"Monday."

"*And?*" Tishy says.

Jenny gets up and walks to Tishy's desk in the outer office. Tishy is known around City Hall for her eccentric DIY wardrobe, though it's her common sense and deadpan delivery that Jenny finds so endearing. At first, Jenny had been disappointed when Noly Spinoly, set to be her mayoral assistant, had moved to Boulder. But Jenny had decided not to hire for that position, giving Tishy a raise instead, effectively making her the mayor's assistant, and it has worked out nicely.

"Well, that is fabulous," Jenny says, admiring Tishy's outfit. "Sushi Day?"

"International Sushi Day. Actually, it's on the 18th. I wanted to take it with me to the Power Rangers convention, so this is a tryout."

"Holy *mackerel!*" Jenny says.

"Ungh. Lame," Tishy says. "Mom joke."

"You've outdone yourself."

Doing something like a twirl to show off her threads, Tishy says, "The plastic grass part of sushi is called *haran*. Bet you didn't know that."

"I didn't."

"The whole skirt is made of haran. Those are yellowtail and eel sushi pieces on my blouse. The earrings are a dab of wasabi."

"I love the hat," Jenny says.

"Doesn't the organza look *exactly* like salmon roe?" Tishy asks.

"You look just delicious," Jenny says. "Are you dressed for a little trip to the basement?"

"What are you looking for?"

"I'm still on the gumball trail."

"Ungh. What happened with Archie?"

"He was, uh, short on details. That's why I want to look through the archives."

Tishy snickers. "Archives? Just boxes." She takes a set of keys from her desk drawer and they head to a wooden door down the hall, which Tishy unlocks. The smell of damp and mildew is strong. Tishy switches on the lights. They walk carefully down the wobbly staircase, Tishy's eels and tunas clicking together.

"How is it organized?" Jenny asks.

"Ha, good one. It's boxes of stuff. That's how it's organized. A few of them are marked."

"How about the file cabinets?"

"Cabinets of stuff. Catch as catch can."

"I'm hoping," Jenny says, "there might a pile of sports clippings somewhere. Let's give it a shot."

For the next hour, they rummage. Jenny's about to give up when she opens a box marked 'AFCE.'

"Huh."

"What is it?" Tishy asks, walking over to Jenny.

"78s."

"Old records?"

"Yeah. And a newspaper clipping."

They inspect the contents.

"Arnold Falls Chamber Ensemble," Tishy reads. "1938. Arnold Falls had *chamber music*? Probably just kazoos."

Jenny laughs. "You're such a cynic, Tishy."

"Arnold Falls and chamber music? That sound right?"

"No," Jenny agrees, as she picks up a clipping from the *Herald-Tribune*. "Wow, this is an interview with Jascha Heifetz."

"Fiddle guy?"

"Yeah. From October, 1936." Jenny skims the article. "Get

this! Heifetz says, 'I had a most pleasant trip recently into the Hudson Valley where I stopped in a town called Arnold Falls, which has a reputation that precedes it. It was a salutary weekend with crisp fall air but the highlight was an evening at their city hall, listening to the Arnold Falls Chamber Ensemble play the Piano Quintet No. 2 in C Minor by Gabriel Fauré. It was exquisite.'"

"Throw that away, don't let anyone see it," Tishy says. "Total buzzkill."

"You're kidding, right?"

"Kinda not," says Tishy. "Doesn't really go with Arnold Falls' vibe. Ask Bender what he knows."

"Good idea. He's as close to a music historian as we have around here."

"Also, he shaved his beard," Tishy says. "He looks so cute."

When she gets back to her desk, Jenny calls Bender.

"Hi, it's Jenny. How are you fixed for Victrolas?"

"Whatdya got?"

"78s."

"Bring 'em over."

TISHY AND WILKY'S EYES FOLLOW JENNY AS SHE WALKS out of the office for a visit with Bender.

Holding up her finger, Tishy mouths "Wait." After a few moments, she says, "I didn't think we'd have a chance so soon."

"You're *surnoise*," Wilky says.

"I hope that means 'awesome,' Tishy says.

"Means, like, you play little tricks."

"It was *your* idea," Tishy says.

"It's a good idea, *non?*"

"Oui."

～

A FEW MINUTES LATER, THE FAMILIAR "WIPEOUT" DOOR chime plays as Jenny walks into the record store/weed emporium Long Strange Trip. Its owner, Bender Hubble, is on the floor with his cat, Humboldt, who is sitting on Bender's lap.

"Cutest fucking picture, you two."

"Twenty-five cents," Bender says. "Nah, swearing charge waived."

"No beard! You look years younger. You working on a map?"

"Yeah, a couple. Is it really the right pastime, though, for a man in his mid-thirties? Creating maps of fictional countries?"

"I love your maps," she says.

"Thanks. How's Wilky?"

"He's doing great. An amazing kid. I am so crazy lucky.

"He's lucky, too," Bender says.

"That's sweet."

"It's true. Okay, show me, dude."

"Don't look at it, just play," Jenny says.

"Hang on."

Bender stands up and he and Humboldt go into the back room. She likes the clean-shaven Bender.

"Oh, that's amazing!" Jenny says as he carries out an ancient record player.

"A Victor VI. Isn't she a beaut?"

"She is. What year?"

"Around 1910, but hard to say exactly."

Jenny carefully passes the record over to him.

"They fit about three minutes per side," he says.

"Don't peek."

Bender winds the crank in silence. They sit next to each other against the wall as the music starts beneath a spray of pops and clicks. Humboldt returns and sits between them.

"Is this Ravel?" Jenny asks.

"Fauré."

They listen to the entire first movement, with Bender flipping the first disc, then replacing it with the second. The piano and the strings intertwine, and it envelops them, hesitantly at first and then insistently. An autumnal chill on this summer day. At the end, she turns her head toward Bender.

"Wow," he says. "That got me."

"That was beautiful."

"Truly. Okay, what's the story?" he asks.

"Guess who's playing?"

"No clue," Bender says.

"The Arnold Falls Chamber Ensemble."

Bender laughs. "Can't be."

"It is. Tishy and I were in the basement at City Hall, looking through the archives for info on gumball. And this was in a box, along with a clipping from the *Herald-Tribune*. Jascha friggin' Heifetz heard them play at a concert in 1936. Might be the same piece. Did you know about this?"

"Nope. Will wonders never cease?"

He kneels by the Victrola. "The label is stamped FW. Maybe this was some kind of private recording?"

"My guess is it was recorded after Heifetz praised it."

"That would make sense. 1937 or '38?"

"That's what I think."

"There were others?"

She nods. "There were several different recordings in the box, all with the same stamp. Couldn't fine anything online about it. I thought FW might mean something to you. Tishy says we should bury them, that chamber music would be bad for Arnold Falls' rep."

Bender grins. "She's got a point."

"And nothing in the basement about gumball, either, at least that I could find."

"So glad you're protecting the frogs."

"There are a lot of people around here who'd prefer baseball."

"If Rufus were still in office, those frogs would already have been bulldozed out of existence," Bender says.

Bender stands up and Humboldt darts to the back.

"What do you want to do with the records?"

"I don't know yet," Jenny says. "Solve their mystery. Softens the town's image, too, don't you think?"

Bender nods. "Let me see what I can figure out."

She kisses him on the cheek and heads back to City Hall.

RUFUS RUBS THE BACK OF HIS NECK AND EXHALES LOUDLY several times. He cracks his knuckles on one hand, then the other.

Ever since he lost his reelection bid for mayor to Jenny, he hasn't been feeling like the old Rufus, the Rufus who felt like he was mayor. He tried, briefly, selling ice cream from a truck, but what are you going to do about winter in Queechy County? Sell the truck, is what he did. Three thousand bucks lost, eleven pounds gained.

And now here he is, having gotten his real estate license just last month, waiting inside a fancy house on Ledyard for an actor lady from *Merryvale*, to give his first showing ever. "I got this," he mumbles to himself, trying to summon up all the confidence he can that this is the path back to success in Arnold Falls.

"YO-DE-LAY-HE-HOO, anybody there?"

He scurries over to the front door, opening it to reveal a brunette in her late 40s — not his usual type, but a looker just the same. He gets a whiff of her perfume as she says, "You must be Rufus, I didn't expect you to be so HAND-some! I'm Fayette. I tried the doorbell but I guess it doesn't work."

She's classy, this chick. And stacked. "You gotta use the knockers. Knocker." He feels a little lightheaded. "Most people have their disconnected doorbells. Doorbells disconnected. It's a superstition here."

"Should I see the house from the porch?" she asks.

"What? Oh, no, come in."

She walks by him into the front hallway. That perfume!

"Yeah, uh, one summer in the 1960s," he says, "everybody's doorbells rang for a week. Something to do with the hail and electrical charges in the air, they think. Put people off doorbells. Newer people have them. Um, this is my first time."

She turns to look at him.

"My first house. Showing."

"Let's get to it! Show me what you've got!" she says.

All this gusto is throwing him off his game. He clears his throat and begins, "The house was built in..." he checks his notepad, "1875 for Occidental Sissboom — the Sissbooms made a fortune in collar stays before they sold to Bartlett. Ox Sissboom was one of the founders of Queechy General."

"What is that?"

"That's our hospital. There are worse places to die." Maybe shouldn't have said that. "Well, over here to the left is the living room..."

As they tour the downstairs of the rambly Victorian, Fayette asks him questions about the house and the town. When they get to the staircase to tour the second floor, Fayette's eyes widen at the arrangement of the steps.

"Nothing to worry about, Fayette. It's a witches staircase. The treads are cut in half and placed at different heights. Everyone knows witches can't climb them. No problem, unless you're a witch. Security feature. You're not a witch, by any chance?"

"Let's test it out," Fayette says gamely.

They both make it to the top.

"WITCH-FREE ZONE!" she trills.

"Didn't have you pegged as a witch," Rufus says.

When they're in the master bathroom, Fayette says, "I'd have to start over in here. It needs a complete overhaul."

"I know just the guy. Does good work. Won't rip you off. Too much."

"How do you know so much about everything?" Fayette asks.

No one has ever said this to him before.

"I dunno, I grew up here, Fayette, and before I got my real estate license, I was the mayor of Arnold Falls."

"Well!" she says. "It's my lucky day!"

He thinks she's flapping her eyes at him. "Let's go out and look at the back yard," Rufus says.

After a few minutes out back they sit on the fieldstone wall.

"Rufus," she says. "I like this house. I may take it. I like this town."

"Everybody loves Arnold Falls," he says.

"I can see why. And I would like to put Arnold Falls on the map."

"It's on maps," Rufus says.

"You're so darling! My best pal in the world is a marketing EINSTEIN and he's worked with other localities to get the word out about their special charms. Branding, you know. Arnold Falls needs to make a big splash."

It occurs to Rufus that a big splash for Arnold Falls could be a big win for him — maybe even a ticket back to the mayor's office.

"And I think," she continues, leaning in to him, "you're just the man to help make it happen. Now tell me more about what Arnold Falls has to offer. Where's the waterfall?"

"No waterfall."

"Poetic license. All right. Any museums?"

"Negative. Well, the Museum of Sex. If that counts."

"How about famous people in history?"

"Lizzie Borden used to visit after the, you know, the chop-chop."

"Sports?"

"There's a Clagger-Chug."

"Clagger?"

"Local drink. We have the Titleholder's Parade coming up in a couple of weeks."

"What's that?"

"It's neat," Rufus says. "You get to march down High Street in the parade if you have a title or you can even make one up."

"So I could be Lady Fayette de la Nouille?"

"Sure. Or let's say you won the Science Day prize in seventh grade. That would work, too."

"Congratulations on that!"

"Thank you," says Rufus. "Balloons and static electricity."

"Are there farms?"

"They're outside of town. Still a bunch of them, yeah. Only a few are real working farms."

"Well, let me ask you. What do people think of when they think of Arnold Falls?"

"We used to have the best red-light district on the east coast."

"What about something more current?"

"We have our own hermit now!"

"A hermit?"

"Yup, I did that. Came highly recommended. He's got a big, bushy beard. Looks just like a hermit."

"Hmmm. Maybe I should look at rentals, too," Fayette says.

Chapter Five

✤✤✤

We're in Nelle's car, destination unknown (to me), singing (of course).

"How about June songs?" she asks.

We sing a bit of "How About You?" — the song that starts "I like New York in June, how about you?" — but neither of us can remember all the lyrics.

"What other June songs are there?" I ask.

"Prince has one called 'June' that starts 'Pasta simmers on the stove in June.' It's an oddball, but a good one," she says. "And 'June Hymn' by the Decemberists."

"Love that song. Gorgeous."

We haven't even gotten to what I would say is the most famous June song: "June is Bustin' Out All Over." And we give it a whirl, though the lyrics don't come easily for this one either. And *that* reminds me: "You've heard the Leslie Uggams version?"

"No," she says, "what's special about it?"

I start to laugh and Nelle glances over at me. "Don't make fun of Leslie Uggams!" she says. "She's totally underrated!"

"Agreed! Haven't you ever seen the video where she goes

up on the lyrics to 'June is Bustin' Out All Over'? at a live show, when she's walking through the audience?"

I sing the 'lyrics' of the Uggams version and when I get to "All the bugs'n out of bushes and the rum an' river rishes/All the little wheels that wheel beside a bill," Nelle cracks up.

"What's the 'dridges' line again?" she asks after I hit the big note at the end.

"Something like 'And the lidda bidda dridges'"..."

And she laughs again. "I don't believe it happened. Show-queen myth."

"Okay, hold on." I play it from my phone and Nelle has to pull the car over to the side of the road she's laughing so hard.

"Well, she goes through all that and she still hits the big note at the end. She sticks the landing. I am in awe," Nelle says, wiping her eyes.

"True, but she does switch the name for some reason from June to Joan: June, June, Joan!"

"That's her training kicking in during an emergency," Nelle says. "Nicer to end on an 'O' sound than a 'U.'"

We're back on the road but Nelle is still chuckling.

"This part of the county is so pretty," I say, admiring the green canopy of trees, backlit to the vanishing point by the late-afternoon sun. I ask Nelle how the album is coming along.

"Still having trouble narrowing down the songs for it."

"You know, I could —"

"I know. I *do* want your help. But I'd rather have it when I'm at, maybe, twenty songs."

"How many songs are still on your list?!"

"Thirty-four," Nelle says.

I pose this question to Nelle a lot lately. Since her boffo concert for Jenny's mayoral campaign last fall, Nils Nyqvist, of the exponentially expanding Swedish clan, has 1) started dating her 2) built a recording studio, in part, to goose her into recording an album.

"Where are you with the little libraries?" she asks.

"Theo is working on them."

"You want to be useful? My back's been killing me so I'm going to order a new mattress. You can help me set it up."

"Sure. And after the little libraries are up and running, maybe I'll work on gumball."

Nelle wrinkles her nose. "What channel is ESPN again?" she asks.

"I know. But it's heritage work for Arnold Falls. Worth something."

"Fair point," she says.

"Will didn't think it was such a good idea either. And now that Alfie Trowbridge is gone, we may never know how to play."

"Oh, he died?"

"Yeah, he had his AHA moment a few days ago. So, will you tell me now?"

"What?"

"Where we're going."

Nelle pushes the door-lock button.

"Child lock? Oh, God. How bad it could be?"

"We're going to a farm," she says. "Fridsy's farm."

"And Fridsy is?"

"Fridsy is a Nyqvist."

"One in a murmuration. What does Fridsy have to offer?"

"I haven't met her. Keep an open mind, Jeebie."

"As I always do."

"No, more than that, please," she says. "When Nils was in Sweden last month, he went to a farm near Uppsala, where he got a demonstration of *kulning*."

"Edge of my seat," I say.

Since Nelle is driving, she can't turn to look at me, but it doesn't prevent her from giving me a swat on my shoulder. "Kulning is an old Swedish tradition to call the cows home," she says.

"Yeah?"

"Yeah. They sing, loudly, across the fields to the cows. It sounds eerie but the cows like it and walk to the singer."

"Has it come to this?"

"What do you mean?" Nelle asks.

"Is this really the best use of our time on a Wednesday afternoon? There are people in the city, right this very minute, at a Broadway show, or an exhibit at MoMA."

"Anyone can do that," she says. "None of them is going to be at a kulning demonstration. Be a sport. Nils was all excited about it and he didn't know that Fridsy actually does it right here in Queechy County. I think the turn-off is coming up."

"Already turned off," I say.

"Funny," she says. "This must be the place."

We pull up to a farmhouse and Fridsy and Nils come out to greet us. My first impression is how huge the farm is. You can't see it from the road so it's a complete surprise. And it's as charming as can be.

I wish I could say the same for Fridsy. Oh, she's good-looking, like all the Nyqvists are — maybe 50 years old, still-blond hair pulled back — but Fridsy has a chip on her shoulder so large that it's probably visible from space: The Great Wall of China, the Amazon, and Fridsy's chip. An imperfect Nyqvist! Jackpot! I mention this to Nelle as we get out of the car.

"Jeebie," is all Nelle says.

Fridsy and her chip offer us coffee and we chat for a few minutes in the kitchen. Let me stipulate that the kitchen is stylish. Even though it has all modern appliances, it's got a Swedish mid-century country vibe. Lovely.

But the chat part unfortunately involves Fridsy and a litany of grievances. The world according to Fridsy involves a lot of *they* do this and that, and how wrong *they* are, and how much better everything would be if *they* only followed Fridsy's corrections and improvements and most of all, her example. She's opposes cars that drive themselves and baby corn. Adamant about baby corn. She doesn't like paisley, either. "I fail to see the point of paisley," she says. "Looks like microbes."

Mercifully, Nils steers the conversation to kulning.

"Kulning," Fridsy says. "Almost a lost art. From the Middle Ages. Nobody wants to uphold the traditions," she says.

In my mind, I roll my eyes.

"The cows roamed free in the warm weather and women, who cared for the cows in large, remote areas, developed a way to get the cows back. The cows listened. Not like men!"

I wonder if this is a clue.

Fridsy looks at the kitchen clock and announces, "It's time for the cows to return home," she says. "Come."

She picks up a cello case by the door and we walk outside, through two smaller fields, surrounded by trees, and then emerge onto a great expanse of farmland, the kind you don't see much any more on family farms. Way down by a pond are the cows, seven of them by my count, all of them resting in the grass.

"It takes quite some practice," Fridsy says, "to get the trust of the cows. I learned everything from my grandmama." As she takes the instrument from its case, she adds, "Nobody uses a cello. That's my special twist."

Without further ado, Fridsy begins playing a wistful tune, seemingly improvised, to which, after a moment, she adds her voice. It's supple and appealing, offering harmonies with the notes from the cello. The music seems to carry far off toward the horizon and it's not long before one cow gets up.

"That's Minna," Fridsy says. "She's the mama. The boss. She knows who she is."

Fridsy continues this somewhat other-worldly serenade, but after a few moments, Minna sits back down. Fridsy tries a different melody, without results.

"They are lazy. Lazy cows," Fridsy says.

Nelle and I are standing off at a distance and I say under my breath to her, "I wouldn't rush back either."

Fridsy tries a more spirited, higher-pitched melody, but soon switches tactics. "Ee-oh, ee-oh, ee-oh," she beseeches, projecting down the valley.

The cows are having none of it.

"Let them stay, they can stay overnight," she says.

"Aren't you worried about bears?" Nils asks.

"Survival of the fittest," says Fridsy.

"Nelle, why don't you try it?" Nils asks. "She's a singer," he says to Fridsy.

"I wouldn't know how," Nelle says. "Fridsy, it's really beautiful, the whole tradition, the sound."

"Takes a *lot* of practice, believe me," Fridsy says.

I just can't help it. I say, "A case of the Chianti, Nelle, if you can get the cows back."

Fridsy shrugs and gives her a be-my-guest wave of her arm. "Don't try to copy me. Let the spirit move you."

"Any spirit moving you?" I ask.

"Fats Waller," Nelle says, clearing her throat.

Nelle plants her feet slightly apart, shoulders erect, and belts it out to Minna and her pals.

Patty Cake, Patty Cake baker man
Makes you music in a rhythm pan

Give it all the heat you can
Serve it right away.

Minna stands up. Hard to tell from the distance, but I'd say she's into the syncopation. The song, which I've never heard before, is brimming with Fats Waller joy.

Now Nelle switches her voice to a wah-wah trumpet and goes back to the first verse, singing "wah-wah" instead of the lyrics. The cows seem to like this. They're all standing up now. Fridsy has a quizzical look on her face.

Do it now, do it now
Wah wah wah
Do it now, do it now
Wah wah wah.

The cows are on the move and I detect a spring in their step. Minna is leading the group toward Nelle.

Show em how, Show em how, yeah
Patty Cake baker man!

Nelle bows to the cows.

"Try something else!" I say to Nelle.

Nelle sings the first verse of Justin Bieber's "Beauty and a Beat."

"You're not considering *that* for the album?"

Nelle shakes her head.

Minna and company put their heads down and turn away.

"They don't like that one," Fridsy says.

"Singing Justin Bieber to cows might be considered animal cruelty," Nils says.

"Agreed. What's another song you were unsure about? Run it by Minna!" I say.

"If Minna is advising on your album, Nelle, we will take royalties," Fridsy says.

I believe this is Fridsy making a joke, and she therefore goes up several notches in my estimation.

Nils looks at Nelle. "Minna will help you. Try one more on your list."

"Talking Heads?" she asks.

Nils nods. Nelle breathes quietly for a moment before she sings "This Must Be the Place" as a gentle lullaby, the way Shawn Colvin did.

Home is where I want to be
Pick me up and turn me around

Minna takes a few steps forward. The herd follows. Everything is strangely hushed. A breeze brushes the grass.

The cows approach. They're now close enough that Nelle can sing it straight to them without projecting her voice. It's lovely and those cows know it. When she gets to "I'm just an animal looking for a home and share the same space for a minute or two," it's so tender I could cry. I'm guessing even Fridsy feels it in her chip.

When the song is over, Minna comes over to Nelle and Nelle massages her shoulder. The other cows crowd around. No one else moves or speaks. I scratch Minna's neck and notice her cinnamon-colored hair and white markings that remind me of the unfamiliar countries on one of Bender's maps. She gives my arm a long, slobbery lick and looks me in the eyes. I see a beautiful, proud mama cow. I wonder what she sees. Then, as we gaze at each other, something passes between us that I don't have words for.

Finally, I say, "Minna. Minna, I'm Jeebie."

She licks my arm again, but slowly this time. When I get goosebumps, I think, okay, now this is getting weird.

"Get a room, you two," Nelle says, and that breaks the spell.

"'This Must Be the Place' is it. You've got your album-closer," I say, glancing again at Minna.

"And a case of Chianti," Nelle says.

"You earned it," Fridsy says, putting her cello back into its case.

NILS HAS STAYED BEHIND TO HAVE DINNER WITH FRIDSY; Nelle and I are driving back.

"You should test all your songs that way."

"I might," she says. "Cow-tested and -approved. Don't you want to apologize to Fridsy?"

"No. Why?"

"Because you decided before we got out of the car that she had a chip on her shoulder that you could see from outer space."

"She does."

"I think she's sweet."

"Both can be true."

"I like that she honors the tradition."

"Nelle, she said 'survival of the fittest' when Nils asked about bears. That's awful."

"I don't think she meant it for a second. Just bluster. And the only bear around here is Stripes and he's practically a lamb. Besides, you don't sing to cows unless you love them. Anyway, she's institutional memory. Or more to the point, a keeper of customs. We need Fridsys."

"I have no idea what you're on about. I need a drink."

"I think you're a Fridsy-in-training," Nelle says.

"That is not funny. Calumny."

It's quiet in the car for several minutes.

"Spill it," Nelle says.

"Minna."

"I noticed. You seemed moooved," she says.

"Shame on you. I *was* moved, but I don't know why. I don't understand what happened."

"Keep going," she says.

"What does that even mean?"

"Just keep going," she says. "Like Leslie Uggams."

"Oh, well, that explains everything."

"Explaining everything isn't my job. I'm a social worker, not a miracle worker."

"Go," I say.

"That's right, just go."

"No, the light's green."

"WHY ARE YOU WEARING THICK, WOOL SOCKS, MARYBETH? It's June."

"My feet are always cold."

"Touch them, Uncle Jeebie," says Sadie.

"Hard pass on that, beloved goddaughter."

"Touch *my* feet."

"No, thank you, Sadie."

"Uncle Will, touch my feet."

Will tickles them and Sadie screams with laughter.

We're sprawled on the two sofas at the Elmore's after a delicious meal wokked by the warm-hearted, cold-footed Marybeth, a kung pao chicken to rival any, with Will's Belgian saison ale the perfect complement. We're not here only for the food and fellowship. Tonight also happens to be the season premiere of "Annie's Farm," the first episode since chef/evil spirit Annie O'Dell's dastardly plan to cook Chaplin for Thanksgiving dinner.

Thwarted by some of Chaplin's many friends, karmic retribution hit her hard for that little scheme: she was coerced by the Bay Leaf Grower's Association into being their spokesperson — after Annie issued defamatory remarks about the herb on that last episode of the season. So, yes, we are ready to hate-watch. Chaplin, Venus, and Serena are in the barn, already tucked in. We wanted Chaplin well away from the television so he didn't have to relive that trauma.

Marybeth and Sadie made Hello Dolly bars for dessert and we're having them now with our beverages. The show's theme music begins and there's that grin, tethered to a whole lot of nothing.

"Welcome to the new season of *Annie's Farmhouse*. I'm so glad to be with you again. We're going to be making two scrumptious dishes tonight. The first is rhubarb pie with the rhubarb fresh from my garden."

"Fresh from the farmer's market," Duncan says.

"From a *real* farm," Marybeth says.

"Annie is a booby," Sadie says.

Unanimous agreement on that.

After a few minutes, Annie has assembled the pie and cosseted it into the oven. She announces to the camera, with what I take to be a tinge of regret, that she'll now make a bow-tie pasta with bay leaf pesto. We lean toward the television.

"I've toasted about half a cup of pine nuts at 350° on a baking sheet until golden brown and then they went into the food processor for a chance to cool down.

"We're adding about three-quarters of a cup of parmesan, and of course I mean Parmigiano-Reggiano, not the sawdust passed off as a noble cheese. I shudder to think of it. I've grated two garlic cloves — fine grate, please — and we'll pulse all that for a minute."

"This is not going to end well," Marybeth says.

"Not well at all," Duncan says.

"Now for the fun part," she says unconvincingly. "We get to add the bay leaves. I've boiled six cups of them for an hour, a good, rough boil, because that's how they like it, and then dried them even more roughly, like a Russian masseuse, a Russian masseuse in a foul mood.

"Into the processor and then we're slowly, slowly adding three-quarters cup of extra virgin olive oil — and I don't need to tell my faithful viewers about the horrors, the true horrors, of lesser olive oil, if it's olive oil at all. Keep a steady hand for a slow drizzle. Add a teaspoon of kosher salt, to taste. And presto pesto! Just spoon on to the bow-tie pasta."

We are transfixed as she takes a forkful of the pasta and eats it. The gravity of this crime hits her immediately: her eyes crinkle, her nostrils flare, the pearly whites clench, lips purse, and her tongue comes nervously out of the mouth to lick her lips, confirming the scope of the catastrophe. She coughs.

"A little went down the wrong pipe!" she says gamely. Her cheeks puff out and she's squinting now, eyes watering. "Yum. Yum-yum. *Yum!*"

She makes a sticky, smacking noise as she says, "That's our show for tonight. Have a delicious week," smiling a sickly, green-flecked smile.

The credits roll and there is a large disclaimer that reads: "Bay leaf pesto is a choking hazard. Do not try this at home."

As you might expect, much merriment all around.

"I'd say we've gotten our money's worth from Annie. Karma is a bay leaf, baby," Duncan says.

"Time for bed," Marybeth says to Sadie.

Sadie reluctantly agrees, giving Will and me a kiss good night.

"Sadie, how's Wilky?" I ask.

"Nothing," Sadie says.

"What do you mean, 'nothing'? Aren't you two pals?"

"He's nice," she says, twisting her foot around.

Marybeth smiles at us.

"Come on, punkin, go change for bed. I'll be up in a little while."

After Sadie heads upstairs, Marybeth says, "She gets tongue-tied when it comes to Wilky."

Duncan says, "Puppy love. It's very sweet."

"We're taking care of Wilky next week while Jenny's in the city," Will says.

"That should be fun," Duncan says.

"I think I might be in puppy love, too," I say. "Or cow love. If there's such a thing. Which I now think there is."

"Jeebie! What the heck are you talking about?" asks Marybeth.

I describe my interaction with Minna and brace for a mockfest. But that's not what happens.

Marybeth says, "It's lovely, Jeebie. You're growing."

"Desophisticating," Duncan says.

"Is that a word?" I ask.

"Maybe, I don't know. But the original meaning of sophistication was a kind of corruption."

"I'm losing my edge," I say.

"No, you're not losing anything. You're finding something," Will says.

"Listen to Will," Marybeth says.

"What if it leads me to bay leaf pesto?"

"You try another recipe," Duncan says.

Chapter Six

❧

"Yelloh, Elks."

"Mange?"

"Speaking."

"It's Sofia."

"They finally shut that bar down?"

"Busier than ever, Mange."

"Yeah, yeah, sure. What can I do you for?"

"Are you missing anything?" she asks.

"Hair, three teeth, my youth. Still got the 'stache. Still got it, baby."

"I know you do, Mange. Is anything missing from the Elks?"

"What are you, Lieutenant Columbus?"

"So you *are* missing something?"

"Maybe."

"Maybe yes or maybe no, Mange?"

"You're a pushy fuckin' broad, you know that?"

"Thank you. Means a lot to me. And it's Columbo."

"Could be that I came in a half-hour ago and found the

Schlitz clock gone. Piece of history that thing is. What's the deal here? You take it?"

"Nope. Something's missing from Argos, too. Just had a hunch."

"What's missing over there?"

"Our powder-blue Princess phone."

"Ohgofuckyourself," he says and hangs up.

Sofia calls back.

"*Yell*oh, Elks."

"Don't you hang up on me again, you miserable slab of rotting flesh."

"Nice talk," he says.

"That phone is actually valuable. One of the first off the line. And has a lot of sentimental value, too."

"So what gives?"

"I don't know," Sofia says. "We've never had anything stolen from Argos before."

"Sure, I believe that. How'd he get in? Second-story man here."

"Jimmied the kitchen door."

"The door to the alley?"

"No, the door to the wormhole."

"You're a riot. Different M.O. Gang maybe."

"Mange?"

"Yeah?"

"A *gang* that wants our blue Princess telephone?"

He sniffs a little. "Little lady has a point. Rotary?"

"The fuck's with you? How would they break in there? Through the wormhole? We haven't had the Rotary in twenty years."

"I meant the dial," Mange says.

"Oh, yeah, rotary. It's from 1959."

"I like rotary. Push buttons? Nah, never did it for me. Gimme a classic rotary. *Especially* in powder blue. Let me know what you find out."

"Sure, Mange. And Mange?"

"Yeah?"

"Blow it out your saggy ass."

She hears him laugh as he hangs up.

THAT EVENING, RUFUS AND DUBSACK WALK INTO THE Elks.

"Yo, Mange. Where's the Schlitz?" Rufus asks.

"Stolen. Came in this morning and it was gone."

"No way. *I* wanted to steal it. I love that clock." Dubsack says.

"Yeah, well, a little piece of Arnold Falls fucking gone. They hit up Argos, too. Sofia told me."

"What'd they get?" Rufus asks.

"Phone."

"Phone?"

"Princess. Princess phone."

Rufus and Dubsack chortle.

"Funniest thing I've heard —" Rufus says.

"— since sending bombs to Plopeni?" Mange says, sliding over two mugs of beer.

Rufus winces. "They needed vegetables," he says.

He'll never it live it down. Arnold Falls' sister city, Plopeni, in Romania, had asked for help from Arnold Falls for various items like drinkable water. So when they requested ammonium nitrate to improve their diet with vegetables, Rufus had sent them one ton of the fertilizer, with his own money. How was he supposed to know that it could be used to make bombs?

Before Rufus had left office, Plopeni's mayor, Mayor Haralambie, pitched him on a satellite event called ArnPlop. He remembered that because it was such a catchy name. But he couldn't make heads or tails of what it would actually be: a place for financial bigwigs to chew the fat, like Davids or Davis or something in Switzerland. He'd said no to the idea and Mayor Haralambie was pissed off — his letters to Rufus afterward made that clear. But the FBI had warned Rufus to ignore any and all requests from Plopeni, so that's what he did. For the most part.

"Did you call the cops?" Dubsack asks.

"I got Mills, if you can call him a cop," Mange says. "I reported it and he says, 'What do you want *me* to do about it?' Never see that again. Maybe I can find something on eBay."

Rufus and Dubsack move to a booth.

"You take it?" Rufus asks.

"No, I told you. I *wanted* to. Wouldn't do that to the Elks."

"Yeah, you would."

"Yeah, I would. But I didn't."

"Listen, I got an idea."

"Your batting average isn't so hot right now, Ruf."

"Just listen. On Tuesday, I gave a whatdyacall house tour to that lady actor, Fayette. Man, does she smell good."

"Oh, yeah?"

"Yeah. Bazoongas, too. So here's the deal. She says to me that her pal does, like, helps towns get the word to tourists. Could be a pot of gold for the town, and a ticket back to the mayor's office for me. Thing is, if Jenny knows I'm involved, she won't do it. So you should be the point person."

"Sure. I can do that. How do they get the word out?"

"I dunno. Something about branding. Those guys just gas a lot. You in?"

"You have to ask?"

Chapter Seven

"Okay, okay. Bup-bup-bup."

Judge Harschly raps the gavel.

"Mute yourselves. Shut off the blabber stream."

He sighs.

"Good evening. I'm Judge Harschly and..."

The conversations in the room continue.

"...the meeting of the town council will...Noise violation in here."

No avail. He sits with his arms folded, looking up ruefully at the framed photos of past council presidents on the walls. "Maple-bacon doughnuts," he says.

The room immediately gets quiet.

Judge Harschly shakes his head. "Unbelievable. The meeting of the town council will come to order. Now, much to my *amazement*, tonight we are discussing a proposal having to do with temporarily changing the name of our town — the very identity — of our blessed plot. Well, blessed plot may be a stretch. Give you that. Throwing out the first pitch is..." — he looks down at his papers — "Dante de Rosa of the DDR Agency in New York City. Floor's yours."

I'm sitting with Jenny, whose arms are every bit as folded as Judge Harschly's. This presentation has made it to the council without her support. She doesn't even know who's behind it, but if there's money in it for the town, she feels obligated to hear them out. She's much more even-handed than I could be.

"Thank you, Judge Harschly. Good evening, friends. I'm charmed by Arnold Falls and my welcome here, having spent the past few days getting to know this beautiful, historic town of yours."

"Did you bring doughnuts?" Petalia Jijanova asks. "Someone mentioned doughnuts."

"No, I'm afraid not. Next time! As Judge Harschly said, I run a marketing agency in the city and I also happen to be an old friend of Fayette de la Nouille, who, you probably know, is starring in the adaptation of *Merryvale*, shooting for a couple of months around town."

"Are you the ones turning the parking garage into a museum?" Petalia asks.

There's a murmur of concern from the audience.

"No, no, not at all. Not a museum man myself."

I see a lot of nodding. Besides Petalia, I note gadfly Phil Fleck, Dubsack, Marvin the Hobo, and Father Burnham in attendance.

"Setting eyes on Arnold Falls, Fayette fell completely in love with it, something I'm sure happens all the time, and she immediately thought of the projects I had done around the country that might work here. Can we have the lights off for the PowerPoint? Thank you.

"The projects in Tennessee and Colorado were similar to what I'm proposing tonight. The first slide is the main street of Pinewood, Colorado. They're dependent on tourism, just as you are, and there's so much competition in Colorado.

Next slide, please. So what we did is match up the town to a product we represent, in this case Pine-Sol cleaner, and Pinewood agreed to change the town's name to Pine-Sol for six months, bringing buzz to the town and to the beloved household cleaner. As you can see, tourism went up dramatically in the following quarters and, since then — next slide, please — the town created the Pinewood Music Festival with the funds from the Pine-Sol promotion. That, in turn, brought in more visitors and more revenue."

"You want us to be Pine Sol, New York?" asks Phil Fleck.

"No, that was a one-off. But I do have other brands that would love to leave their mark on Arnold Falls. It's a win-win kind of thing."

What palaver.

Dante gives more examples of successful public-private partnerships around the country, as he calls them, and the grumbling makes it clear that the audience is skeptical.

"How much?" someone asks.

Dante says, "There's a range. The devil is in the details, of course. But figure —"

"The devil take the hindmost," someone interjects.

"Needs must when the devil drives," Petalia says.

"Idle hands are the devil's workshop," adds Father Burnham.

"Devil's advocate!"

"Between the Devil and the Deep Blue Sea."

"The devil you know."

"Went Down to Georgia," says Phil Fleck.

"An apple a day keeps the devil away."

"*Doctor!*"

"Does someone need a doctor?"

"I'm a doctor!"

"You are not, sit down!"

Jenny and I look at each other.

Judge Harschly raps the gavel. "Must you? *Must* you? Please let the gentleman continue."

Taking this detour in stride, Dante says, "To answer the question of how much, it could be in the two-to-three-hundred-thousand dollar range. Not to mention the ongoing income from all the exposure in terms of tourist dollars. Could you use the money?"

It's maple-bacon-doughnut quiet. Jenny looks at me as if to say, "We could do a lot with that money" and I nod.

"My firm currently represents two brands that would be a great fit with Arnold Falls. Next slide, please. The first is something new from an old faithful sort of product. That seems like a perfect metaphor for Arnold Falls."

The room waits expectantly.

"It's called Emollimax, by the makers of Vaseline."

Jenny whispers in my ear, "You have got to be fucking kidding me."

"Emollimax is patient, Emollimax is kind. Emollimax is there for you," Dante continues, "Emollimax, by the makers of Vaseline, is a salve that could have tie-ins with your great hospital..."

"Great hospital? Hasn't done his homework," I mutter to Jenny.

"...doctors' offices, pharmacies, and every medicine cabinet in every home. Next slide, please. It could be put in party-favor souvenir packets for tourists to take with them."

Judge Harschly looks like he's doing a deep-breathing exercise.

"So we'd be Emollimax, New York?" someone asks.

"No. You'd be Emollimax, by the makers of Vaseline, New York."

"Zip code stays the same!" Dubsack calls out.

Jenny turns to look at Dubsack. *"Rufus,"* she says to me. "He's behind this somehow. I should have known."

"The other option is an old family favorite. It says comfort, home, and hearth. Next slide, please. You've just entered the town of I Can't Believe It's Not Butter!, New York."

The room reacts loudly. Judge Harschly raps the gavel.

"Mr. de Rosa. Your two choices are certainly lubricious and there's an argument to be made that that's apropos for Arnold Falls. For the rest of you, I'm going to open up the floor to general discussion. Keep it on topic. Do you think you can do that? One at a time?"

Heads nod.

"Very well. Let the record show I said 'very well' *trepidatiously.*" Judge Harschly sits back in his chair, folding his arms again.

"How long would the promotion last?" Jenny asks.

"Both are for six months," Dante says.

Father Burnham asks, "Should we sell the soul of this town for a couple of hundred thousand dollars?"

This gets a resounding *"Yes!"*

"Hell, yes!" someone says.

"Hell, yes!" the crowd agrees.

"Amen."

"A-fucking-men."

Judge Harschly gives an obligatory gavel rap.

"Emollimax or butter?" Dubsack asks.

"Not butter!" someone says.

"Why not butter?"

"It's not butter. That's the whole point. You can't believe it, but it's *not* butter."

"I believe it," Petalia says.

Judge Harschly rubs his temples.

"How much, again?"

"Figure about two-hundred thousand," Dante says.

"Two-fifty!" someone shouts.

Applause.

"Three!" from the back.

"Three-five!"

The crowd cheers.

"I'll go four."

"Sold!"

Judge Harschly pounds the gavel. "Nope, nope, nope, *not* sold, *not* an auction. Mr. de Rosa, you've given us all a lot to think about. Thank you very much. I ask any of the council members, if you're *compos mentis* and you know it, clap your hands. And then make a motion to adjourn, for the love of God."

As we file out, Jenny says, "I'm going to pick up Wilky. He's with Marybeth and Sadie. Want to walk me?"

"For a bit," I say. "Are you Team Emollimax or Team I Can't Believe It's Not Butter?"

"I'm Team This is a Terrible Idea. It's embarrassing."

As we leave the crowd behind, it gets quiet in that summer-evening way, which is to say not actually quiet (crickets, again), but soft and sweet.

"You'll never guess what Tishy and I found."

She tells me about the 78s and the unlikely story of Arnold Falls' foray into chamber music. "You have to hear them, Jeebie. What we heard was beautiful."

"That seems more unlikely than being I Can't Believe It's Not Butter, NY."

"Agreed. Maybe mention it to Nelle. I'd love to get her take."

"Okay. What time should I come get Wilky tomorrow?"

"How about three? I have a 3:30 train," Jenny says.

"By the way, there's no charge for child-sitting, of course. But I assume parking ticket forgiveness is implied for, shall we say, a year?"

~

"HERE'S YOUR NINJA NINJATO, WILKY MY MAN," SOFIA says, setting down the drink in front of him on a cocktail napkin. Wilky and I are sitting at Argos' bar having an early dinner.

Wilky grins. "Thank you, Sofia."

The cocktail looks very much like a Shirley Temple, smartly rebranded.

"What is Uncle Will's surprise?" Wilky asks. "Will you tell me?"

"What do you think the answer to that is, Wilky?"

"I think...no."

"Correct. I wouldn't tell you if I knew, because it's a surprise. But I don't know either," I say.

Sofia hands me a glass of Txakoli, a bubbly Basque white wine that's nice in warm weather. "Do you gents know what you'd like?"

I look at Wilky.

"Hamburger, please."

"Penne alla vodka?" Sofia asks me.

"Yes, m'lady."

"Where's Will tonight?" Sofia asks as she pokes the order on the computer screen.

"He's at home working on some kind of surprise."

"His home?"

"Our...my...be gone with you," I say.

Sofia reaches over to rub my head.

After dinner, Wilky and I walk back from Argos. I look at

this happily chattering kid and think what a delight he is. Jenny's told me some of Wilky's history — that he was raised by his mother, who worked in the front office of a fancy resort. His mom was at work during the hurricane, he was sheltering at a neighbor's house, and the whole front of the hotel collapsed. Wilky was placed in a crèche, which is what they call an orphanage. His resilience and optimism are hard for me to comprehend.

"What do you think Uncle Will has planned for us?" I ask him.

"He said don't eat dessert. He makes dessert."

Will is not downstairs when we get home, but I hear him shout "in the back." Wilky zooms past me and out the screen door. He does a little jumping dance at what he finds: Will has built a firepit with paving stones and the fire is going strong.

"You've been busy!" I say.

"You don't mind, do you?" he asks.

"Of course not," I say. "It's great."

"Not as great as the s'mores we're going to be having. How was dinner?"

"Good," I say.

"As-way e-hay a ood-gay oy-bay?" Will asks me.

"Es-yay," Wilky says.

"Too smart, this one," Will says.

"What is s'mores?"

"My favorite dessert," Will says. "And we're going to make them together. Grab a stick."

Will has set out a whole mise en place with graham crackers, marshmallows, milk chocolate squares, and thin birch branches that he's apparently just whittled.

"Okay, Wilky. We're making s'mores which they call s'mores because you will want s'more."

Wilky smiles at this.

"They're like a sandwich, so just follow along with me."

And in no time, we are feasting on the gooey things. Three happy campers.

"How is it going with Sadie?" I ask.

"We're too young to get married," Wilky says with marshmallow all over his lips.

"Well, for now she can be your sister."

Wilky's face changes completely. His upper lip trembles.

"No," he says.

Will sits next to Wilky and puts his arm around him. "What is it?" he asks.

Wilky shakes his head.

"Tell us, Wilky," I say.

"Mirlande is my sister," he says.

"You have a sister?"

He shakes his head and tears stream down his face.

"She died."

"In the hurricane?"

"Before."

"Was she older or younger than you?" I ask.

"Three years older," Wilky says.

Will takes the s'more he's been working on and hands it to Wilky.

A minute passes. Wilky finally says, "Cancer. Leucémie."

"Leukemia?" Will asks.

Wilky nods.

"I lost a younger brother," Will says.

"À cause de?" Wilky asks.

"Drugs. Prescriptions drugs for pain."

Wilky hands him back the s'more.

"Let's share it," says Will.

"I love s'mores, Uncle Will," he says quietly.

Later, when Wilky is asleep, Will and I lie in bed talking.

"Why didn't Jenny tell us that Wilky had a sister?" I ask.

"I don't know. It's way, way too much for Wilky to take on," Will says.

"He's had to grow up too fast," I say.

"He's still a little boy."

"When I went in to say good-night to him, he told me how sad Mirlande had been in the hospital. Like he was the big brother."

"I'm so glad he's got Jenny," Will says.

"And us. Bridget wants to be a god-parent, too. Not sure *that's* a good idea. The kid's suffered enough."

"You are terrible," Will says. He kisses me.

"S'more," I say, of course.

Chapter Eight

"No! Oh, no!"

Trudy comes running out to the back porch. "What's the matter? Out of Clagger?"

"Martha!" Bridget says.

"Is she not well?"

"No, look!"

"Where's her mobcap?"

"It was there yesterday."

"You didn't wear it today?"

"No! I think it's been stolen!"

"Bridget, no one is in the market for a mobcap."

"*I* was."

"No one *else*. Although, now that I think about it, I did see that actress in *Merryvale*, the one who's playing a character supposedly like you..."

"I can not be imitated," Bridget says.

"True. But I watched a minute of filming this morning and she was definitely wearing a mobcap."

"I *am* a trendsetter. Do you think it was Martha's?"

"Doubtful that a production company would steal a costume."

"Two weeks ago there were zero mobcaps in Arnold Falls. And now there are *two*? Occam's razor. I will go to see that Fayette! I will not have Martha Washington disrespected."

"Oh, boy," Trudy says.

A short while later, Bridget arrives at Fayette's trailer and knocks on the door.

"Come in, DARling," she hears. When Fayette sees Bridget, she says, "Oh. I thought it was Trevor. Who are you?"

"I am Bridget Helen Roberts!"

"BRIDGET!" Fayette says warmly. "I have been dying to meet you. I'm Fayette. Come in! Sit."

"I'm here on behalf of the First Lady. *I think you know what I mean.*"

"Would you like some coffee or tea?"

"No, thank you."

"You're so lovely looking. BEAUTEOUS!"

This is not how Bridget expected the encounter to go. And her perfume is divine.

"I know you're one of the most sought-after agents in the theater," Fayette says.

"Sought-after? I don't...yes, well, I suppose you could say that."

"I just did! Please, sit down."

Bridget sits in the chair near Fayette.

"The writer, Alec Barnsdorf..."

"Yes, I know him," Bridget says.

"He says that the characters in *Merryvale* aren't based on real people in Arnold Falls. Only that he took the *flavor* from Arnold Falls."

"I *would* be a delicious seasoning," Bridget agrees.

"I know a BOUQUET GARNI when I see one! There's

so much I'd like to know about you, Bridget. I'm going to be called to the set soon, but let's get together, *entre nous.* Tomorrow's Friday. How about after-work? I'll be finished by six or so."

"We could meet at Argos," Bridget says. "That's the Joe Allen's of Arnold Falls. Right on High Street."

"Let's say 6:30 at Argos?"

Bridget stands up. "Yes, Fayette, see you then."

At that moment, there's a knock at the door and Trevor Aitken, the assistant director, walks in.

"Here you go, Fayette. Oh, hello, Bridget!"

"We were just having a lovely, little sit-down," Fayette says.

"We're going to need you in five. I had wardrobe wash the mobcap," he says, handing it to Fayette.

"That's my mobcap!" Bridget says.

"Giles saw you wearing it at the farmer's market and thought it would be great for Fayette's character."

"It belongs to Martha Washington. Did Giles steal it from my porch?" Bridget asks.

"No, Bridget," Trevor says. "Of course not."

"Then *she* must have stolen it!" Bridget says, pointing to Fayette. "I thought as much!"

"I did no such thing!"

"I *denounce* her!" Bridget says to Trevor, pointing at Fayette.

Fayette says, "Well! In my own trailer! I denounce *her*, in NO UNCERTAIN TERMS!"

"Trevor, Giles needs you," comes from Trevor's walkie-talkie.

"Please don't quarrel, ladies. No more denouncing. I'm sure we ordered the mobcap online."

After he leaves, Bridget says, "May I see it, please?"

Fayette hands over the mobcap. Bridget studies it carefully.

"Uh-huh. Mm-hm. Well, I see this is *not* the mobcap that belongs to Martha Washington. Shabby workmanship. It's a rather unlikely turn of events that you have a mobcap and I, at the moment, do not. However, I withdraw my denunciation."

"Tomorrow at Argos?"

"See you then," Bridget says, closing the trailer door behind her.

It's quiet when Nelle walks into the Chicken Shack, a lull between breakfast and lunch. She waves to Sal. He waves and points toward the back. Nelle finds Doozy sitting in a booth, wearing her Red Sox baseball cap, finishing a cup of tea.

"You look adorable in that cap. Who are they playing tonight?" Nelle asks.

"Orioles. Away game," Doozy says.

"What's the matter?" Nelle asks.

"Nothin'. Why?"

"Something."

"Okay, something," Doozy says.

"You want me to drive us?"

"I can walk," Doozy says, getting up from the booth.

"Back in a while, Sal."

"It's muggy," Nelle says as they walk to the museum. "So?"

"Shoulda said no to this whole idea."

"Why? It's going to be a wonderful tribute to Miss Georgia. What's wrong with that?"

"Nothing's wrong. The past is the past, that's all. I gave

them all them boxes of stuff about my mama. I don't know what it's in there. Never really went through it."

"Are you worried they'll find something about Miss Georgia you don't like?"

"Naw. She was the madam of a house. Not a lot of surprises after that. I know who she was. It's a lot of fuss."

Nelle isn't sure what to make of this.

"Many more people will get to know who she was. If there's something you don't like, just tell them and they'll change it. There's Darnell waiting for us."

Darnell Pressley hugs them as Doozy asks, "Why you not Chesty Biddle? She's more fun than you."

"I'm in business attire, Aunt Doozy," he says. "No drag at my day job. I'm excited for you to see what we've done."

They walk into the museum, where there are people preparing for the show's opening, a few weeks away. Theo Nyqvist comes over to greet them. Darnell says, "Theo is doing the construction and painting."

At the entrance to the exhibit, they pass a docent training tour, consisting of Petalia Jijanova and Marvin the Hobo, getting up to speed by a member of the staff.

Doozy looks up at the big sign over the door: Georgia on My Mind: The Life of Linah Alverett. Nelle puts her arm through Doozy's arm and they walk into the exhibit.

Darnell says, "Not everything is finished yet, Aunt Doozy. But this should give you a good sense of it."

"Dark in here," Doozy says.

They look up to the wall straight ahead where there is a large portrait of Miss Georgia.

"Where'd that come from?" Doozy asks.

"Theo painted it," Darnell says.

Doozy nods.

"The show is arranged more-or-less chronologically."

"How did you figure it all out?" Nelle asks.

"Aunt Doozy had so many boxes full of Georgia's letters and photos, a couple of diaries."

"Diaries?" Aunt Doozy says. "She didn't keep no diaries."

"She did," Darnell says. "We found two. Many years apart. She wrote very well, especially considering she didn't have any formal education. Shall we get started? Linah Alverett was born in 1904, in, or maybe near, Rutherfordton, North Carolina."

"Did she ever live in Georgia?" Nelle asks.

"No, she didn't," Darnell says.

"So why did they call her Miss Georgia?"

Doozy says, "I think she picked it. Sounded better than Miss North Carolina."

"Linah was born to John and Easter Kendrick. Or it could be Ester. It's written both ways. We know now that your grandfather wasn't just a sharecropper, as we assumed. He had a small printing plant."

"Yeah, I think he did," Doozy says. "And she was Easter."

"Okay, good. That settles that. This is the first photograph we have of Linah. She's probably twelve here. It's outside his shop."

"Look like a tomboy," Doozy says.

"I think you can see she's going to be a great beauty," Darnell says.

"Maybe," Doozy says.

"She probably worked in the fields with her mother or in the printing plant or both. Then, in June 1921, she leaves the South for good. Right after the Tulsa Massacre."

"Where'd you get that? They was nowhere near Tulsa."

"That's true. But it caused a lot of people to get the hell out of the South."

"In my family, too," Nelle says.

"Mine, too," says Darnell.

Doozy reads the summary on the wall.

"Could be, I guess," Doozy says. "She never talked about that."

"She spoke with her feet, Aunt Doozy. We know she got herself to Kingston, New York. She was only seventeen. This is just a guess, but there's a cousin named Grady who turns up a lot in the papers. We think she may have traveled with him. There was family in Kingston."

"Uncle Grady, that's right."

"The next year, 1922, Linah buys a house in Arnold Falls from a friend of the family for $550, almost nothing, even then. It was pretty run-down. On this wall is a photo of it as it was. Two years later, you join the world."

"Aunt Doozy! What's your given name? I have no idea!" Nelle asks.

"Harriet. Harriet Alverett. Don't even think about it." Doozy inspects the photo. "That's the house. Where she get the money?"

"That one I can answer. She says in a diary entry that she used the money her father gave her when she left. The diaries are over here in this case. We know that across the back alley lived John and Rose Delaney, who will give birth, in 1930, to —"

"Emma Rose!" Doozy says. "Glad she finally turned up."

"The bordello opened in late 1924 or early 1925 and stayed in business until the raid in 1958. The Valley Observer — it was called the Gazette then — ran pictures of the raid, and we have those, too. Lots of photos in the next room of the house and the ladies, even a few johns. One of Chester and you. A picture from 1944 at the Chicken Shack. Looking fine, Miss Doozy. The two rooms after that are all about the Great Northern Migration. Your mama was part of it, Doozy. It took courage to get out of the south. That journey out was full of danger.

"This wall has pictures of her with all kinds of folks, famous and every-day. Good Lord, she knew everybody! And over this way, some photos of Miss Georgia in the '80s and '90s, before her death in 1994. I love the one over here of the two of you."

"Yeah, that's nice," Doozy says.

"It's a wonderful exhibit," Nelle says.

"You did good, Darnell," Doozy says.

"So glad, and relieved. The last room isn't ready yet, so we'll leave that as a surprise, but I think you'll like it a lot. You'll be back for the opening?"

"I guess," Doozy says. "Past is the past but here it is again. It'll be in the past, too, 'fore you know it."

Nelle looks at Darnell and shrugs her shoulders.

FAYETTE AND BRIDGET ARE SEATED AT A TABLE BY ARGOS' large front window. Manny has just dropped off two Manhattans and Bridget continues her story about the time she saw a play in London and wept openly during the tragic second act in a theater full of Brits who did not condone such behavior.

"I broke the stiff-upper-lip law," Bridget says.

"How did you become an agent?" Fayette asks.

As Bridget speaks, Fayette is trying to get a read on her. Her character in *Merryvale*, Luba, is broadly sketched; Bridget has more shadows to her. A kindred spirit, maybe.

"Who's your agent?" Bridget asks.

"I have a lawyer. I don't use an agent. Or manager," Fayette says. "LONG story."

Fayette has a sudden urge to share that long story, but

she's distracted when she looks up to see *Merryvale*'s director, Giles Morris, walk into Argos, with his assistant director, Trevor. They stop by the table.

"So nice to see everyone getting along," Trevor says.

"Don't stir the pot," Fayette says.

"Are you having fun?" Bridget asks Giles.

Giles smiles. "Not as much fun as *Sound of Music* night."

"I'm available for day work," Bridget calls out as Giles and Trevor sit down at the far end of the bar.

"That young man makes a beautiful nun," Bridget says. "*I'd* date her."

Fayette asks what *Sound of Music* night was and Bridget explains about the rescue of the much-loved turkey Chaplin last November, Chaplin's unrequited feelings for Bridget, his public demonstrations of affection, and that unfortunate chase sequence on Thanksgiving morning. Fayette eats up every bit of it.

"I had no idea the turkey story really happened!" Fayette says.

"Chaplin and I are still good chums. Another thing you should experience," Bridget says, "is the Titleholders Parade on July 3, if you want to get a feel for the town. I have to ask you. What fragrance are you wearing? It's divine."

"It's called Persona. I just love it. Here, I always have a little travel vial of it. Take it."

"Thank you so much, Fayette!"

"Nothing at all. You mentioned Martha Washington. Was it really her mobcap?"

"'Might have been her mobcap' is what they said."

"But who would want it?" Fayette asks. "I mean, who would want to steal it?"

"That's just it. It's not in fashion, though I think the time is right for them to come back in style. I paid four figures for it."

"We must get to the bottom of this mystery!"

They clink glasses.

"I hear you're a sleight-of-hand artist? Is it true?"

Bridget hands Fayette a box of Throat Coat tea.

"I use it ALL the time! I have a box with me," Fayette says.

"This is your box."

"How did you do that?"

"I am Bridget Helen Roberts," she says, sipping her cocktail.

"Well, let me lift some ideas for my character. Show me what's in your bag?"

Bridget pulls out the stash. "Today, I have my wallet, house keys, a Magic 8-Ball, a packet of Corn Nuts, a sample of Witness Protection face cream, and my hail pail."

"I need to get a hail pail," Fayette says, picking up the hail pail and then the Magic 8-Ball. "Will I have an interesting time in Arnold Falls? Look! 'Signs point to yes.'"

"I could have told you *that*, Fayette," Bridget says merrily. "Fair warning about the face cream: it freezes your face for an hour."

"And what are these? Corn Nuts? Never had one. May I?"

"Yes, but they are —"

Too late. Fayette has popped a Corn Nut into her mouth.

Fayette gives a loud yelp. Argos gets quiet. Giles and Trevor run over to the table, Sofia comes from behind the bar. Manny hovers. Bridget can say only "tooth, tooth." Trevor and Giles escort Fayette out to Trevor's car.

After the commotion dies down, Bridget sheepishly pays the bill. After brief consideration, she puts the box of Coat

Throat tea Fayette has left on the table into her bag and walks out.

"I'M GETTING A PERMANENT CROWN IN THREE WEEKS. There's a temporary crown on now. They had to rearrange the shooting order for a couple of days. Thank you for the gladioli."

"You're welcome," Bridget says.

Fayette looks up at Trevor, who is leaning against the makeup table, looking at Bridget.

"Bridget," he says. "I'm sure you know now that Fayette didn't steal Martha's mobcap. The mobcap being used by the production is one we ordered from hoaryhats.com for $59.99.

"I know it's not the real one. I saw it when I was here last week. No craftsmanship."

"When we arrived on the set this morning," he continues, "the...let's call it the Merryvale mobcap...was missing."

"Are you accusing *me*? Well, that is a fine how-do-you-do! As if I were a...Well, I can see your point. I have a motive. And the skills. But I didn't take it."

"You did take my box of Coat Throat tea."

"You left it on the table."

"But you had already taken it from my bag," Fayette says.

"Technically."

Fayette sighs. "I'm afraid I have to denounce you again. *DE*-NOUNCE."

"Didn't anyone warn you about me?" Bridget asks.

"Everyone," Fayette says.

Bridget nods and walks out of the trailer.

Chapter Nine

❦

"And then she says, 'I'm afraid I have to denounce you again.' I denounced her first!"

Bridget is telling us the story of the missing mobcaps with her usual relish. We're sitting outside in our backyard, Will and I, Bridget and Trudy, having drinks before the inaugural firepit barbecue.

"Since when do you go around denouncing people?" I ask.

"When someone steals your mobcap, it's the least you can do. The point is, we don't need *Merryvale* interfering with Arnold Falls. We have enough to deal with. Imagine a character named *Luba*, chased by a turkey, dressed in a mobcap! If it weren't true it would be ridiculous."

"Not sure that logic parses," I say.

"You know what I mean," she says.

"I'm actually a little confused," Trudy says. "Someone took Martha's mobcap. It seemed like it might have been *Merryvale*, because now they have a mobcap, too. Or they had one. But both mobcaps are currently missing. Is that right, Bridget?"

"Right."

"So," Trudy continues, "neither of you took the other's mobcap."

"Right."

"Then who took the mobcaps?"

"And *why?*" adds Will.

"*Precisely! Exactement!* I see someone is using his little gray cells," Bridget says, in a flamboyant imitation of Hercule Poirot. "That is what I ask myself! *Pourquoi*, indeed!"

"Is there an answer to this? Because I'm getting hungry," I say.

"And something else doesn't sit right to me," Bridget continues. "A character that bears a lot of resemblance to me, without my permission."

"That's showbiz! You, of all people, should know that," I say. "What's the character's name again?"

"Luba."

"*Luba?* Well, anyway, for such things, your friend, Hercule, might recommend insouciance. Works for me."

Will puts the London broil on the grill.

"Do you know Tonda Tolay?" Bridget asks me. She asks it so innocently that I suspect an ambush.

"I've never met her. I saw her in the revival of *Dreamgirls*. She's great. Why?"

"I ran into her coming out of Fayette's trailer. It's her first day of shooting and she's playing one of the leads in *Merryvale*. From what she said, her character is a gay social worker and singer who loves Motown, and helps save the town from a cement factory."

"But that — that's like — that sounds like some freakish combination of Nelle and me!"

"That's showbiz. Try a little spritz of insouciance," she says, patting my cheek.

"I can deal with that."

"There's more," Bridget says. "Her character's name is Giblet."

Will bursts out laughing and I suddenly feel highly souciant.

Trudy says, "I think you should feel flattered, Jeebie."

"You mean *Giblet!*" Bridget says.

Trudy ignores her, turning to me. "You're part of the fabric here. That should make you feel good."

"We're a team. Luba and Giblet," Bridget says unhelpfully. "Corn on the coblet, too!" she says as Will puts the cobs on the grill. "A perfect summer dinner, Willet."

"What part of the fabric I am is a bit of a sore spot at the moment," I say to Trudy, ignoring everything that emanates from Bridget Helen Roberts.

"I think you need a project," she says.

Will looks up at me.

"You're right, Trudy. I thought AF should have little libraries and Theo is building four of them for the town."

"Wonderful, Jeebie. Good for you," Trudy says.

"I'm still mulling other ideas," I say.

Bridget says, "If you ever need any help getting to someone for something, my Rolodex is yours."

"Thank you, Bridget. That's very kind."

"Did you say you have some of that lovely Chianti?"

I did not say that. She really is a piece of work.

We enjoy the evening, almost as much Bridget enjoys the Chianti. After they leave, Will and I are cleaning up when he asks me,

"Everything all right?"

"Yes, fine. Why?"

"You're not upset about Giblet?"

"No, not at all. It's funny."

"You didn't eat much of the London broil."

It's probably the wine, but I suddenly have tears in my eyes.

"What is it?" he asks. He comes over and puts his arm around me.

"Minna."

"Minna? Oh. Minna, the cow you met."

"I don't...I couldn't. The corn and the salad were delicious."

"That's fine, Jeebs. It's okay."

I nod my head. We sit on the couch together quietly.

Will asks, "Do you want to stop eating meat?"

"I think so."

"Okay. I'll go vegan with you," he says.

"Really?"

"Yes, really," he says.

"Can we call it plant-based?"

"Sure."

"I don't know this Jeebie," I say.

"I do," he says simply.

I WAVE TO THEO NYQVIST AS HE PULLS UP IN HIS SUV (which, I probably don't need to tell you, is a Volvo). He bounds out of the car — blond, strapping, all that — with a big smile for me. He pops the hatchback and pulls out a little library cabinet and a long post.

"Built in record time, Theo. And it's beautiful!"

It really is beautiful. The first of the little libraries has a glass-paned door and stencils of birds perched on books and tree branches.

"Happy to do it. And I owed you anyway."

"For what?" I ask.

"You got me into Höôôs in Tribeca."

"That was nothing. Just a phone call. How did the date work out?"

"The food was great. No second date. I think she couldn't get over the fact that I used to perform in the circus."

"Her loss," I say and mean it. You see the problem right there. The Nyqvist conundrum. Insufferable as a general principle, yet Theo is charming, Nelle's happily dating his brother, Nils, and their mom, Susanne, is lovely, too, so it can be hard to stand on principle. I'll probably end up besties someday with Fridsy.

We're installing this first little library just off High Street by the sock monkey store, which is perfect because this one is for kids' books. Theo hammers the post into the ground and begins attaching the cabinet, as stringy-haired, chronically-disoriented, 3D-Roz-Chast-figure Petalia Jijanova walks toward the store.

"It's Sunday, Petalia. They don't open until noon."

"I need a sock monkey now," she says. "What are you doing?"

"We're setting up little libraries in AF. Theo built it — isn't it nice?"

"We have a library," Petalia says. "I heard they want to turn the parking garage into an art museum. I'm against that."

"Petalia, do you own a car?"

"No. Why?" she says.

"Then why...Never mind. The parking garage isn't changing."

"What are you turning the big library into?" she asks.

"We're not turning it into anything," I say.

"What a waste," she says.

I see Theo grinning, which is the only thing that stops me from strangling her.

In desperation I try, "Petalia, I think one of your cats might need you!"

"Which one?"

"I don't know which one."

"It's probably Squibbles. She wants a sock monkey. I'll just wait here until they open."

The good news is that Theo has finished with this library and we hop into his SUV to drive over for the second installation, leaving Petalia waiting for the sock monkey store to open. I ask what else he's working on and he tells me about the painting he just finished of Aunt Doozy's mother, Miss Georgia, for the upcoming exhibition.

"I hope Aunt Doozy liked it," he says.

"I'm sure she did, though Nelle said she's been a little cranky about the show."

"Nils told me the same thing," he says.

"I met your — whatever relation she is to you — Fridsy."

"She's a cousin once-removed. I think. I heard about Nelle's kulning performance. Nils said Fridsy took it pretty well."

"She did. Fridsy doesn't make a great first impression, to be honest."

"No, she doesn't," Theo says.

"But she's growing on me."

"That's good. I like her a lot," he says.

"And I'm smitten with Minna."

"Who's Minna?"

"Who's Minna! She's the mama cow. I feel a...I don't what it is...a strong connection with her."

"For real?"

"For real."

"She was studying me. And then she showered me with kisses."

"Cows are good judges of character," he says.

I look at Theo. Not a trace of snark on his face.

"Hey, if there's ever an Arnold Falls baseball team, Minna could be the mascot," he says.

"You mean if there's ever an I Can't Believe It's Not Butter baseball team."

He laughs. "Rolls right off the tongue. The next library is supposed to go at this corner, right?"

We spend the better part of an hour installing the other three libraries, including a stop for coffee. I ask Theo what else he's working on. He tells me that he wants to redo the welcome sign by the main entrance to the town, the one that used to say Welcome to Arnold Falls until about ten years ago when people started noticing that the letters A, R, L, and the D were slowly fading out. Eventually it was determined to have been a nitpicker (a nitpicker with sandpaper), making it clear that Arnold Falls does not have, and has never had, a waterfall. The sign now reads:

Welcome

to

no

Falls

After we're finished, he drops me back at my house with a cheery wave, a sweetheart from beginning to end, but don't quote me on that; I'll deny it. The rest of the day is taken up with getting the books I've collected so far into their new homes.

∾

"It's here," Nelle says when I answer my phone.

"I'll be right over," I say.

"You read my mind," Nelle says when I get to her apartment, eyeing the bottle of Chianti in my hand. "Did you —"

"I did. The distributor had to order more. Soon."

You'll remember that I owe Nelle the wine for calling the cows home.

"Which mattress did you end up going with?" I ask.

"The queen from Right Side of the Bed."

"Did you —"

"Yup, they took the old one," she says.

"I see we're using telepathy for our communication tonight. I sense you're ready for wine," opening the drawer where she keeps the corkscrew, then taking two wine glasses from the cabinet. As I pour, I ask, "How's work?"

"Three new cases at the end of last week, all difficult, which, before you say it, is the basis of social work. Maybe we can do some good with all of them, but not clear yet."

I say, "Cheers to giving it your best shot," and we clink. "Where —"

"Here," she says, opening the hall closet and dragging the box out.

"Do you have —"

"Drawer next to the sink. I like this game."

I get the scissors and begin cutting the packing tape.

"What's new with you?" she asks.

"I think I may be —" but I can't bring myself to say it, so I mouth it.

"My telepathy is cutting out. You may be what?"

I mouth it again.

"Going to Fiji?"

"Going vegan. Plant-based."

"Don't tell me," she says. "Minna!"

"Minna."

"That is very cool, Giblet," she says.

"It feels right."

I start pulling the plastic-wrapped bed-roll while Nelle holds the box.

"Theo and I installed the little libraries yesterday," I say.

"Nils told me," she says. "How do they look?"

"Beautiful. He always does beautiful work."

I cut the plastic and Nelle pulls it from the roll, putting it next to the front door.

"Wait 'til you see the painting he did of Miss Georgia for the exhibit," she says. "They did an amazing job of bringing her back to life. So much history."

"Speaking of history, Jenny wanted me to tell you about something she found."

"More?"

"Yes, please."

Nelle refills our glasses.

I tell her about the 78s from the Arnold Falls Chamber Ensemble.

"Any theories?" she asks.

"Bender's working on it. Jenny said the pieces were beautiful."

We carry the mattress into her bedroom and lay it on the frame.

"Test," I say.

We both lay down on it.

"Oh, yeah," Nelle says. "Yeah, baby!"

"That is comfy," I say, as we lay on our backs, staring upward. "You have a spider."

"Spiders are good."

"You're Giblet, too," I say.

"How am I Giblet?" Nelle asks.

"The character is a mix of you and me."

"Terrifying thought," she says. "Do you think you'll grow old here?"

"On your new mattress?"

"You know what I mean."

"I genuinely have no idea. Do you?"

"No, I don't know."

"What's got you thinking about this?" I ask.

"Aunt Doozy."

"Ah."

"And Wilky, too. Doozy was born in 1924. If Wilky lives to be the age she is now, it'll be the year 2103. Isn't that weird?"

"Yeah. Did you just work that out?"

"Last night when I couldn't sleep."

"Well, now you have a new mattress. Only thoughts of unicorns and daisies. It's in the warranty."

Chapter Ten

✤✤✤

Wilky is sitting on the window seat of Jenny's office on the second floor of City Hall, overlooking High Street. Jenny watches him from her desk — he's deeply engrossed in her iPad, wearing headphones that look larger than his head, listening to the audiobook of *Charlie and the Chocolate Factory* (taking a break from *Harry Potter*) — and thinks how peaceful he seems, like any kid with no particular history. She walks over and kisses him on the forehead. He smiles without looking up.

Tishy walks in and says, "You've got a busy morning."

"Mr. Emollimax and who else?"

"Mr. Emollimax, by the makers of Vaseline."

"Shoot me now," Jenny says. "I love today's outfit. What's it called?"

"Morse code," she says, sucking on a lozenge. "All curse words. Mr. Emollimax, by the makers of Vaseline, is in a few minutes. Archie the Fourth wanted to stop in, too."

"*Archie?* Why?!"

"He didn't say."

"Oh, no!"

"He's not so bad."

"It's not that. F— where's the f-word?"

Tishy points to the dots and dashes on her left shoulder.

"What's the matter?" she asks.

"I have to tell you something but you have to promise..."

"Jenny, you know me. Do I spill secrets?" she asks, chomping the remaining lozenge.

"You did on Rufus."

"Ungh. Higher purpose."

"Okay, but this is bad."

"What, did you kill someone?"

"Yeah, kind of," Jenny says, lowering her voice, glancing at Wilky, who remains hunched over the tablet. "Archie. Archie the first."

"You killed Archie?"

"Shhh!"

Jenny tells Tishy about her visit to AHA with Bridget.

Tishy says, "You don't know that you killed him. He died that week."

"That day."

"Well, he was 104. Fluke that he made it that long. Never ate a vegetable in his life. And Bridget did it, if anyone. You're just an accessory," she says, expelling a cough-drop splinter. "I almost forgot, the painters are starting this morning, too."

Jenny sighs.

"They're taping around the windows first."

"Tishy? What do you think we should do? The town wants a ball field."

"I want a pony," Tishy says, looking to the doorway. "Your ten o'clock is here. With a plus-one."

Jenny taps the f-word on Tishy's left shoulder.

"Good morning, Mayor," Dante says, walking in with Dubsack.

"Good morning." Jenny says. She raises her eyebrows at Dubsack.

"Sherpa," he says.

"That's my son, Wilky, lost in an iPad," Jenny says to Dante.

"Glad to finally have the chance to sit down with you, Mayor Jagoda," Dante says.

"Okay, sit down," Jenny says.

"I hope you've given some thought to signing the Emollimax, by the makers of Vaseline, agreement. It's a clear favorite around town —"

Jenny says, "You know, Mr. de Rosa, part of my job is to protect the things that make Arnold Falls Arnold Falls. A lot of the appeal to visitors is that our past remains part of our present, for good and for ill. And while we could do a lot of things with the money that's involved here, I'm not going to sign the agreement. I can't let Arnold Falls turn into some kind of comedy, not even for six months, not even for a quarter-million dollars."

Dante is about to respond when Dubsack says, "Say, Mayor, I heard you and Sticky Fingers McGee were the last people to visit Archie just before he went to his reward. Nice of you to visit him and all. His family and mine go way back. I know Archie would want you to keep an open mind about this contract."

Jenny looks at Dubsack and says nothing. She taps her pen on the desk. She looks out the window. After a few moments, she signs the agreement and hands it, stone-faced, to Dante and stands up.

Dante starts to speak, but Dubsack cuts him off, almost pushing him out the door.

"Pleasure doing business with you, Mayor," Dubsack says over his shoulder.

After they're gone, Tishy comes in with tea for Jenny.

"Thanks, Tishy."

"Strange bedfellows," Tishy says.

"I feel a little sick about this," Jenny says.

"What is tollboot?" Wilky asks, taking off his headphones.

"Tollbooth? You have them on highways. You pay at them to drive on the highway. Why?"

"Sadie's mother read it to her and she likes it."

"*Phantom Tollbooth*," Tishy suggests.

"I'll get it for you. How 'bout you read it to me?"

Wilky nods happily.

"Incoming," Tishy says.

Archie IV is standing at the doorway.

"Wilky," Tishy says. "Can you come help me for a few minutes?" He puts down the iPad and follows her out.

"Come in, Archie. I'm so sorry for your loss. Come in, sit down."

"Thanks, Mayor. He was one-of-a-kind."

Jenny braces herself.

"I heard you and Bridget were the last to see my great-grandpa alive. Wish I could have been there to give him a shot of Clagger to send him on his way. That's what he would have wanted."

"Is this a setup with you and Dubsack? I just signed it."

"Huh? Signed what? What's Dubsack got to do with anything? His family and my family aren't on what you call speaking terms. Not for years."

"So you meant what you said about a shot of Clagger?"

"Definitely! You know what he was like."

"There might have been...a little Clagger involved."

"Yes! Psyched to hear that! Couldn't bear to think of a dry

send-off. Can you picture his last drink is a glass of milk or juice? That would have killed him!"

He laughs and Jenny smiles uncertainly.

"He probably shoulda gone out like Elbridge Bartlett's Farewell Wassail, but you don't always get to pick your swan song. Listen, I've been looking through his stuff for anything on gumball. I did find one thing."

He hands a sheet of paper to Jenny.

"The Dugout!" Jenny says. "He kept saying something about the dugout, that you drink in the dugout. Now I get it! They wanted a pub at the baseball field, called The Dugout!"

"Not really surprising," Archie says. "A little beer and Clagger to pump up the crowds."

"Painters are here," Tishy shouts from her desk.

Three guys come in. One says, "Sorry to disturb you, Mayor. Just taping the windows. We'll be out quick."

Jenny's eyes land on the painter with the bushy beard.

"Aren't you, excuse me, aren't you the hermit?"

"Marvin the Hobo," he says.

"But..."

"Was a hobo, now a hermit. You people are fixated on this."

"By what stretch of the imagination are you actually a hermit? You're here in my office, working as a painter."

"Much virtue in work. You politicians don't get that. It's not cheap being a hermit. Now, if you don't mind, I'll get back to some character-building work," he says, taping a window.

"Well, I gotta be off," Archie IV says.

He shakes Jenny's hand.

"Thanks, Archie. Really glad you stopped by."

"I'll give you a shout if I find anything more."

Tishy brings Wilky back into the Mayor's office. "Tell her, Wilky!"

"Me and Tishy talk —"

"Tishy and I were talking..."

"Tishy and I were talking and she ask me if we play base-ball at home. Other home. I tell about vitilla."

"Go on, honey," Jenny says.

"It's a game on the street."

Jenny googles it as she asks, "What kind of ball?"

"From the top of a big water bottle."

"Really? How about the bat?"

"The stick of escoba."

"Broomstick," Tishy says. "Googled it. Sounds like Quidditch."

"How many bases?"

"Home base and first base and third base," Wilky says.

"No second base?"

"No."

"Weird. I like that. Oh my God, this sounds so Arnold Falls! Ah, I see," Jenny says, looking at the screen. "So the top of the water bottle is like a big cap."

Wilky nods.

"You are the best Wilky!" she says, going over to hug him.

"Chicken Shack? Can we?" he asks.

Jenny nods.

Tishy clears her throat.

"You, too, Tishy. Lunch is on me."

The painters look at Jenny. "Maybe tomorrow, guys."

TRUDY LOVES SEEING PICTURES OF BRIDGET AS A YOUNG girl, even then brimming with mischief in her eyes. Bridget has told her that her adoptive parents had always been kind to her and so never had much interest in her biological family history. When Jenny adopted Wilky, though, and Bridget spent time with that lovely, little boy, it brought a lot of questions to the surface. The DNA test was part of her effort to learn more.

"Read it to me again," Trudy says.

Bridget reads the letter in her hand.

Dear Ms. Roberts,

Thank you for your participating in Begat's DNA testing service. Our mission is to offer insights into your past through our robust DNA database.

As noted in our previous letter to you, we are unable to furnish you with test results. Initially, we thought that the sample was canine or feline DNA and, as I mentioned, we do not test dogs or cats at this time. Nor do we have offer testing for non-homo-sapiens primates. Our algorithm compares your DNA to the data sets we use as reference. In your case, the results were anomalous enough that they were flagged both times.

After the second run, a researcher took a closer look and she believes you may be descended from the Denisovans, a group of hominins, previously thought to be extinct. Are your molars especially large? That's very Denisovan. In any case, we have refunded your testing fee and wish you good luck from your friends at Begat.

Your sincerely,

Edward W. Foley

Begat DNAmbassador

"I'm sure it's just a mistake," Trudy says.

"It's upsetting," Bridget says. "I don't have human emotions!"

"Oh, don't cry, sweetheart," Trudy says. "You're still the same wonderful, irrepressible woman I married."

"Am I?" Bridget says, blowing her nose. "I need to read about the Denisovans."

"It probably explains a lot about why you are...the way you are," Trudy says. "It's just an added dimension. It makes you even more special."

Bridget grins at this, then dissolves into girlish giggles.

"You're right! I'm a Denisovan! Not like you common sapiens."

Trudy starts laughing, too. "Coming soon, my new book: *I Married a Denisovan*."

"Check my teeth! My molars! I think they *are* on the large side!" Bridget uses a finger to pull back her cheek skin. "Look, how are they?"

"Huge! Enormous! Bridget! That's why you can eat Corn Nuts!"

This strikes them as funny all over again, and they fall into the sofa, laughing at the way of the world.

THE BACK DOOR TO THE COURTHOUSE TAKES ONLY SECONDS to crowbar open. Except for illuminated exit signs, the building is completely dark. There is no camera system to worry about, as a previous scouting had revealed, so the burglar switches on a small flashlight and walks up the steps onto the main floor hallway.

Listening intently and hearing nothing, the hooded figure points the flashlight at each door. The target is somewhere in this long hallway, but all the doors look alike so the flashlight illuminates each nameplate until it stops on the one that reads Honorable Lionel Harschly.

All that's needed for entry is a screwdriver, which the thief produces, quickly gaining entry to the office and, a few moments later, into the judge's inner chamber. The desktop has several books on it and two framed photos, but is otherwise clear.

Top left drawer? No. Top right? Yes, there it is. Into the bag.

Using the same route in reverse, the intruder exits the building into the warm, summer night.

JENNY HAD SEEN ONE OF THE FLYERS AROUND TOWN FOR Arnold Falls' first hot yoga class. Key points: Hester "Chesty" Biddle (aka Darnell Pressley, from the Red Light Museum) would be the instructor and the series was called Chat N Stew. Jenny was in.

So here she is in the boiler room of the courthouse basement early on Monday morning, unrolling her yoga mat, greeting her fellow Chat N Stewers — about a dozen people for this first class. Jenny's priorities are refreshingly unambiguous these days. Number one by a mile, take care of Wilky. Number two, her job as mayor. A distant third, take care of herself. Chat N Stew is her first stab at the third priority in months.

It's so hot in here, warming up seems unnecessary but she does it anyway. As she stretches her head to the right, someone comes and sits down to her left. When she stretches her head to the left, she sees it's Dubsack.

"Nice leggings," Jenny says.

"I got nice legs," Dubsack says.

"Why are you here?"

"Doctor's orders," he says.

"What's wrong with you?"

"Little this, little that."

"High blood pressure? Guilty conscience?" Jenny asks.

"Decline to answer."

"Who's your doctor?"

"Jantzen."

"*Jantzen?* He's an infectious disease specialist."

Dubsack shrugs. "I get a discount."

"Good morning, everyone," Chesty says. "Welcome to the first Chat N Stew. I'm going to finally answer the *burning* question of whether hot yoga and drag mix. Meanwhile, let's all have some fun. This class is going to be pretty loose, chatting is encouraged, just please set your phones to vibrate. Not great cell service here anyway. We'll leave the door open so the carbon monoxide can escape.

"Let's begin. Stand in the center of your mat. Feet together, toes and heels touching. Interlace your hands under your chin. Now, we're going to start with a deep breathing pose. And here we go. Deep breath in the nose...drop your head back, long, slow out."

After a few breaths, Jenny says during an exhale, "Even though I signed the agreement, I happen to know that you and Archie's family haven't spoken for years. I also know that Archie IV was happy that Clagger was involved in his great-grandfather's sendoff."

"Time for some balancing," Chesty says. "Feet together, toes and heel touching. Body weight on your left leg. Right thigh up, parallel to the floor, now grab your foot. Get that leg up there and grab the bottom. Hold that foot."

"Too bad you didn't know that before you signed it," Dubsack says as he struggles to keep his balance.

"If I were you, I'd watch my step," she says, giving him a quick shove. He tumbles over.

After he rights himself, he looks at Jenny and does a little bow. "Namaste."

"All right, now it's time to move on to triangle pose," Chesty says. "Arms up over your head, right foot steps out to your right, big step. Hips forward, bend your right knee, left hand stretching upward."

Jenny is facing the door and sees Judge Harschly march by. He stops and walks to the boiler room doorway.

"*Gavel?*" he asks sharply.

"Hot yoga," Chesty says.

He storms off.

Just then, Jenny's phone vibrates. She looks at it and says to Dubsack, "Tishy texted that Judge Harschly's gavel was stolen. Sounds like something you'd do."

"Now bend your right knee, right hand stretching upward."

"Definite no. Sounds like one of the thefts going around," he says, grunting.

"What thefts going around?"

He tells her about the Schlitz sign stolen from the Elks and the Princess phone missing from Argos.

"Not the powder-blue Princess!"

"Deepest sympathies."

"No one told me about this."

"Check into the mobcaps, too," says the woman behind them. Jenny turns.

"I'm with *Merryvale*. Our mobcap is missing, and so is the one belonging to — I forget her name."

"Bridget," Jenny says. "What the hell is going on?"

"Now let's get into a Supta Vajrasana. You start by sitting between your heels, knees together, your feet facing up. Hands holding your feet, lower your back. Go slow with this one."

"Sadist!" Dubsack says to Chesty, sweat dripping on to his mat.

"My pleasure is your pleasure," she says.

Jenny skips the pose, sitting for a moment, and wonders why anyone would take Judge Harschly's gavel. Senseless crimes have a whole different meaning in Arnold Falls, she thinks, mopping her forehead.

Chapter Eleven

❧❀❧

"**D**arlene veggie burger for me, please, and fries with vinegar."

"Veggie burger?! Who *are* you?!" Jenny asks.

Jenny wanted to meet me across the river at Darlene's to discuss some development that she didn't specify.

"I know. Talk to Minna."

"Who's Minna?"

"My new cow pal."

I explain my experience at Fridsy's a couple of weeks ago.

"Good for you. I'm trying to eat less meat, too. What about cheese?"

"Cheese is a struggle. Addictive."

"Tell me about it," Jenny says.

"How's my godson doing?"

"He's so easy it makes me nervous."

"He'll have his moment when he's a teen."

Jenny fills me in on Wilky's suggestion for vitilla.

The waitress brings us our iced teas.

"Have you given up on gumball?" I ask.

"I killed Archie," Jenny says.

Unfortunately, I'm taking a sip of iced tea and there's no choice but to do an actual spit-take.

As I mop it up, Jenny explains her trip with Bridget to see Archie at AHA.

"Okay, you didn't kill him," I say. "At worst, some questionable judgment. Look, if Archie IV is fine with it, you should be, too. Is that why you asked me to lunch? To confess to murder? You know I'll dime you out."

"No. There's something going on that's weird."

"Weirder than killing Archie?"

She brings me up to speed on the series of burglaries: Bridget had told me about the mobcaps but the Schlitz sign, the powder-blue Princess phone, and Judge Harschly's gavel are news to me.

"Judge Harschly's gavel? That's poking the bear," I say.

"It's bizarre," Jenny says. "What do you make of it?"

"The obvious suspect is Bridget, since purloining is her pastime. But this doesn't sound like Bridget at all. Plus, why would she steal Martha's mobcap?"

"For attention?" Jenny asks. "Munchausen by proxy?"

"I'm not a doctor, but I doubt taking a mobcap from your own mannequin fits the clinical definition."

"Well, what then?"

Suddenly, I remember Nelle's comment about Fridsy being a 'keeper of customs.'

"One thing that occurs to me..."

The waitress brings over our lunches. I take a bite of my veggie Darlene burger expecting the worst. It's delicious.

"The thing is that they're all part of Arnold Falls. Little bits of Arnold Falls," I say, as two chickpeas drop from my sandwich onto the plate.

"You mean, little bits of Emollimax, by the makers of Vaseline."

"You didn't!"

"I did," Jenny says. "I'll tell you about that in a minute."

"Okay. Well, all I can think is that the objects have value to people here. They're tangible things that differentiate Arnold Falls from, say, Blue Birch Corners. Part of the local character. Does that make sense?"

"Kind of," Jenny says. "I can't understand, though, who would want to steal them. What would you *do* with them? And Judge Harschly is *pissed* about his gavel."

"Something with *Merryvale*?" I ask. "That's a whole show that tries to portray a version of Arnold Falls' world. Though that doesn't make a lot of sense. Why would they steal stuff?"

"More to come, huh?" Jenny asks.

"Yeah," I say. "Seems likely."

"We can't put cameras everywhere," she says. "I'm not sure what to do about this."

"What does Chief Williams say?"

"He doesn't think it's a high priority." Jenny says.

"We need a honey pot."

"A lure?"

"Right," I say. "Let me think about it."

"Are you eating dessert?" Jenny asks.

"Oh, yeah."

We order strawberry-mint doughnuts and coffee.

MERRYVALE WAS SCHEDULED TO FILM AT NOON IN THE northern end of the Farmer's Market lot, so the market has shut down early. That gives us an early start for Fridsy's farm and gives Will the chance to meet Minna (and Fridsy). I've warned Will about Fridsy's chip and he's come armed with strawberries for her and apples for the cows. Nelle's looking forward to some serious kulning, seeking help from Minna and family to narrow down the song selections for her album.

We're discussing the perplexing string of burglaries as we pull into the farm — what possible reason anyone would have to go after mobcaps and Judge Harschly's gavel and all the rest — when Will says suddenly, "You didn't tell me it was clothing optional."

The conversation stops. After a moment, we realize what he means: there is Fridsy, sitting in a rocking chair on her porch, without a stitch of clothing. Starkers. When she sees us, she jumps up, awkwardly Charleston-flapping, and scurries inside.

"I didn't notice her chip," Will says.

In seconds, she's back outside, clad in a peony-print kimono, no trace at all of embarrassment. I introduce Fridsy to Will.

"I like your kimono," he says.

"It's a yukata," she says.

"What's that?"

"It's similar to a kimono but it's less formal and you wear it in summer. I picked it up years ago in Tokyo when I was flying."

"You were a *stew?*" I ask.

"Yes, I was with SAS for about ten years."

"I bet you were a party girl," I say, not believing that at all.

"Yes, I *was* quite the party girl," she says. "Almost got fired several times."

"I bet you were a *rocking* party girl," Nelle says.

"Yes, true," Fridsy says.

I'm shuffling the pieces of Fridsy in my mind to take in this new info. Something else is different about her.

"I have some lingonberry kombucha that's just ready. Would anyone like some?"

We go into the kitchen and she pours for us. Oh, I know: her hair isn't pulled back.

Nelle takes a sip and says, "That's delicious. Fridsy, would you be willing to give the kulning demonstration, the real thing, to Will?"

Fridsy agrees, picks up her cello, and we head off to the big field. The cows are down by the pond again.

"It's early in the day, so they won't be eager to come home."

"That's okay," Will says. "I'd just like to know what it sounds like."

"The cello is my jam, not traditional," she says, taking the instrument from the case.

Her *jam*? I wonder if we're being pranked. Maybe Fridsy has a twin sister, a chip-less double who was a party-girl stew and likes to hang out naked on her porch.

"I listened to a few YouTube videos," Will says, "but it was hard to get a sense of it."

"*YouTube!*" she scoffs. "No place for a kulning education. Listen."

That has a Fridsy ring to it.

Just as it unfolded last time, Fridsy creates an ethereal sound with her voice and cello, only this time, the cows dutifully stroll back toward the barn. Will looks entranced.

Fridsy stops suddenly and says, "That's how it's done. Traditionally. Nelle has a different way."

"Are they working cows?" Will asks.

"Working!"

There's a sputtering sound, like a car trying to turn over. And now we know what Fridsy laughing sounds like.

"No, no. Minna wouldn't *dream* of doing a day's work. Anyway, I don't want working animals. I want a sanctuary for them."

Nelle asks, "You mean like one of those sanctuaries for unwanted animals?"

"Yes. Exactly. But I'd need help if I took in more animals and it gets expensive with all the food and vet visits. Well, maybe someday. Come on. Let's work on your album."

"How do you know if they like a song?" Will asks.

"You'll see. They can't stand Justin Bieber."

"I'll show you," Nelle says to Will. She sings a few lines of "Beauty and a Beat" again and the cows begin walking back toward the pond. Then she tries out "The Power of Love" and the cows bleat loudly. Celine Dion is a no.

"Maybe they don't like Canadians," I point out.

"I'll bet they'd like Joni Mitchell," Will says.

"Sing 'Help Me,'" Fridsy says.

And sure enough, the cows have a change of heart and hang on every note.

Nelle pulls out the list of songs from her bag and says, "Okay, Minna, and all you guys. This is the list."

She starts with "Grazing in the Grass," which the cows bop along to, or maybe I'm just imagining it. I sit down near them, and think about what Fridsy wants to create.

I feel Minna's lick on my arm when we were here last time, and her eyes watching, *observing*, me. Fridsy is stretched out on the grass, her head resting in her hand. Will is soaking in Nelle's voice, and looking to the cows for their reactions. The sun is warm on the back of my neck. It would be wonderful if this farm were a sanctuary. As I listen to Nelle and look at Will and Fridsy and Minna, it occurs to me that, in a way, it already is.

After she finishes the song, Nelle makes a note on her paper that must say something like 'cows pleased.' I love that about Nelle, very diligent and organized in her pursuits. She goes through the songs she's considering, giving each at least one chorus.

A butterfly sails past and I think, well, someone is laying this on a bit thick: now we're in a Disney movie. But during "Lean on Me," Minna lets out a big cow fart, and I realize we're not. Nelle laughs, stops, and crosses the song off her list. When Nelle finishes pasture-testing the maybes, we have an after-party in the field, just four humans and seven cows, apples and strawberries.

I get Minna to myself for a moment, so I ask her if she'd like to share the farm with other animals. She licks my arm again. Without thinking it through, I ask Fridsy if *she'd* be open to the idea of a fundraiser to create a sanctuary, and she says yes.

Oh, God, I knew it! Didn't I tell you? Just like that. Now I'm friends with Fridsy. What is happening to me?

"WHAT ARE YOU DOING?"

"I'm in the car with Will and Nelle, on my way back from Fridsy's farm. It's the mayor," I say to my fellow passengers.

"Come right now to the Elks," Jenny says.

"Really?"

"Just come."

Ten minutes later, I darken the Elks' doorway.

Jenny's at the bar and I take the seat next to her. I say hello to Rufus, who is on the other side of Jenny, and to Mange, with his flourishing mustache, the Exalted Ruler of the Elks (also its bartender).

"What are you drinking?" Mange asks.

"Bud, please," I say. When in Rome and all that.

"We came up with an idea to lure the thief," Jenny says.

"We want our Schlitz sign back," Mange says. "No questions asked. Although I got a question. What kind of dirtbag would steal our sign?"

"It wasn't Dubsack, if that's what you're thinking," Rufus says to me.

"Why would I suspect Dubsack?" I ask.

"No reason. He wanted the sign, is all I'm saying," Rufus says.

"So, using the idea you had of a lure," Jenny says, "this is what we thought: Bridget wears a new mobcap during the Titleholders Parade."

"We're fresh out of mobcaps, Jenny."

"I know. Coming to that. Bridget wears the mobcap during the parade and then we put Martha, with mobcap, on the steps of City Hall to honor the Fourth of July."

"How does that help?" I ask.

Rufus says, "Here's where I come in. This thief likes mobcaps. We know that 'cause he's ripped off two of them. So I'm the night watchman. I'm across the street that night. I'll see who the perp is, write down their name, and give it to Chief Williams in the morning. Pretty good, right?"

"Okay, well. Worth a try, I guess. What do you want me to do?"

Jenny says, "Your wardrobe mistress friend, the one who works on Broadway shows..."

"Preston. What about her?"

"Could she whip up a mobcap?"

I'm not sure this plan has been well thought through. "Why not the costumers on *Merryvale*?"

"They're not allowed to do outside work when they're in production."

"A likely story." I pick up my phone and call Preston Davis

and ask about her mobcap chops. She agrees to knock one out, peach that she is, and overnight it to me.

"My work here is done," I say, finishing my Bud.

Jenny nods her head to Mange and he pours another for me.

"Not quite," Jenny says. "Bridget doesn't want to be in the parade."

"She loves wearing the mobcap."

"It's not that. She says she's sworn off parades after the chase scene with Chaplin last Thanksgiving."

"Even for Bridget, that is ridiculous. Such a drama queen," I say as I call her. "What's this about not walking in the Title-holder's Parade? Uh-huh. Uh-huh. Yes. Right. Okay. Yup. Okay." I put the phone down. "She'll walk."

"How did you do it?" Jenny asks.

"She loves my Chianti."

"I think the town could reimburse you for the bottle."

"Not bottle. Case."

THE BEST PLACE TO WATCH THE TITLEHOLDERS PARADE, MY favorite of Arnold Falls' many parades, is near the stand where Judge Harschly emcees the event. That way, you get to hear not only the titleholder's claim, but also Judge Harschly's asides, which get less *sotto voce* every year. We're sitting on the curb, Nelle to my left, Will to my right; I'm in the middle of the happiest s'more sandwich I can imagine.

As a parade, the concept couldn't be simpler: if you have any distinction, any kind of title, earned, honorific, self-iden-tified — anything whatsoever, no matter how loosey-goosey — you, too, can march down High Street with your fellow titleholders. It started in 1930 as a pick-me-up during the

Great Depression and the parade route has always been the same: two blocks long. You're announced at the front end and you're applauded by the spectators and fellow titleholders at the back end. Confetti — sparkly these days — is the projectile of choice.

I see Fayette and Trudy take a spot on the sidewalk across the street and I wave to them as Judge Harschly leans into the microphone: "Hello and all of that. It's July 3 and here we are again, as luck would have it, celebrating Arnold Falls' *many* overachievers." Under his breath: "*Judge Harschly is struck by lightning.*"

"And so I proclaim the start of the 88th Annual Titleholders' Parade!"

He picks up a stack of index cards and reads from the first: "Kicking things off, we have Jenny Jagoda, proudly marching as the First Female Mayor of Arnold Falls, with her son, Wilky."

We whoop it up for them.

"Jenny rocks!" Nelle shouts. "Wilky rocks!"

"Bringing a daily *spark* of life to City Hall, Arnold Falls' Most Fashion Forward, Tishy Mustelle. Tishy is wearing a fetching, red-and-black jump suit, made of jumper cables, helping her power through the day."

Lots of cheers.

"It wouldn't be a parade without Bunny Liverwurst, the Last of the Liverwursts. (*She'll clean your clock at the poker table. A ruthless woman.*)"

Bunny calls over to Judge Harschly: "I heard that. And you still owe me thirty bucks."

"Moving on, a perennial favorite, Rufus Meierhoffer, Winner of a School Science Day Project, 1993 (*SMH, as the kids say*)."

"Next, Dr. Emil Jantzen, CMO of Queechy General, the

196th Best Hospital in the State of New York (*slipping again this year and absolutely no sense of shame*)."

Someone down the block blows a vuvuzela.

That's a big decline for QGen. Can that be? Judge Harschly's right. Dr. Jantzen shouldn't be marching to announce that his hospital is one of the worst in the state.

"The *New York Times* called the Chicken Shack's fried chicken the best north of the Mason-Dixon line, but we all know it's the best anywhere. Representing the Shack, Aunt Doozy!"

Long, sustained cheers.

"And here he is again this year, Ouch Macgillicuddy, for the most times charged and brought before yours truly. Hello, Ouchie. (*Stunning incompetence as a crook. Couldn't break his way into a paper bag.*)"

"Go Ouchie Mac!" someone shouts.

"Please welcome Bridget Roberts, who holds two titles this time out. She not only has the Largest Collection of Air Sickness Bags in Queechy County, but she is also Arnold Falls' Dame of Mobcaps. Today, she's wearing a special, monogrammed edition that belonged to Martha Washington. You can see it up close through the holiday when Martha graces the steps of City Hall in her millinery finest."

"Enjoy the Chianti!" I shout. Bridget doffs the mobcap.

"A new entrant for 2018, please welcome Marvin the Hobo, Arnold Falls' First Hermit-in-Residence. Follow him on Instagram, TikTok, and Snapchat, @MarvinTheHobo. (*Yes, ladies, he's single.*)"

"Beloved by just about everyone in Arnold Falls, a rare accomplishment in itself, give it up for Chaplin, the first turkey in Queechy County to complete the therapy turkey course."

Crowd goes wild as Chaplin struts his way down High Street.

Judge Harschly flips through the index cards. (*Only a couple dozen more to go unless a hailstorm grants us clemency.*)

After the parade, we mingle with the sparkle-covered Titleholders and I seek out Jenny while Will and Nelle are chatting.

"Did QGen really drop to 196th?" I ask.

"Yup. From 127th three years ago."

"How many hospitals are in the state?"

"Two hundred and fourteen."

I knew Jenny would know that.

"Does QGen have a pediatric oncology unit?"

"Yes. Why are you asking?"

"Because I just had an idea. Do they have any music or arts program or anything like that? Where artists come in and perform?"

"I don't think so. Not any more. What brought this on?"

"Wilky."

"Oh."

"He told us about Mirlande. He said how sad she was in the hospital."

"He's talked about her more with you than he has with me."

"Well, we sort of stumbled into it. The point is, it would be unconscionable that with all the artists and performers around here, if there weren't a program for them."

Jenny scans the crowd for Dr. Jantzen. "He must have left. Let me call him."

As she calls, I watch Chaplin on a collision course with Bridget. Duncan and Marybeth have told me that Chaplin is still pining for Bridget, but pointedly ignores her whenever he sees her. Poor guy's pride is wounded. But Bridget doesn't like to be ignored, so when he walks right past her, she says, "Hel-looooo, handsome tom."

That's all he needed. He zooms back toward her, emitting exceedingly loud gobbles, Bridget gives out a loud yelp, and they're off, gobbling and whooping down to the river.

"No. I just spoke with Jantzen. No arts program at the current time," Jenny says to me.

I am speechless.

Will and Nelle walk over to us.

"Come on," Nelle says. "I want to show Will that meadow we found when we took a walk near Arnmoor, remember?"

"Of course," I say. "Okay. You coming with, Mayor?"

"Nah, I've gotta get back to my desk. That reminds me, though. I need to have a structural engineer inspect Arnmoor. That old loony bin is being held together by its ghosts. And I have to make sure Martha makes it safely to the front of City Hall. Anyway, have fun," she says.

We walk up High Street toward the northern end of town, stopping to chat with various and sundry. As we pass the cross-street where the sock monkey store is, I look over to the little library Theo installed. It's now tagged with graffiti and the door's been ripped off, smashed into pieces.

I'm speechless for the second time. And sucker-punched.

Without a word, we go to check on the three other little libraries. Two are fine; one has been tagged and the books are strewn on the ground.

"Why would they make people so angry?" I ask.

"Jeebie, honey," Nelle says. "It was a good idea. It's just that not everyone needs books. Sometimes they need money, food, a job. And they're pissed off. And it's not the answer they're looking for. And they feel like people don't under-stand their world."

"You're defending them?" I ask.

"No, baby. I'm not. I'm just saying it's not personal, even if it feels that way."

"Okay," I say, not sure if I mean okay or not.

Will says, "Minna needs you."

"For what?"

"She needs some new companions."

"The sanctuary, you mean."

Will nods. "Just think, lots of new animals for her to hang with. Less Fridsy, more friends."

I finally smile. "Definite upgrade. And did you know that Queechy Gen has no arts program — nothing — for the kids with cancer?"

"That's a disgrace," Nelle says.

"It's fixable," I say, picking up the books scattered on the grass.

THAT NIGHT, WHEN WE'RE ALL TUCKED IN, WILL TAKES out his phone and begins typing.

"What are you doing?"

"Mind your business," he says.

"Tell me."

"I'm going to run off with the FBI guy I dated that one time."

"Not Ash Plank!" I say.

"Oh, yes, Ash Plank! I am going to ask him to marry me," he says, taking his pillow and gently smothering me with it while I shake with the giggles.

Chapter Twelve

Fridsy is laying on her beloved, old waterbed, reading the second book in the *My Brilliant Friend* series, when her phone beeps. She's on two dating apps and figures it's someone hitting her up, but it turns out to be from Jeebie's boyfriend.

Dear Fridsy,

Thank you so much for letting us hang out at your farm and for introducing me to the beautiful tradition of kulning. The farm is really a special place and if you do turn it into a sanctuary, it will be great. That's why I'm writing: Jeebie is excellent at pulling off events like the benefit idea he had. But he may need a little coaxing to get him going. Flattery works wonders with him :)

Will

Putting down her phone, Fridsy nods several times, the bed bouncing along as she does. That is a good boyfriend.

RUFUS IS SITTING ON THE FOLDABLE CHAIR HE'S BROUGHT from home, under the low-hanging awning of Winstian

Antiques. He's dressed in dark gray sweats and a black t-shirt for his night watchman gig. I'm rocking the special ops vibe, he thinks. "Lookin' dangerous, Rufus! Seal Team Stud!" is how he imagines the compliments will go.

The fireworks for the Fourth at the waterfront have been over for half an hour and High Street has cleared out. Rufus glances across the street at his charge and decides Martha's code name will be Hoochie Mama. If he can catch the thief of Hoochie Mama's mobcap, the Elks will probably get their Schlitz sign back, and he'll be the club hero for years, and probably mayor again in a landslide, and, who knows after that, but Governor Meierhoffer sounds pretty good.

He puts on his headphones, connected to a small, old-school radio. The Dodgers-Pirates game is in the third inning and he settles back in the chair. Dodgers are up, three-two. A few minutes go by when he sees Jim Ebbens across the street, admiring Hoochie Mama. Guy who raises chickens and ducks into all these crimes? Nah. Ebbens continues up High Street without looking back or doing anything Rufus considers suspicious. He writes down Ebbens' name anyway.

The pitcher for Pittsburgh was throwing some wild balls at the bottom of the fourth; still, the score's the same at the top of the fifth. Wait, what's this, what's this? Someone with suspicious hair is walking slowly by the City Hall steps. He/she passes, stops, and walks back. Rufus pulls off the headphones and his chair squeaks. Damn. The person looks over. That hair, kinda stringy. It's that chick, weird name. She's walking over. He writes down: 'hair, coming over.'

"You look sketchy sitting there," she says.

"I — What are you doing on High Street at —" he looks at his watch — "nine-forty at night? I know you. You're always at the town meetings asking stu—, asking questions."

"I'm Petalia Jijanova."

He writes down 'Name: Polly Something.'

"I used to be the mayor," he says.

"I know," she says, She pulls out her phone and starts taking a video of him.

"It's too dark for that. Won't come out. Hold on, why are you taking a video of me? You're the one under suspicion."

"I have to go home and feed my cats."

"I have more questions for you," Rufus says.

"Maybe another time," she says and walks down High Street.

'Hiding something,' he writes down and then erases it, changing it to 'Cats, how many?'

He sits back, with his headphones back on, half-listening, half-dozing. They're in the top of the eighth, when he hears, "Clagger?"

"Sure, would never say to no that," Rufus says. He takes a swig from the bottle extended to him.

"Keeping an eye on Martha?"

"Can't confirm."

"Have some more. Make the time go more quick."

"Don't mind if I do."

When he opens his eyes, Rufus has no idea where he is. He's achy all over. His watch says just past six. In the morning? He's thirsty. His head hurts. He's on High Street, across from City Hall, that much he's able to figure out. He calls his wife.

"Why am I on High Street?"

"It's six in the morning, Rufus. You were on some stakeout. I'm going back to sleep," she says and hangs up.

He stands and stretches. Oh. Oh! God damn it to hell. Martha Washington. He can't remember her code name but he sees she's hatless and knows that is wrong, very wrong. He was listening to the game — and then nothing. He picks up a piece of paper that reads:

J. Ebbens

Hair, coming over

Name: Polly Something

Cats, how many?

He can't remember any of it, except that he was on a mission and, judging by how he feels, Clagger may have been involved. He declares the mission aborted, folds his chair, and walks unsteadily back home.

FROM BENDER HUBBLE'S VANTAGE POINT, THE TOWN LOOKS as quiet as Christmas morning. It's early on July 5th, a time when Arnold Falls is traditionally nursing hangovers, and he's sitting at his desk in the octagonal room beneath the cupola and widow's walk atop his house. A series of windows wrap around the space and he can see the entirety of Arnold Falls with a few-second circumnavigation.

Last week, he converted the 78s that Jenny found into digital tracks and he's just finished listening to all of the music from the Arnold Falls Chamber Ensemble. He can't contain himself, so he calls Jenny.

"Dude, are you sitting down?"

"Bender, I'm lying down. It's 6:30."

"I forgot it was so early."

"Is this good news or bad news?"

"Good. Well, I — actually, why don't you come over?"

"Can it wait until 8:30? Wilky goes to day camp."

"Okay, come over then. The back door's unlocked; I'm up in the octagon."

Bender hears Jenny coming up the stairs. When she

appears, he says, "Morning, Jen. Help yourself to coffee and brownies."

"Are the brownies —"

"Nope. Straight-up brownie goodness. Not doing much weed these days."

After she gets her provisions, she sits on the bench near Bender's desk. "Have you listened to them?" she asks.

"Yeah, unbelievable! I don't know all of the pieces, but man, they are good. This is what was scrawled on the sleeve of one the LPs: Weir, Jeter, White, Johnson. First thoughts?"

"This brownie's delicious, that's first. Well, I think of Bob Weir, because of you. I mean, you named your record store after the Grateful Dead lyric. And Jeter, obviously Derek Jeter. You're a big Yankees fan, something I'll never understand about you. White and Johnson — I dunno. Obviously, the records were here long before the Dead and Jeter."

"I thought the same things," Bender says. "Weird coincidence. But this is a whole other playing field. I think that the violinist was Felix Weir. Leonard Jeter was the cellist. I think it's Hall Johnson on the viola and Clarence Cameron White the other violinist."

"Have I heard of any of them?"

"Probably not, but they were all fine, respected musicians a century ago. And they were all black. The Arnold Falls Chamber Ensemble was all black. The FW stamp is for Felix Weir. If I'm right, it's really an important piece of history. And especially these days, with Black Violin sort of picking up the baton, as it were."

"Black Violin?"

"Two guys, classical and hip-hop mashup. They're amazing."

"Wow! Why...why don't we already know this about this chamber ensemble?"

"I don't think it was a regular thing. Maybe a one-time only group. These guys had played together in different quartets. And the newspaper clipping?"

"About Jascha Heifetz?"

"There was definitely a connection between Jascha Heifetz and Clarence Cameron White because later on, Heifetz recorded a piece by White. That's as far as I've gotten. What I can't figure out is why they were in Arnold Falls. Even if it was a one-time-only kind of thing — why Arnold Falls?"

Jenny says, "Maybe..."

"Maybe what?"

"Miss Georgia."

"Yes! Yes! You're right!" Bender says. "Of course! She knew so many people, from so many places. That's the link. I'll bet you're right!"

"We should check with the Red Light Museum to see if they came across anything that might tell us more," Jenny says, looking at her watch. "I've got to get going."

Bender says, "I'm going to check it out. Hey, you can't go to City Hall with a brownie mustache," he says, grabbing a napkin to wipe it from her upper lip. "'Dignity, always dignity.'"

Jenny laughs. "I love that movie," she says, and takes off down the stairs.

Chapter Thirteen

"**F**ruit and toast, please."

"With your chicken and waffles?"

"No, just fruit and cinnamon toast."

"Tss-tss-tss-tss."

"I'm not kidding, Aunt Doozy. I'm...eating differently now."

"Eat whatcha want, thatcha don't want, don't eat," she says. "What 'bout you, Fizzy?"

"Omelette and hash browns, please."

After Doozy walks back to the kitchen, Fridsy says, sipping her coffee, "She's always called me that. I like it. The name fits me."

I bite my tongue. I have a lurch of uncertainty about this whole idea of Fridsy/Fizzy and her sanctuary, so I sit back and ask, "How do you see this sanctuary operating? Tax exempt?"

She gives me a long look of appraisal before discussing, quite fluidly it seems to me, what she wants to do and how she wants to get there. I ask a lot of questions and I'm about to ask another when she cuts me off:

"Why are you doing this?" she asks.

"I'm just asking questions."

"No, that's not what I mean. They're good questions. Why would you consider helping me?"

"Minna," I say. "She got to me."

Fridsy nods. "That's a good answer." After a few moments, she says, "You're still unsure."

"It would be a lot of work."

"Jeebie, I hope you'll help me. I don't think it will happen without you."

"You're perfectly capable," I say.

"Sometimes people find me a little brusque. I know, hard to believe. Anyway, I don't have your skills. Minna needs you. And so do I."

I am such a pushover. And the truth is, I *do* want to do it.

We get down to details of the fundraiser, setting a date of Saturday, August 18, and discuss our wish-list of performers. That would include Hullaballoo — the circus is in Austin at the moment but maybe the family members will agree to a rare return engagement. Fridsy is going to work on that. Of course, we'll ask Nelle to sing, if her ladyship can conquer her performing-live aversion. I'd call it an obligation since it is Fridsy's bovine denizens who've been instrumental (ha!) in song selection for her album. And the mariachi band Queechy Caliente always makes for a good time.

Aunt Doozy brings over our food and we take a break to eat. It occurs to me that working with Fridsy is almost pleasant. Nelle will be glad to know that Fridsy's chip hardly crosses my mind.

"Why do you want to run a sanctuary for animals?" I ask.

"Because they need one," she says.

"I thought you were going to say because you like animals more than people."

"Yes, as a rule. Though I like children."

"Did you know that QueechyGen has no arts program, nothing, in the kids-with-cancer ward? I just found that out. That is criminal."

"Is Popsy Siddons-Swain still there?"

"Who?"

"Popsy Siddons-Swain," she says, spitting at me. "Sorry. All those Ps and Ss," launching another round of fire.

"Is she from the esteemed Siddons-Swain family, that no one's ever heard of until now?"

"I couldn't say. She's their finance director. I was a candy striper there for a long time. Then Popsy Siddons-Swain gets hired, about four years ago. Killed the candy striper program, can you imagine?, and all the volunteer programs, just to save on one salary. She did a lot of other questionable things, too. It's been downhill from there."

"QueechyGen went from 127th to 196th in the ratings of hospitals in three years."

"Not surprised," Fridsy says.

"Are you saying there's a connection?"

"Possible. I made a complaint about her last fall but never heard back."

I wonder if Jenny knows more of the story. Nelle might know something, too, through her social work contacts. And just as I have that thought, in walk Nelle and Nils, who grin when they see me with Fridsy.

"The power of kulning," Nils says.

"Pull up a table if you like," Fridsy says.

"Be right there with coffee," Doozy calls over.

Nelle looks at me. "No chocolate *chip* ice cream?"

I avoid her eye and say, "I am plant-based now, as you know."

"We're working on the benefit for the sanctuary," Fridsy says.

"You're singing," I say to Nelle.

"Do I have a say in the matter?" she asks.

"No," Fridsy and I say in unison, which we follow with a high-five. Nelle looks amused at our newly-minted conspiracy.

As Doozy pours coffee, she says to Nils, "Tell your brother I liked the painting of my mama."

"He should be here any minute if you want to tell him yourself, Aunt Doozy."

I ask Nelle, "Have you ever heard of Popsy Siddons-Swain?"

"No. Why?"

I explain as Theo comes into the Shack and slips into the seat waiting for him.

"Coffee, Theo?"

"Yes, please, Aunt Doozy."

"I like what you painted. You got my mama right."

"That means a lot," he says, his cheeks flushing. "The last room of the exhibition is ready now. Come see it. It's amazing."

Doozy nods and goes back behind the counter.

"To answer your question," I say to Nelle, "Popsy is a bad, bad egg. Theo, if there were an arts program at the hospital, for kids with cancer, would you paint with them?"

"Of course. There's no program like that?"

"No."

"Why not?"

"I am going to find out."

Trevor Aitken swans into the Shack with Fayette de la Nouille. He takes one look at our group and says, "It's the Algonquin Round Table!"

"We do have a table," I point out. "We're only missing the talent and wit."

Trevor introduces Fayette to those of us who haven't had the pleasure. I watch her study our faces. What is that, I wonder? Checking the perimeter in some way. There's a story there. I've heard Fayette has a big footprint, but for the moment she's demure as an ingenue.

"Can we join you?" Trevor asks, giving Nelle a kiss.

"Absolutely," I say. "You're not filming today?"

"Giles had to go collect an award, so we're off until tomorrow."

"Is he still wearing his hair in a stupid bun?"

"No, I'm happy to report, Jeebie, that he's wearing his hair commando."

"A party without me?" Bridget says.

Apparently, Bridget and Trudy were in a booth at the back all this time, because they suddenly appear on their way out.

"Did you get your permanent crown?" Bridget asks Fayette.

"Last week," Fayette says. "Good on the dental front."

"Well, *I* have big molar news: I'm a Denisovan!"

This stops conversation in the whole restaurant.

"What do you mean, you're a Denisovan? Like a Neanderthal?" I ask.

Unfortunately, Bridget is in cheek-patting range, and she pats my cheek.

"No, Jeebie. Neanderthals were rough around the edges. Denisovans are a whole other kettle of fish."

"You still died out."

"We're back, baby!" she says.

"Bridget sent out her DNA to be tested," Trudy says. "They think she might have — be — Denisovan."

"Look at my molars!" Bridget says, hooking back her cheek for me to see.

"That's okay, Bridget. I believe you're Denisovan. I'm just

surprised none of us thought of it. I'm starting to think our meeting is adjourned," I say to Fridsy.

Bridget and Trudy bring over chairs, and town gossip-trading begins shrewdly, incrementally. Before long, Jenny turns up with Wilky and they drag over another table. Doozy comes over with a fresh pot of coffee and Jenny asks her, "Do you remember hearing about a chamber music group that performed in Arnold Falls a long time ago? Around 1938."

"Say what?"

"They called themselves the Arnold Falls Chamber Ensemble but that may have be have been just a whim, because we think they only performed live once. They were an all-black chamber ensemble."

"Naw. Classical? Naw. What's happening with baseball in the park?"

Jenny tells Doozy about Wilky's suggestion of vitilla and explains how it works.

Doozy nods at the broom and the bottle cap equipment. "Sounds good. Fit right in here."She calls out to the people sitting at the tables by the French-door entrance, "Open them doors," which everyone knows translates as: Doozy is having a momentary episode of flatulence.

"This young man is brilliant," Bridget says, referring to Wilky.

In her unsubtle way, she's trying to charm Wilky, angling for a godmother gig. At the same time, she looks, what? Sincere about it. I have no idea if she's made the Denisovan thing up, but with Bridget, it could easily be true. Still, she seems pretty human to me.

"Jeebie?"

"Sorry, what?"

"Theo just asked if you want to rebuild the libraries," Nelle says. "Do I need to buy you an ear trumpet?"

"No ear trumpet necessary, thank you. I don't know, Theo. That's very sweet of you. But I'm afraid they'll just get destroyed again."

"I can make them more vandal-proof. They could still look nice," Theo says.

"Let's talk about it."

"Just say the word," he says.

"Jeebie has trouble accepting things freely offered," Fridsy says.

I'm about to respond to this not inaccurate observation when Marvin the Hobo walks in and my tablemates urge him to join us.

He sits down and says to Bridget, "I finally tried the Jimmy Nardello peppers at the farmer's market. You are right, they are excellent. Thank you for the tip."

"I'm glad you enjoyed them," Bridget says. "The last time we met, communication was difficult."

"An hour for that stinking face cream to wore off," Marvin says.

"To wear off, yes."

I see a quizzical expression pass over Trudy's face.

"The new frame is terrific," Nelle says to Theo.

"What new frame?" I ask.

"Around JFK," Nelle says.

We look up to the photo of JFK at the Resolute desk, the only adornment on any of the Chicken Shack's walls. Theo explains that the Red Light Museum asked to use the picture in the exhibition and Doozy had agreed to Theo building a new frame for it.

Theo says, "The back of the image has an inscription."

"From?" I ask.

Theo smiles.

"No!"

I jump up and take the photo off the wall, bringing it to the table. I turn it over to reveal a white rectangular card, enclosed by glass, with The White House, Washington at the top. It reads, 'To Georgia, Lem speaks so highly of you. With best wishes, John F. Kennedy.'

Doozy is talking to Sal behind the counter. I call over to her.

"Change your mind for chicken and waffles?" she asks, walking towards our group.

"Did you know all this time that the JFK photo was signed to your mom?"

"Yeah. But forgot about it 'til the museum asked to borrow something that was from the Shack. Wasn't going to give them no recipes. Anyway, stays here until the show opens. What you all looking at?"

"So what's the tea, Aunt Doozy?" Nelle asks.

"No tea. Ma knew Lem-something, friend of Kennedy."

Trudy says, "Lem Billings. One of JFK's oldest and closest pals."

"A client?" Trevor asks.

"It would definitely have been platonic with Miss Georgia," Trudy says.

"Yeah, Lem liked the boys," Doozy says. "But he was a friend. He sent it to my mama early that year. 1963. After Kennedy died, we hung the picture up here."

I put the photo back in its spot.

Rufus comes into the Shack, sniggering with Dubsack. He sees our congregation and goes silent.

Jenny doesn't miss a beat. "Rufus," she says. "I didn't get the whole story about Wednesday night. What happened to the decoy mobcap on Martha?"

"Oh. Well, what happened is…it went down like this."

Our group gets quiet and waits for Rufus to come up with something.

"Okay. I'm hidden under Winstian's awning across the street from City Hall. Lot of suspicious people all around. Danger in the air. I was on high alert. Musta been three in the morning when I spotted a shadow. A shadow moving. Suspicious for sure."

"What happened then?" Jenny asks with a straight face.

"Then, I took out my binoculars."

"I thought you were across the street," I say.

"Affirmative. I remembered that. Put 'em away again. Kept very still. No creaking chair on my watch."

"Well, who was it?" Bridget asks.

"Fair question," Rufus says. "Asked myself the same thing."

"And what did you answer?" Nelle asks.

"His face was covered!"

"Then how do you know it was a he?"

Jenny should have been a prosecutor.

"I have a tactical background. It was a dude, trust me. Or a chick dressed as a dude."

He doesn't have a tactical background. He might have had a subscription to *Soldier of Fortune* magazine.

"Then what happened?" Nelle asks.

"Then? Then the perp grabbed Martha's hat. Then I gave chase."

The idea of Rufus giving chase is met with such a skeptical silence that he has to back-pedal.

"I mean, I started to give chase, but after the perp grabbed Martha's hat, he, or she, ran around the corner, um, and turned to give me a ninja pose, no fooling around, and then I lost him. Or her." Rufus, face flushed, looks at his watch. "I gotta be somewhere," he says, and beats a hasty retreat.

Dubsack gives a "so-so" wiggle of his hand for Rufus' explanation and then follows him out.

"That seemed plausible," I say to the group.

"We need to solve this crime spree," Jenny says. "Solve it, Jeebie."

"Me? Okay. We're looking for a dude, or a woman dressed as a dude, trained as a ninja, who collects 18th-century ladies hats, gavels, and Princess phones. Over to you, Jen."

Everyone is looking at me expectantly, apparently thinking that I can somehow actually solve this.

"You all know I do voiceovers for a living, right? I'm not a detective."

They're hanging on my every word and I have no idea why.

"Well, then I would say we need someone to patrol tonight because the thefts seem to be increasing in frequency."

I don't know if this is even true but everyone's nodding at me, so I say, "Do I have any volunteers?"

"I'll ask Chief Williams to loan us an unmarked car," Jenny says.

I'm about to say that any car not a police car is unmarked but Jenny's ahead of me on the appeal of this.

"Oh, yes, I'm up for an adventure!" Bridget says, looking at Trudy.

Trudy says, "Bridget, you are utterly unqualified to investigate. What if he's dangerous?"

"He's not going to think we're the po-po because it's an unmarked car. Nothing to worry about."

"Count me out," Trudy says.

"Anyone want to accompany me?" Bridget asks. "Ride shotgun with a Denisovan?"

Fayette raises her hand.

"Great," I say. "Bridget and Fayette handle night patrol. Trudy, will you ask around and see if there's anything to the theory that it's someone from Blue Birch Corners?"

"What theory is that?" she asks.

"I heard they were unhappy that *Merryvale* pulled out of filming there," Trevor says.

"On it," Trudy says.

Doozy comes over and says, "All right, I'll take orders now for anyone still wants something."

As Doozy goes around the table, I give out a few more investigative assignments, munching on my cinnamon toast, followed by a coffee chaser. The conversation moves to various theories of the case, none of them remotely plausible, though not-remotely-plausible has a different cadence in these parts.

Annie O'Dell runs into the Shack out of breath.

"They're after me!" she cries.

No one says anything to her, so I take pity.

"Who's after you, Annie?" I ask.

"Bay Leaf Growers! Those people are ruthless. They didn't like my bay leaf pesto. Is there a back door here?"

Doozy walks her out.

Nelle, Nils, and Theo go to the register to pay. As they leave, Nelle calls over to me, "Let me know what you want me to sing at the benefit."

"Let me know when painting classes start," Theo adds.

Then I text Will: "Wish you were here at the Shack. Bay leafers after Annie. She's on the run. Handing out assignments for solving the rash of thefts. I have no idea why people think I can solve crimes."

He responds, "It's not crime-solving they look to you for. Bossing people around is your superpower. I should know."

"Funny. See you at home."

Chapter Fourteen

❧❧❧

Bridget and Fayette are scanning the horizon. The headlights of their unmarked car reveal brief tableaux of late-evening Arnold Falls but no signs of disorder, no hint of a criminal mind at work. Bridget drives slowly, and while she and Fayette chat, their eyes remain steadfast on the stores, houses, alleys, and doorways of Arnold Falls on this warm, Sunday evening in July.

They had met behind the police station two hours ago with Chief Williams, who had handed them the keys to an unmarked car for their neighborhood-watch shift. As they drive, momentarily suspending their conversation, Bridget reflects that the police department's 1983 Chevy Impala was perhaps not ideal for their mission since the car bangs and rattles loudly. Worse, Chief Williams has a loose interpretation of an 'unmarked' vehicle: 'Rugs and Plugs' is emblazoned on each side of the car, 'Carpet Steaming and Ear Piercing by Peggy' on the hood. And it isn't a pleasant ride: even Fayette's perfume can't mask the smell of stale fast food.

"I feel like we're in a film noir scene," Fayette says.

"I was thinking more along the lines of *Police Squad*."

Bridget glances over and sees that Fayette doesn't understand the reference.

"Leslie Nielsen as Frank Drebin?" Bridget asks, still no lightbulb. "Where did you grow up?"

"Oh, we moved around a lot."

"But where were you born?"

"In London," Fayette says.

"For a minute, I thought we might have grown up together. You look so familiar."

"I get that a lot," Fayette says. "I have that type of face. How does it feel knowing you're Denisovan? How Denisovan are you?"

"They didn't say. It was a bit of a shock at first. Now that I've had time to think about, it does seem to explain a lot. And I'm starting to feel a strong Denisovan affinity. A lot of pieces have fallen into place."

"Identity isn't a destination, it's not a past or future. It's who you are along the way."

"I couldn't agree more, Fayette."

"How COMPLETELY dull it would be if you knew you were fated to be the exact same person ten years from now. Did you ever think you'd be right here, right now?"

"If you mean," Bridget says, "driving around at night with you, undercover, in Peggy's old beater, looking for someone stealing Martha Washington's mobcaps — no, the thought never crossed my mind."

"The case in point," Fayette says.

Bridget pulls the car over and stops the engine. "This is Benedict Arnold Park. Trudy and I had our first date here. Let's get out and have a look around. A park at night is a good place for a perp to lurk."

"Is there a statue of Benedict Arnold?" Fayette asks.

"No, though there is one of Hezekiah Hesper, the town's

founder. Not a very impressive statue, smoking a pipe, a very louche pose. But he was D-List as founding fathers go."

They get out of the car, which, even after the engine is shut off, continues to make sputtering sounds. Chief Williams had supplied them with two flashlights; they switch them on and begin searching the perimeter.

"Oh!" Fayette says when she sees the eyes of a deer in the woods.

"Yes, lots of deer. And look how many stars!" Bridget says.

After a few minutes, having found nothing suspicious, they start to walk back toward the car.

"Where's the statue of the founder?" Fayette asks.

"Right over there," Bridget says, pointing her flashlight.

"Right over where?"

"Right —"

Bridget walks closer to where the statue should be.

"Hm. That's odd. Hezekiah Hesper seems to be on the lam."

THE NEXT MORNING, BRIDGET, JENNY, AND CHIEF Williams meet in Benedict Arnold Park.

"I suspect Hezekiah Hesper is wearing Martha's mobcap this very minute!"

"Bridget has a point, Chief. All this seems related somehow," Jenny says.

"Agree. Can't make heads or tails of it yet. I'm gonna issue a BOLO. Be on the lookout for Hezekiah Hesper. Sounds like a BOLO from a different era."

Chief Williams walks over to his cruiser and calls in the alert.

"I loved talking with Wilky on Saturday. He is the most charming child," Bridget says.

"I'm very lucky," Jenny agrees.

"You know, a child can never have too many god-parents. If you're in the market, Trudy and I would be honored to audition."

Jenny smiles. "You don't have to audition, Bridget. I know your many virtues."

"And vices! Don't forget those! Much more interesting." Bridget says.

"We're still settling in to everything but the offer is very kind."

"It's a standing offer. And Jeebie is a perfectly good choice for godparent, in his way, but there's no love like Denisovan love."

"I'll keep that in mind," Jenny says.

"I don't work on holidays. We can talk later about who would be the featured godparent."

Chief Williams walks back to them and says, "Archie IV just reported a break-in."

"No!" Bridget says. "Not Clagger!"

"Afraid so," Chief Williams says. "Six cases."

"A dark day for Arnold Falls," Bridget intones.

I tell her about my conversation with the hospital.

"That is funky," Jenny says. "Seriously funky. Let's pay a visit to Dr. Jantzen. I'll call him."

~

Dr. Jantzen is evidently taking a personal day at home. He greets us at his door with tongue depressors, which is his idea of a warm welcome.

"Did you know," he asks, "that in the summer, the Eiffel Tower gets six inches taller? It's true! Now, why would that be?"

"The metal expands," I say.

"It's because the metal expands!" he says, ushering us into his study. He's dressed nattily for someone working from home.

"Gustave Eiffel died while listening to Beethoven's Fifth, which seems like a fine choice. Please, sit. Now, Beethoven died during a thunderstorm and I'd prefer that to Arnold Falls thunderhail any day. Poor old Roy Sullivan. He's the fellow from Virginia hit on seven separate occasions by lightning. He was a park ranger, so there was some occupational hazard in there. There's a book from 1957, I think it is, by C. B. Colby, called *Park Ranger: The Work, Thrills and Equipment of the National Book Rangers*. Or maybe it was 1956. I think it was 1956. That's up there with my favorite books."

Jenny and I had come prepared for Dr. Jantzen's free associations, which can go on for quite a while if unchecked, and this one seems especially loopy, so Jenny fakes a loud sneeze.

"Now, if you think you might be contagious..." he says.

"Allergic to grass," she says.

"Ah, grass. Tall fescue is starting to rival Kentucky bluegrass as..."

"Dr. Jantzen, we came to see you because Jeebie has an idea for QueechyGen and I think it's an excellent idea."

He starts to interrupt but Jenny plows on.

"Wouldn't it be wonderful if the pediatric oncology unit had artists and musicians come in to perform and spend time with the children?"

"Arnold Falls has many wonderful performers. I went to a balalaika concert last year..."

"Yes," I add, "we thought that it's odd there is no volunteer program now, nothing for those kids. It's really not right. We understand Popsy Siddons-Swain is no longer with the hospital."

All of a sudden, the wheezy raconteur clamps up, his face tightens, his eyes look off into the distance. There is a long and uncomfortable pause.

"Dr. Jantzen?"

"Yes, Popsy is no longer with the hospital. She left."

"When did she leave?" I ask.

"What? Oh, April."

"Have you hired anyone to take her place?"

"Take her place?"

"She was the CFO," I say. "And she eliminated the volunteer supervisor and the whole volunteer program."

"We have had to tighten our belts," Dr. Jantzen says.

"Who's the new CFO?" I ask.

"We're using the bookkeeper until we find...find someone."

"I'd like to start a program for those kids, Dr. Jantzen," I say, running short of patience.

"Yes, of course. There's no money for it."

"I don't need money for it."

"Yes, good."

"Are you all right, Dr. Jantzen?" Jenny asks.

"Thank you for coming in," he says. "See the receptionist on the way out to schedule a follow-up."

Jenny and I look at each other and stand up, as Dr. Jantzen appears to have gone into power-saving mode. We wait until we're back on the sidewalk before we speak.

"What the holy hell was that?" Jenny asks.

"No idea. Wow."

As we walk past Bunny Liverwurst's house, next door to Dr. Jantzen, there's a rapping on the window. It's Bunny, waving to us to come in. A few moments later, she's opening her front door, wearing a maroon track suit circa 1980, not the fetching house coat she had on when we visited during Jenny's mayoral campaign. No corn-cob pipe this time, either.

"I saw you going to visit Emil. He's in a bad way. Come in. I've played poker with him every Friday for years and I've never seen him like this. How did he seem to you?"

"He seemed normal. Well, that's not the precise word," I say. "But like he always is. Until we mentioned Popsy Siddons-Swain."

"No one was supposed to know, because they were colleagues and all, but they'd been carrying on for a while now."

"Carrying on, meaning they were in a relationship?" Jenny asks.

"Yes, he was smitten with her. And she just up and left. He can't understand why. Poor Emil. No word in months from her. I need a bowl. Come in."

Bunny gets her corn-cob pipe from the hall table, fills it with tobacco, and takes a long draw. "Why were you asking for her?"

"I want to create an arts program for the kids with cancer ward but Popsy cut the volunteer program and fired the director." Something about Bunny's expression makes me ask, "You didn't like her, did you?"

Bunny shakes her head. "Nope."

"How come?" Jenny asks.

"First thing, who calls themselves Popsy Siddons-Swain? I know, I'm Bunny Liverwurst, but I didn't pick it."

"It could be a fake name."

"There you go!" she says. "There you fucking go! And second" — she takes a puff of her pipe — "something way-the-fuck-off about that dame."

"But Dr. Jantzen didn't see her that way," Jenny says.

"Nah, like I said, he was smitten. She was after his money, I guess. Poor Emil. He doesn't even have that much. Well, good riddance. Last time you were here was when you were running for mayor. How do you like being mayor? Told you not to do it. Something must be way-the-fuck-off about you, too," she says with a raspy laugh.

When Jenny and I are back outside in the glaring, midday sun, she says, "This isn't the whole story."

"Agreed. It's not a breakup story at all. I have to go home and grab my overnight bag."

"Where are you going?" she asks.

"Into the city. I have an early call tomorrow for a Life-Lock ad. We need to keep on this, Jen. Something is fishy. Popsy Siddons-Swain..."

"...seems suspicious," Jenny says, finishing my thought.

"Surpassingly suspicious."

"Sounds like we're hissing," she says.

"Appropriate for a villain," I say.

Chapter Sixteen

Will texts Nelle: *Bike ride after work? Jeebie's going to the city.*
Definitely. 5:30, Midden Park path?
Great! See u then.

NELLE AND WILL SPEED ALONG THE BIKE PATH ENJOYING the full, midsummer bloom.

"Swimming hole?" Will asks.

"Where?"

"Coming up. Want to?"

"Hell yeah."

"This is it," Will says, turning onto a narrow opening through the trees.

He drops his bike, strips off his clothes, and jumps into the water before Nelle has taken off her helmet and fanny pack.

"Any time, grandma," Will shouts.

"Shut up," Nelle says, laughing.

They swim and splash and finally rest against the bank as the late afternoon sun streams through the trees, warming their faces.

"How's the album coming along?" Will asks, raking his hair back on his head.

"Getting there. The cows helped."

"It's killing Jeebie that he's not more involved."

"I know. But I want it to be my thing first, you know what I mean?"

"I do," Will says. "His bossiness is a gift and a curse. He just needs to feel connected, that runs deep with him."

Nelle looks at this lovely, lanky, man with the poker face that occasionally lights up and gives the game away. "He's so lucky," she says, looking at Will, who just smiles back at her.

"What do *you* need, Will?"

"I need to go have a beer at Pearson's Tavern."

"You sound just like Jeebie. God, don't do that. Answer the question."

His green eyes cast around for a moment as he collects his thoughts.

"I need a bigger horizon. I want to see the world. With Jeebie," he says. "I've hardly been anywhere."

Nelle nods her head slowly. "Yeah. I get it. You'll do it. Plan it."

"I have. Paris and Rome. For starters."

"Good plan," she says.

As they dress, Will asks, "You up for a drink?"

"Yeah, lead the way. I've never been to Pearson's."

It's another five or so miles to get to the tavern and by the time they arrive, they're dry and thirsty.

"Sweet place," Nelle says of the small stone structure that

looks like it's been around since Colonial times. It's not quite as charming inside, though the fireplace must be nice in the winter. Nils would love it.

"What's the latest on the hospital?" she asks, as they carry their beers to a table. "I like this idea of an arts program for those kids."

"I didn't get the whole story because he was rushing to get his train. The CFO shut down the volunteer program."

"Popsy Something?" Nelle asks.

"Yeah, Popsy Siddons-Swain. She's no longer working at QueechyGen. And, she and Dr. Jantzen were an item."

"That sounds like a mess."

"Yup. Jeebie thinks there may be a connection between her and the hospital's decline in the ratings."

"Something's going on."

"I think so, too," Will says. "I had one idea that might help. But I'm not sure I should do it."

"Say," Nelle says.

"Well, you remember that dinner at Pumphrey's when you were with Jeebie's parents and I was with —"

"Of course. You were with the FBI guy."

"Yeah. Ash Plank. I thought I might find something out from him."

"Why would the FBI be involved?"

"If there were wire fraud, let's say. She was the CFO and now she's vanished."

"You think there's money missing? That could be right. But Ash isn't going to tell you anything about an investigation, if there is one."

"I can read between the lines."

"You're still in touch with him?"

"We're Facebook friends. The only thing is…"

"Jeebie," Nelle says.

"I think he'd get over it. Especially if I got some info."

"It's a longshot."

"Yup," he says, and pulls out his phone.

Another thing I love about this guy, Nelle thinks. He's got a spine. She watches him take a deep breath, then message Ash Plank.

When they're biking on the way back into town, Will signals Nelle to stop. He takes out his phone.

"'Call me,' it says."

"You want to call him now?"

"No time like the present."

Nelle sits on the grass as Will ambles in circles, talking to Ash Plank. She looks up at him but can't read his face. When the call is over, he says, "I asked him, 'Do you have an investigation going on in Arnold Falls?'"

"He said, 'I can't talk about anything like that. Which investigation?'"

"I said, 'How many do you have? Something medical-related?'"

"He said, 'We always keep an open file on Arnold Falls. Not standard, just easier that way. I wish I could be more help TO you. You've always been so HOSPITABLE to me.' That's what he said. So I guess he's telling me two. And one has to do with the hospital."

"You are a rock star," Nelle says.

Will grins. "Let's see if Jeebie thinks so."

"When is he back?"

"Tomorrow afternoon."

"Wait, if there are *two* investigations, what's the other one? It can't be all the mobcaps and beer signs and stuff that's being stolen. The FBI wouldn't be involved in something that small."

"Beats me. Race you back into town," Will says.

"Grow up," she says, and then speeds off hooting, taking an early lead, as the evening sun dips below the horizon.

Chapter Seventeen

"**S**ounds like you had a good time," Will says. "Except for the train part."

"They need to improve their air conditioning," I say. "Stuffy doesn't begin to describe it."

I had vetoed a drink on the porch because it's too humid, so we're sitting on the sofa together, enjoying the chilly central air. "You missed me," I say.

"You have to ask it, not state it," Will says.

"It's a fact," I say. "Or is it not?"

"It is," he says. "I went on a bike ride with Nelle. She's coming over Friday night for dinner," Will says.

"Great. Where did you bike?"

After describing the ride, he says, "And Nelle and I were talking. And, uh..."

"Sing out, Louise!" I say.

"What does that mean?"

"What does that mean! It's a line from *Gypsy*!"

"Oh. Anyway, I had an idea that I ran by Nelle and she thought it was a good idea."

"Go on."

"I thought it would help to know more about what's happening with QueechyGen and Popsy Siddons-Swain. So I...texted Ash Plank."

I feel my stomach do a quick backflip.

"Jeebie, I'm not interested in Ash Plank. You know that."

"Have you never seen *Gypsy*?!" I ask.

"No. Is it good?"

"I'm questioning our compatibility."

"No, you're not. You're changing the subject."

"What happened with Ash Plank?"

"He said there are two investigations in Arnold Falls, one at the hospital."

"He told you all that? What kind of FBI guy is he? Big talker."

"He didn't say it in so many words."

He relates the phone call to me. Good thinking on Will's part. Smart to follow the money.

"You're not mad?" Will asks.

"Excellent detective work. What I don't understand is how you can be gay and never have seen *Gypsy*. Disturbing."

He takes my hand and pats it.

"It's okay, it's okay, it's okay," he says.

"What do you mean, okay?" I ask.

"I mean, okay boomer."

"RIGHT THERE. IT LOOKS LIKE A TEAPOT."

"Where?" Nelle asks.

"You see Saturn?" Will asks.

"Yeah."

"Go down to the left. The teapot is at an angle, ready to

pour," Will says as he draws an outline with his finger. "The Milky Way's the steam."

"Oh! I got it now," Nelle says.

"Sagittarius," Will says.

We're out in the backyard after dinner, sitting in the Adirondack chairs, looking up at the stars, taking turns using Will's telescope. Saturn, Antares, and Mars seem close tonight.

"It's amazing," I say, "that Bender's great-uncle figured out that there are galaxies beyond the Milky Way, isn't it?"

"A personal connection to *beyond*," Nelle says.

We mull this over a for moment.

"Your turn on the scope, Jeebs," Will says. "See if you can find any aliens."

As it happens, I *am* on the lookout for aliens. Nothing wrong with that.

"Mock me all you want. I'd like to be here for the biggest news day of all time. Everyone thinks Will is so sweet," I say, as I adjust the telescope's focus. "A few days ago, he called me a boomer."

"You *are* a boomer," Nelle says.

"I'm too young to be a boomer. But I still got 'ok, boomer-ed.'"

"For cause," Will says. "I didn't know a reference to some musical."

We're quiet for a bit, when Nelle says,

The frail white stars moved slowly over the sky.
And now, far off
In the fragrant darkness
The tree is tremulous again with bloom
For June comes back.

"What is that from?" I ask.

"Summer Night, Riverside," she says. "A poem by Sara Teasdale. I love that the stars are frail."

"I could stare at them forever," Will says.

"Ah!" I say and run inside to get my iPad.

When I come back out, I ask, "You don't have an album opener yet?"

"Nope."

"Okay. Check this out. 'The Sweet Sky' by Laura Nyro. I don't think anyone's ever covered it."

The song starts playing.

"Yeah, I sort of remember it," she says, nodding.

After a few seconds, she's singing along. Ha! I knew it!

And then Will starts doing fingersnaps on the offbeat. Nelle nods. I want in, so I try some background vocals. Will surprises me by adding his voice, using a falsetto that I've never heard before. I join him up there in falsettoland and now we're handclapping along to Nelle and Laura. Three drunken fools on a summer night.

"We're the Pips!" I shout.

Will produces a harmonica and plays a perfect shuffle during the bridge.

We bang out the final choruses and from the way Nelle is singing the hell out of this sweet, happy song, I know this could be her album opener.

As we catch our breath, Nelle gives me a thumbs up. "Bubbly?" she asks.

I nod and Will goes into the house to get it, saying, "I sang out, Louise!"

I sit on the arm rest of Nelle's chair. She puts her arm around my shoulder and we gaze upward. The darkness is fragrant indeed, and summer is sweet. I point to the space station passing. Not a shooting star, but it'll do.

~

THE NEXT MORNING, I FEEL A WARM, DRY BREEZE COMING through the open window and I wake up with "The Sweet Sky" in my head.

Will comes back from the bathroom to give me a kiss. A minty kiss.

"No fair, you already brushed your teeth," I say.

"Life is unfair. Accept your fate," he says, softening the blow with another kiss. "Today's E-Day," he adds, reminding me that this afternoon, Arnold Falls will become, for six months, the town of Emollimax, NY.

As Will gets ready for the farmer's market, I ruminate over the imminent identity switch for Arnold Falls. The Emollimax team had decided to drop the 'by the makers of Vaseline' part, persuaded that it was too cumbersome and that locals would be forced to come up with snappier, less-flattering nicknames. This whole thing, this commercial rechristening, strikes me as, well, folly is the nicest word I can think of. I know Jenny and the Council will put the money to good use. But still.

After a late lunch, I walk over to Midden Park. Jenny had put out the word that before the Emollimax ceremony at 3pm, there would be an informal game of vitilla, to see if the town wanted to adopt it as their baseball alternative. Wilky has helped Jenny rustle up broomstick handles and water jug caps and she's learned from Wilky that the rules are flexible, which was all to the good.

As she and Wilky set up the field, players and spectators start arriving. It's Nelle and Nils, bartender Sofia, and Wilky on one team and, on the other, Officer Wanda Velez, Dubsack, Marvin the Hobo, and City Hall fashionista Tishy, who is dressed, more or less, as Wally the Green Monster.

Home base is one of the methane pipes. There are three fielders plus the *lanzador* (the pitcher) and as the game gets underway, it quickly becomes apparent that the mechanics of connecting broomstick to flying bottlecap are trickier than anyone, except Wilky, had anticipated. It all makes for a fun, if low-scoring, game ending in a 1-1 tie.

Afterwards, everyone crowds around Wilky to applaud him for the idea. Bender hoists Wilky up on his shoulders. I walk up to Aunt Doozy and ask her what she thought.

"Good. Doozy-approved," she says.

Will arrives, having finished his farmer's market duties.

"How was vitilla?" he asks.

I fill him in as we head toward the Emollimax festivities, where they've set up a tent for the speeches (essential when you factor in our issues with hail). Nearby, we read the small sign next to two large cauldrons being warmed by super-sized cans of Sterno, which states that one of Emollimax's many uses is aromatherapy. I have to be honest, it does smell wonderful: a heady scent of eucalyptus and rosemary and maybe some verbena.

"Eucalyptus is highly flammable," Will says.

Down from the tent and the cauldrons, closer to the river and the railroad tracks, is a nice spread: I see stacks of pepperoni sandwiches and boxes of doughnuts from Darlene's. A couple of suits, presumably from Emollimax, are standing with Dante de Rosa and Fayette, being interviewed by the *Observer*'s Ginger Abrams. There is a local news crew from Albany as well as Giles Morris, the director of *Merryvale*, talking to his cameraman.

"What's Giles doing here?" Will asks.

"Probably shooting B-roll footage for *Merryvale*. That big electric sign is a horror."

"They're called Electronic Message Centers."

If you're on the train pulling out of the station, you won't be able to miss its messages: Greetings from Emollimax, NY! and You're Leaving Emollimax, NY. Come Back Soon!

It looks like the event in the tent is about to start, so we head over and stand at the back. Father Burnham begins with a benediction, something about renewal, but then he veers, unwisely, into blather about 'the divine hand guiding Arnold Falls.' He, of all people, should know that the line between church and state is one of the few things sacrosanct in Arnold Falls. In any case, the leap of faith required to believe that Arnold Falls, of all places, is being guided by a divine hand, is a leap this crowd is unwilling to make. Father Burnham gets rhubarbed.

Theater tradition has it that townspeople onstage are supposed to say "rhubarb" over and over to each other when a plausible crowd noise is needed for a scene in a play or musical. Someone passed this vital information to our actual town residents and now rhubarbing is a preferred protest of unwelcome speech. And when I say *someone* passed along this vital information, I will say, in my defense, I had no idea how enthusiastically the custom would be adopted.

After a few moments of rhubarbrhubarbrhubarbrhubarb, Father Burnham pauses, then trims his remarks to the bone, finally sitting down to tepid applause.

Jenny's next. Given her feelings about the whole stunt, I know she'll keep it brief, too. As she begins speaking, I see out of the corner of my eye that a train is pulling out of the station heading north. But instead of accelerating, it comes to a full stop between the river and the food stations that have been set up on this side of the train tracks.

"We need to make sure Arnold Falls thrives in the twenty-first century," she is saying as the train begins blowing its horn.

Oh, brother, bad timing. Jenny used to date one of the train engineers on the NYC-to-Albany route, and whenever he sees her, he gives her a toot. Or several. This time, though, the horn is persistent and people start turning around, looking toward the cronking train.

After a collective gasp, the cry goes up: "Stripes! Leave them, Stripes!"

The crowd bolts out of the tent toward the food tables as Stripes, the black bear easily recognizable by his striped snout, is dispatching doughnuts like nobody's business. The bear sees his time at the buffet table is limited (now *there's* a homily suitable for Father Burnham) and grabs three boxes of doughnuts and a tray of pepperoni sandwiches before considering his exit strategy. He can't hold it all at once, so Stripes decides to go with the tray of sandwiches and one box of doughnuts as the crowd closes in. He ambles off cheerfully toward the woods. The train continues north.

The humans, having rescued most of the doughnut stash, are understandably relieved — the atmosphere turns festive and chatty. It becomes clear after a few minutes that they're not going to get people back into the tent, so the final speaker, the head of the Emollimax division, decides to meet people where they are, which, as ever in Arnold Falls, is by the doughnuts. He begins his talk.

He's an unpleasant chap and a blow-hard, overselling Emollimax, absurdly proud of the fact that it contains botanicals, selling it like snake oil to a town of rubes, touting its manifold uses: taken by mouth it settles the stomach, calms nerves and tastes delicious! Applied to the skin, it promotes healing, moisturizes and quells itches!

"As you can smell from here, when heated, it is a comforting air freshener!"

Whatever testing was done on this product, I guarantee it

didn't include mixing off-gassed methane and heated pots of Emollimax, something that occurs to me when I see the cauldrons by the tent suddenly shooting up big puffs of yellow, oily flame.

I tap Will's shoulder.

"Um," I say.

He turns around and then springs into action. My hero. He runs toward a fire extinguisher next to the steaming essential oils.

The Emollimax guy has stopped mid-sentence and watches Will with a look of alarm on his face. Everyone turns to see what's happening.

What's happening is that a large cloud of flaming Emollimax and methane grease is drifting into the tent and upward. There is a collective holding of the breath. It doesn't take long for the top of the tent to pop off with a boom, sending a sallow cloud up and away.

The crowd applauds the pyrotechnics, shouting out "woohoo" and "awesome" before returning to the pepperoni sandwich table and the doughnuts. I wonder if the town's insurance covers a tent-popping. On the plus side, Arnold Falls has never smelled this fresh.

I hang around waiting for Will while the fire department investigates. As the food runs out, the crowd thins. When we're finally heading off, I turn back, noting that someone has already hacked the Electronic Message Center. It now says: Do Some Molli!... Killer Mollitov Cocktails at Happy Hour!...If you lived here, you'd be living Down on the Pharma by now... RIP Arnold Falls (1803-2018).

And then it starts thunderhailing. I don't believe in a divine hand, though I'd say if there are any spirits hovering over Arnold Falls, their feelings about Emollimax are unambiguous.

∿

Unambiguous is also the word for the reaction on the AF message board. Yes, sentiment was for the rebranding (or at least for the money it would bring in), but that was theoretical sentiment. Now that it's happened and nothing has magically transformed the town, there's bellyaching, second-guessing, and gainsaying online at the AF Community Board. If you know anything about AF, it shouldn't surprise you at all.

Offroad: that tent blowed up real good.

DudeAbides: AF has been over for a while. Now it's Emollimax.

Username MYOB: #TeamStripes

ModernMajorGeneral: Divine hand guiding Arnold Falls lololololololololol

ChocolateFrosted: We're now named for an OINTMENT.

WhoMe?57: If Emollimax brings in more business, okay. But let's see cui bono.

Petalia: I'm worried about the parking garage. Does anyone have info?

We've established Petalia does not own a car so I can not explain this obsession of hers.

GabbyGadfly: Even Hezekiah Hesper has fled, can't blame him.

Fleck: Come back, Arnold Falls

PolatinosRule: A pot of gold for Arnold Falls. You're welcome.

Dubsack taking a bow.

Patel: Vitilla looks fun.

Username MYOB: Agree.

There are about a dozen more, all pro-vitilla, until the thread devolves into Red Sox bashing/defending. Jenny will be glad about the vitilla support. Wilky, too.

Chapter Eighteen

"Are you sleepy?"

"No, Mayormama."

They're driving back after the game at Fenway, listening to a classic hits radio station. Jenny glances at Wilky.

"You had fun?"

"Yes, you know that!"

"Which do you like better, baseball or vitilla?"

"No. Too hard."

"What did you enjoy most today?" Jenny asks.

"We win, 5-2," Wilky says. "And the X-man's homer in the first inning. And having you all day to myself."

That's the best thing he's said to her. Maybe the best thing anyone has ever said to her.

After a few minutes, Jenny decides to broach the subject of Wilky's sister.

"Jeebie said you brought up Mirlande with him and Will."

"We talk about her a little."

"You can talk about her with me any time you want."

"I know," he says. "It just make me sad."

They're quiet for a few minutes.

Jenny sings along to "Everybody Wants to Rule the World" on the radio.

Wilky says, "You know what also make me sad? Your singing. Terrible."

∾

DRIVING BACK FROM THE FLEA MARKET IN QUEECHYVILLE, Bridget is looking through her purchases, while Trudy, as she drives, is basking in the efflorescent greens of the midsummer trees, before the inevitable scalding of August.

Bridget holds up an object. "The amethyst color of this glass insulator makes it the crown jewel of my collection. And the pink on this Braniff sick bag! I love the text on it, too: 'This litter bag is for your convenience. You may take it with you if you desire. It can also be used for airsickness should the occasion arise.' They're not saying you *have* to take it with you, only if you desire."

"Do you think you would have been one of those people?"

"Which people?"

"Who would desire to take it with you for your convenience?"

"Of course! And I'd been trying to find the Havana Capitol souvenir building forever. A recast, but still. Big flea market day."

"Are you looking forward to *Merryvale* tomorrow?"

"Giles says it's quite a small part. I don't even know who I'm playing. But, yes. It should be fun. I'll enjoy a scene with Fayette."

"Making a scene," Trudy says.

"Always a possibility."

"You have a little crush on her?"

"No, Trudy. Not at all. Only you, my love. I do like her.

She was cast to play a character like me, so I guess there's a natural affinity. But there's also something intriguing there, some mystery."

"What do you know about her?"

"That's exactly it! Details are sketchy. I did find out she was born in London."

"Should we stop at Higganum's and get corn?" Trudy asks.

"Of course. You may take me with you if you desire."

Chapter Nineteen

When Bridget was offered a small, two-episode part in the *Merryvale* series by its director, Giles Morris, she'd gotten it into her head that she needed a personal assistant for the gig and asked if I would do it. Bridget didn't need a personal assistant for day work, but she insisted she did and told me to name my price. I asked for four bottles from the case of Chianti that I gave her for participating in the Titleholders Parade.

"I'm sorry," she had said. "There was no claw-back clause in that agreement."

"Bridget," I'd said. "Can you think of anyone besides me, within a hundred-mile radius, who would agree to be your assistant, at any price?"

"All right. I'll give you three bottles."

And so, against my better judgment, here we are at the wardrobe trailer, Bridget having arrived early for her 9 a.m. call, brimming with eagerness. We don't know what role she'll play, all we know is the plotline involves Merryvale being used as a location for a fictional town called Lower Hacklesbury, for a series of the same name. To recap for anyone losing the plot, Emollimax, nee Arnold Falls, is the location for the real Merryvale shoot in which Merryvale has to deal with the filming in *their* town of a series called Lower Hacklesbury. It addles my brain.

Bridget has told me many times about her salad days in New York, getting acting jobs before she became a junior agent at the Flora Agency, and she seems happy to get back in the game. The trailer door opens and out steps a woman who introduces herself as Kara, the wardrobe supervisor.

"You must be Teller #2," Kara says.

"Teller #2?! I thought I'd be playing a named character."

"Well, it's Teller #2. You're Bridget, right?" she says, giving a script to Bridget.

"I am Bridget Helen Roberts! How many tellers are there?"

"Just you."

"Well, then I should be Teller #1 of course! Jeebie, please tell Giles I cannot perform until this is straightened out. I'll be in my trailer."

"You don't have a trailer," Kara points out.

"Who negotiated my contract?" Bridget asks.

"You did," I say.

"Well, I will *never* use her again!"

Giles himself walks up at that moment and Bridget becomes noticeably more docile as he begins to describe her scene. He stops himself and says, "Let's just head over to the bank and we'll rehearse it. They should be ready for us. Good, you've got the script. It's only a few lines to memorize."

"Jeebie, see to my costume, please," Bridget says.

They're shooting the scene at our own Renegade Bank on High Street, which now has a temporary sign over it claiming it is First Lower Hacklesbury Bank & Trust. The minute we enter, Bridget grabs a large handful of the free pens the bank has in a stand by the door, and tosses them into her bag.

The bank is far from its usual somnolent self: there are throngs (relatively speaking) of people, large, square lights on tripod stands, and several craft service tables, to which Bridget makes a beeline and diminishes the supply of everything bagels by one-hundred percent. Her scoop technique with the sugar substitute packets by the coffee urn is adroit and she briskly adds three dozen or so Ferrero Rocher wrapped chocolates to her arsenal. Even if she doesn't actually say "Something to give out at Halloween," trust me, I know her.

She hands the stash to me.

"Bridget, this bag is now full of stolen goods."

"It's fine, I have an account here. But keep a low profile."

I follow her to the table on which the real bank, Renegade, places its enticement goodies for new customers.

"Bridget, I'm not going to be an accessory to your crimes. Don't leave me holding the bag." She takes it from me and immediately adds to it two cans of maple syrup from the gift table, a snow globe, two boxes of English breakfast tea, three aluminum tea caddies, a travel iron, and a potted dieffenbachia that's just there for decoration.

Next, she goes to the area to fill out deposit and withdrawal slips, where the bank kindly leaves a jar of dog biscuits. Bridget turns it upside-down into the now-bulging tote.

"Giblet, darling," she says to me under her breath. "I'm going to need another bag."

I notice that Fayette has arrived and we're about to get down to business. I hand Bridget her blue-blazer costume, she hands me back the bag, and Trevor brings Bridget to her seat behind the teller window.

Trevor shouts, "A-team walking in!" which I think is movie talk for actors to take their places. "Quiet!"

Giles says to Fayette and Bridget, "Let's just run through it. Take it from your line 'next,' Bridget. Here we go."

"Next!" Bridget says so loudly that there's an echo throughout the bank.

Fayette approaches the teller window and says, "Good morning. I'd like to close my account, please."

Bridget says, "And you are?"

Giles interrupts, saying, "Bridget, the line is 'I'm sorry to hear that. May I have your name?'"

"What did I say?"

"You said 'And you are?'"

"Well, Giles. I do think mine has a more authentic ring. Have you been in a bank lately?"

"It may be authentic, Bridget," he says patiently, "but remember, this is Lower Hacklesbury."

Bridget nods. "Excellent point. Not the Hacklesbury way."

"Let's try it again," Giles says.

"Just a moment. There are so many paper clips on this desk, it's hard to concentrate. Jeebie, bag please."

She brushes all the paper clips with the side of her hand into the bag, along with the Furby next to the phone, before handing it back to me.

"Bridget, when you're ready. And you can just say 'Next.' You don't have to shout it. A little friendlier."

"Note taken," she says. She clears her throat.

"Here we go," Giles says.

"Ooo is next on moy loine, luv?" Bridget asks in an iffy Cockney accent.

Giles stops her. "Bridget, the teller is American."

"Ah, it didn't specify. I was trying to make her sound friendlier."

I see Fayette looking at Bridget but I can't quite read her expression: amusement?

"She can be nice and chill and American," Giles says. "Take it again."

"Next," Bridget says in a low, sleepy voice.

"Good morning. I'd like to close my account, please," Fayette says.

"Sorry to hear that." Bridget takes a long pause before asking, slowly, "May I have your name?"

"Bridget? Pick up the pace." Giles says.

"I think she may have a little ketamine problem," Bridget says.

"No, Bridget. Teller #2 has been clean for years," Giles says.

"Good to know! Good for her," Bridget says brightly.

"Let's try it again."

I wonder why Giles is being so patient with Bridget and then I remember that she helped him land the director gig for his first movie, his *award-winning* movie. Fayette, on the other hand, seems somehow activated, like she wants to get in on the game.

"Next!" Bridget says.

"Good morning. May I have a paper clip?"

Bridget says, "I'm sorry, the bank no longer gives out paper clips."

"Complimentary Furby?"

"That promotion ended in 1999."

"In that case, I'd like to close my account, please," Fayette says.

"I'm sorry to hear that. May I have your name?" Bridget says.

"Mrs. Sedgewick Trumble," Fayette says.

Bridgets types it on the computer. "May I see some ID?"

Fayette hands a driver's license to Bridget. Bridget studies it carefully, holding it up to the light, looking at the back, then re-examining the front, comparing it with Fayette's actual face, holding it up again, snapping her finger at the plastic, before returning it to Fayette, who snatches it back from her.

"Nothing personal, Mrs. Trumble, but you do have a suspicious look about you. You can't be too careful these days."

"Shameless. You're a shameless ham," Fayette says.

Bridget pretends to answer a call.

"You think you can out-ham me?" Fayette asks.

Bridget holds up finger while she finishes her 'call.'

"Let's try it again," Giles says.

Bridget 'hangs up' the phone, then clears her throat commandingly.

"Next!" Bridget says.

"Good morning. I'd like to close my account, please," Fayette says.

"I'm sorry to hear that. May I have your name?" Bridget says.

"Mrs. Sedgewick Trumble," Fayette says.

Bridget types it on the computer. "May I see some ID?" Glancing at the card, she says, "You're Sedgewick Trumble's old ball and chain."

"NAY!" Fayette says loudly, startling Bridget. "Ball and chain *was* I, in sooth. NO MORE!"

She sounds like some insane Irish, practically-toothless charwoman and I'm not sure what else.

"'Twere a nannikins ol' Sedgewick seen, not a crack afore he waggled his last fiddle-de-dee. KILLED him, I did."

This bit of nonsense gets a laugh from the cast and crew, so Bridget jumps on board.

"Cackled him, didja?"

"Not the only swaggering lump to get his 'ead on a tray. No luck 'ave I with 'usbands."

"'ow many gone?" Bridget asks.

"All of 'em, if ye must know," Fayette replies.

"Lost count, eh? Well done, luv. A gargle for each on me."

Fayette and Bridget have now made each other laugh and the whole crew seems to be enjoying this divertissement.

"All right," Giles calls out. "Maybe say a few words of the script, ladies. Let's get some of this for posterity. Action!"

From the sound guy: "Sound!"

The lead camera: "Rolling!"

The guy with the clapboard: "Take 1 scene F"

Giles yells, "Background. Aaand action!"

"Next," Bridget says.

"Good morning. I'd like to close my account, please," Fayette says.

"Killed another one, 'ave ye?"

"Sedgewick were no prize," Fayette says.

"Now for the bad news," Bridget says. "Ee left ye with ne'er a farthing."

"I need some dosh, the rozzers are on me tail. Come on, give over some cash."

"Then the rozzers will be after me, too."

"Just enough to get me on my way," Fayette says.

"Can't."

"Come on, old crone, hand it over NOW!"

"Old crone!" Bridget says, slapping the large, red button on the wall to her left. Suddenly there's a loud bell ringing.

Giles yells "Cut!", the actual Renegade bank manager comes flying out of his office, and I see out the window that

Arnold Falls cops are racing from the police station across the street into the bank.

"Bridget! Why did you do that?" Giles shouts, finally losing his composure.

"You can't go around robbing banks," Bridget says, handing me the bag of items she has, in fact, stolen from the bank.

Bridget is escorted out by Arnold Falls' finest and I follow her onto High Street.

"Under the circumstances," she says to me, "we may have to renegotiate the three bottles of wine. But help yourself to pens. And can you give me an everything bagel for the road?"

Chapter Twenty

Bender is reading an email when he hears a loud alarm go off. He walks out onto High Street and sees it's coming from the bank. After watching for a few minutes, he calls Jenny.

"News from the street," he says. "I just saw Bridget being marched out of the bank to the police station."

"No! Archie IV was *glad* about it!" Jenny says quickly.

"Huh?"

"Nothing. I'll tell you later."

"I just got an email from the Smithsonian," Bender says. "About the chamber music records. I called and left a message last week."

"You cold-called them?"

"Not exactly. Helps to have Hubble as a last name. They have the Space Telescope named after my great-granduncle so I know some people at the Air and Space Museum. They put me in touch with their African American History and Culture museum. I emailed the Collections Manager and she just wrote back."

"Go on."

"She says she's excited to hear about the discovery. They're working on an exhibit for next year about black classical music and this could be a significant addition if we were willing to loan the items. But maybe we should donate them if they're interested. I also told her about the exhibit on Miss Georgia. She seemed interested in that, too. Let's talk more later. You might want to check on Bridget."

Jenny walks from City Hall to the Police Station and finds Chief Williams pouring himself coffee.

"Cup?" he asks.

"No, thanks."

"Any update on the hospital investigation? FBI's keeping it close to the vest, even from me," the Chief says.

"Haven't heard anything in the last couple of days. What's going on with Bridget?"

"She rang the alarm at the bank. We may charge her with Filing a False Report."

"You're holding her?"

"Yeah, she's gotta learn one of these days. I told her she was gonna go before Judge Harschly and she'd probably have to post bail."

"Let me see her," Jenny says.

The Chief leads the Mayor into the holding room. Bridget is gazing downward when she walks in, but perks up when she sees Jenny.

"Oh, Jenny, hello! Some silly misunderstanding here. I may need someone to post bail."

"What about Trudy?" Jenny asks.

"She refused," Bridget says. "She seemed cross with me about the whole thing, I have no idea why."

"Bridget, you know it's a crime to do that? It's a false alarm."

"That may be," Bridget says, "but it would have been a

far worse crime to film that scene as it was written. Besides, I'm the one who discovered the terrible theft of the statue. That statue was on the National Register of Historic Places."

"Absolutely not true," Jenny says.

"I'm a Denisovan. I don't know your customs. I'd like to file a change of venue motion. I'd like to be tried in Merryvale. Or Lower Hacklesbury."

Jenny sighs and looks at Chief Williams.

"All right," Chief Williams says. "Go, Bridget. Just don't do anything. Nothing. Just stop doing things."

"Right you are. Quiet as a mouse. Not a peep from Bridget Helen Roberts! Thank you, Chief, thank you, Mayor," she says, turning over a nightstick to Chief Williams.

"Whose?" he asks, closing his eyes.

"Velez," Bridget says.

"WHAT TIME IS YOUR APPOINTMENT?" NELLE ASKS, looking up at the black Kit-Cat Klock on the wall.

"Not 'til ten."

"Where's the office?"

"At the hospital."

Nelle is in Doozy's home, only the second time she's been here, and the first visit had been brief. She's sitting at Doozy's kitchen table.

"Lordy, that smells good," Nelle says. "Apple pie?"

"Apple cheddar."

"Is this your annual checkup?"

"Yeah, annual, 'cept it's every six months now. Thanks for giving me a lift. Too hot to walk and no air conditioning in my car."

"Of course. Aunt Doozy, don't you want to think about getting a new car? You can afford it!" Nelle asks.

"Naw, not the point. That Chevette and me, that's a fight, see who can last the longest. Here you go. You want ice cream with that?"

"No, just like this."

"Iced tea?"

"No, thank you. Oh, God, Aunt Doozy, that's delicious."

"Good."

"Aren't you having any?"

"Maybe later," Doozy says.

She's not going to have any later, Nelle thinks. She made this pie for me. As she's savoring each warm bite, Nelle tries to imprint everything she's sees. The white tablecloth with hand-sewn cherries, the pale-yellow walls, a well-worn, enamel bread box with a roll-top. She recognizes the O'Keefe & Merritt stove from the 1950s, because it's similar to the one Aunt Myra had. Everything is so tidy, impeccably clean, and out of a different era. She could have a piping-hot pie resting on the sill of an open window and it would seem just right.

"Do you think your mama would have liked having a show about her life?" Nelle asks.

"You sure you don't want any iced tea?"

"I'm sure," Nelle says.

Doozy sits down at the table.

"She'd be surprised. You know, things was out in the open, but not *that* out in the open."

"How much do you think about your Ma?"

"Every day. Her and Chester."

"Did you ever wish she didn't run a house?"

"Naw. It's just the way it was. She was always trying to provide for me, I know that."

"You don't know who your father was."

"Naw."

As Nelle looks at her, Aunt Doozy drops her eyes.

"Oh!" Nelle says with her mouth full of pie. "Is that, is *that* why you were so down on the exhibit?"

Doozy says nothing.

"You didn't want to find out who your father was. You were afraid it would turn up somehow in your mama's things. I'm right, aren't I?"

"Could be. I'm too old for all that, Nelle. Too late in the day."

"News you can't use," Nelle says. "I can understand that."

"I know you can. But what you remember of *your* father is good, ain't that so?"

"Yeah," Nelle says. "It is."

"My pa? He could be...he coulda been any kind of thing. More pie?"

Nelle smiles and shakes her head.

Doozy gets up and goes into her bedroom. Nelle puts the dish into the sink, runs water on it, and walks into the living room. It's also perfectly neat, with two photos on the wall over the sofa: one of Miss Georgia, and one of Chester, not quite smiling, dressed in his khaki uniform and garrison cap. A fine-looking man he was, killed in 1944, a member of the 761st Tank Battalion.

Doozy returns, saying, "He trying to look all tough in that picture. Chester never went ten seconds without smiling. Come sit down on the sofa. I want you to have this," handing a small box to Nelle.

Nelle looks at Aunt Doozy, while Doozy lights a candle.

"Open it. Go on."

"What a gorgeous necklace!" Nelle says.

"I wanted to give it to you on my birthday but there was

too many people and we got off the track with me calling that park my park."

"Oh, Aunt Doozy, I don't need gifts from you!"

"Never mind that. It's alexandrite. What color you see? Hold it near the candle."

"Red. Crimson red."

"Come with me," Doozy says, blowing out the candle. They walk out to the back porch. "Now what color you see?"

"It's green!"

"Alexandrite, that's my birthstone," Doozy says. "Changes color. Let's sit out here. Little story with that thing. I'm not sure I remember all the details zactly, but anyway, something like this. Guy named Kunz, George Kunz, did minerals, you know, whatchamacallit..."

"Gemstones?"

"That's it, gemstones, for Tiffanys. Friend of my mama's. When I was born, he gave her this stone with the alexandrite, to celebrate me turning up in June. Mama had it made into a necklace. That's a rare gem, I guess, because it came from them Russian mountains and it's three carats. It don't do nothin' 'cept change colors, green to red and back again. Don't bring luck, got no curse. One thing, though, is when someone who's owned the stone dies, it turn blue."

"Really?"

"I didn't believe it either. My mama told me when Mr. Kunz die, I musta been eight or nine, it was blue for days. And when mama died, same thing. When I go, take a look at it. See if it still work."

"You're not going anywhere, Aunt Doozy."

"Not today. 'Cept the doctor. Anyhow, I wanted you to have it."

Nelle doesn't trust herself to speak so she takes the necklace, her eyes looking up at Aunt Doozy, and wraps it around her neck, gently clasping it.

Doozy nods and walks into the house, returning with the pie, now wrapped, and hands it to Nelle.

"Come on, let's go," Doozy says.

Nelle doesn't want to leave the porch. She doesn't want the moment to end. Not for an apple-cheddar pie, not for an alexandrite necklace, not for anything in the world.

WITH DOOZY ENGROSSED IN A COPY OF *PEOPLE* MAGAZINE (A Property Brother's Dream Wedding!) in the doctor's office waiting room, Nelle returns to the lobby. Is she imagining it or does everything about the hospital look shabbier than when she was here last? She stops at the directory board and scans the list as she runs her fingers over the necklace from Doozy: Popsy Siddons-Swain's name is still there, room 403.

When she gets off the elevator at the fourth floor, Nelle goes down one corridor and then another, finally locating the right room. The door is half-way open, so she pokes her head around the corner. A man is standing with his back to her at a desk, riffling through a cardboard box. He senses her presence and turns around, startled.

"Hello," he says warily.

"Hello," Nelle says. "You're Ash Plank."

"That's true. Who are — you're Nelle Clark."

"Also true," Nelle says. "We know each other's names and yet we've never met. I know who you are because I was with Jeebie that time you and Will Shaffer had dinner at Pumphrey's. How do you know me? Am I on the FBI Watch List or something?"

"No," he says, sitting against the back of the desk. "I've

seen the video of your concert last fall. A lot of times. You're amazing."

"Thank you."

They look at each other for a few moments, trying to decide what to make of the situation. He's handsome, Nelle thinks. In an old-fashioned, square-jawed way. But not so sure of himself.

"Why are you here?" Nelle asks.

"Shouldn't I be asking you that?"

"If you're any kind of agent, yeah, I guess."

"I'm not an especially good agent, to be honest. That's why they give me Arnold Falls."

"So?" Nelle asks.

"Financial irregularities," Ash says. "Now you."

"Well, Jeebie, he's the guy that Will —"

"I know who he is," Ash says.

"He wants to start an arts program for the pediatric oncology unit but Popsy Siddons-Swain had stopped all volunteer services. And the hospital's rating has gone way down. And Jeebie called to speak to Popsy Siddons-Swain and got suspicious about the way his call was handled and so we're trying to figure out what's going on."

"I'm trying to figure out the same thing. Nothing good, is the preliminary report. I shouldn't say more than that. Ongoing investigation and all that."

"Come on, Ash, spill it."

"Couldn't. I'd get fired."

"It's just you and me. I'll sing for you," Nelle says.

"Huh?"

"I sing, you sing."

"Now?"

"Yeah."

"You're not allowed to bribe the FBI."

"Give it a rest. Deal?"

"I really shouldn't," he says.

"You can pick the song," Nelle says.

"I dunno," Ash says.

"Yeah, you know," Nelle says.

He nods. "That Stevie Wonder song you sang."

Nelle sings a short version of Stevie Wonder's "If You Really Love Me." Just as she's getting to the final chorus, Ash looks to the doorway. Nelle turns and sees Will. She stops singing.

"I don't think I could explain what is going on at this moment in this room, if you gave me a thousand tries," Will says. "Hi, Ash."

"Hey, Will."

"Hi, Nelle," Will says.

"Ash is going to sing for us. Like a canary," she says. "Over to you, Ash."

"You sing great, Nelle. Anyway. Okay. This Popsy is bad news."

He lives up to his end of the bargain, explaining that Popsy Siddons-Swain opened the money spout by going through a subsidiary, MedRegional, as payers for wire transfers to herself. And she used credit cards in the name of MedRegional. Nelle raises her eyebrows at Will. His theory of wire transfer crimes was right on the money.

"Throw in bank fraud, aggravated ID theft and forged securities," Ash says.

"How much?" Nelle asks.

"Getting close to a million. That we know of. Forensic accounting is going through it. We gotta keep it quiet until we know more. No charges yet."

"Where is Popsy now?"

"That's the big question. Unclear. We're working on it."

Nelle nods. "I've gotta go pick up Aunt Doozy. She's at her doctor's office downstairs. You coming with me Will?"

"Yep," he says.

"Thanks for the song, Nelle. Nice to meet you. And good to see you, Will."

"You, too, Ash. Thanks."

Nelle links her arm in Will's and walks him out into the corridor to the bank of three elevators.

"What are you doing here?" Nelle asks.

"Same as you. Snooping around," Will says.

The bell rings for the center door, which slides open, releasing one Jeebie Walker into the hallway.

"Now it's a party," Nelle says.

Will says, "I thought you were helping Bridget today."

"Police escorted her from the set."

"No!" Nelle says.

"Oh, very much yes. Nice necklace. New?"

"Aunt Doozy. I have to pick her up now and take her home."

"I was going to see if I could speak with the head of pediatric oncology but I thought I'd poke around first about Popsy."

Will says, stepping on to the elevator, "Nelle sang a song for Ash Plank, the hospital's missing a million dollars, and Popsy's taken a powder."

The elevator door closes.

∾

COME CHECK ON YOUR BOYFRIEND. HE'S DOWN WITH MINNA *but doesn't seem very happy.*

Will reads the text from Fridsy and gets into his pickup.

When he pulls into the driveway of the farm, he notes Fridsy is once again on the porch, this time fully clothed.

"I just happened to notice him down there," tapping her finger toward the pond. "I told him he could come visit anytime."

He smiles at her and sees, way off in the distance, a group of cows lying down, although one of them doesn't look like the others.

When he reaches the pond, he sees Jeebie in nearly fetal position. Two of the cows announce Will's arrival and Jeebie looks up, his eyes red and watery.

"What's happened?" Will asks, kneeling next to Jeebie.

Jeebie starts to say something but it's mixed with sobs and tears and sniffles, so Will can't make sense out of it. He's never seen Jeebie like this.

"Hang on, hang on," Will says, sitting cross-legged. "Here, rest your head here." Will strokes Jeebie's hair. He looks over to Minna and sees she's watching closely.

"How did you know where I was?" Jeebie asks.

"Fridsy texted me."

"Why is Fridsy texting you? I don't understand *anything*," Jeebie says, his voice quavering.

"Tell me," Will says.

"After I saw you, I went to talk to the director of the pediatric oncology unit. She wasn't available and you're not supposed to just walk in there, but I know one of the nurses, and when I explained what I wanted to do, they let me hang out with two of the kids for a little while."

"How was that?" Will asks.

"It was good. But t-terrible." Jeebie dissolves into tears again. "Zoey and Makayla."

"You're going to do something for them," Will says.

"I know. But what can I do? So little and it's so unfair."

"Anything else on your mind?"

"No. But why should kids have to suffer like that? And Popsy took all that money. And the hospital is falling apart and those kids aren't getting even a singalong. As if they don't matter. Makayla has neuroblastoma. What kind of world does that to a child? She's so sweet. They're ten and eight years old. Nothing makes sense. I'm friends with Fridsy. Inexplicable. Minna thinks I've lost it. Do you think I've lost it, Minna? And I have something on the down-low with a cow. And I'm plant-based. And when I put up the little libraries they get vandalized. And you're going to start grad school and you'll probably fall in love with your advisor."

"The advisor I want is a woman," Will says.

"Her brother, then," Jeebie says.

Will gently wipes away Jeebie's tears.

"Jeebie. You've got this. Go back to the hospital. Spend time with Makayla and Zoey. Talk to the head of the unit. Tell them what you want to do. Then do it. You'll make a big difference. Theo already offered to rebuild the little libraries. Take him up on it. And I'm not going to fall in love with my advisor or her brother. Okay?"

Jeebie nods.

Just then, Fridsy appears with a tray for lunch: bread, cheese, fruit, and chilled white wine. She sees Jeebie's face and puts the tray down on the grass without a word and walks back toward the house. The kindness sets Jeebie off again and Will holds him tightly while he cries it all out.

Chapter Twenty-One

Zoey and Makayla rock. That becomes increasingly evident as I hang out with them this morning, after my meltdown yesterday. They're not saints, they're kids. But still, amazing kids. Even though they're way ahead of me on the latest in pop culture, I do my best to keep up, and we watch videos, and tell little stories and somehow I can make them laugh. I still feel what I felt when I was so low at Fridsy's farm. I feel all of it. But I also feel angry about it and there's nowhere to go with that anger, except here, and do whatever it is I can do.

Eventually the head of the unit, Dr. Sharma, comes out. I like her straight away, especially her empathic eyes. We go sit by the windows and I tell her what I'm planning.

"Listen, do it," she says. "Just go ahead. I'll back you up."

"We don't need any money," I say.

"That's good. Because there isn't any."

"Popsy?"

"Yes, but it's more than that."

"How so?"

"We're a small hospital. Only a hundred beds. As complicated as hospital bills are, the big-picture math is simple. For-profit hospitals have to make a profit. And we've been struggling. If what I'm hearing about Popsy is true, it could be a fatal blow."

"A fatal blow?"

"Meaning we'd have to close. Or get bought out. But probably the former."

"Where would the patients go?"

"They'd have to travel to Albany. A big hardship for many. And of course devastating for Arnold Falls and the surrounding communities."

An intern walks by checking his phone. Dr. Sharma smiles at him and changes the subject while he's in hearing distance.

"The open lounge area down at the end of that hall is a good place for performers. We'll get everyone who can to sit close, otherwise they can listen from their rooms, or maybe their doorways. Music of all kinds is good. Well, not all kinds. Use your judgment. Stuff they can participate in, crafts, painting. If you're not sure, you can ask me. You've got be careful with stuff like paint — nothing with toxic fumes, things you might not think of."

"Baking?" I ask.

"We do have a pretty big tabletop oven in the staff room. You can use it."

"If the hospital's going to close, should I even do this?"

"I can't answer that for you," she says, clasping my hands. "Whatever happens, what you want to do can only help."

"I was a wreck after I was here yesterday."

Dr. Sharma nods. "I can't say you'll get used to it because you won't. Come cry on my shoulder when you need it," she says, and walks into her office.

I sit by the window and consider that whatever happens with the hospital is out of my control. What I can do is try to bring a little joy to these kids. And whatever I feel about what is happening to them is beside the point. Will calls and says, "Meet in the back yard for a drink? I've renamed the summer ale Sad Giblet in your honor."

This makes me both laugh and tear up at the same time. I'm a mess.

"Okay, but there's something I have to do first. I'll be home soon."

I go hang out with the other child on the ward at the moment, a boy named Jace. We don't talk much because he doesn't seem up to it. After I while, I say, "I'll see you later, Jace," and I get a little smile from him, I think.

Zoey and Makayla are sitting together at a table, drawing.

They nod when I ask, "You want me to read a story?"

Zoey goes to the bookshelf and picks out *The Adventures of Nanny Piggins*.

It's a charmer, the story of three children and their nanny, who is a pig. I use all my skills from voiceover work to create a memorable Nanny Piggins, and she does sounds somewhat piggish, somewhat nannyish, and somewhat Carol Channingish. In any case, it does the trick: every time Nanny speaks, Makayla and Zoey crack up.

My work here is done. For today.

Chapter Twenty-Two

T rudy has always liked the idea of summer Fridays: the season and the day of the week teaming up to say slow down, smell roses, drink gin and tonics. In the past hour, she has done all three. She and Bridget are comfortably ensconced in Adirondacks chairs, their feet up on footstools, under the afternoon sun, Trudy's mind wandering where it will.

She sees Bridget pull out another Denisovan book from her bag: this one is called *Pretty Little Lying Denisovan Girl, Gone Extinct*.

"Denisovan *fiction* now?" Trudy asks.

"That's all that's left," Bridget says, sipping a glass of Chianti.

Trudy picks up today's crossword puzzle and fills in six clues without breaking a sweat. The seventh, *Wear-off*, she's not sure about, but she gets two verticals that give her the answer: drag ball. As she writes it in, something tugs at her about this. Not the answer, the clue. *Wear-off*. It makes her think of The Shack for some reason. And then she remembers.

"Bridget, when all of us were having breakfast at the Shack together, did you notice Marvin the Hobo said, 'It took a long time for that face cream to *wore* off.'"

"He's a hobo, not a copy editor," Bridget says.

"I taught ESL for six months in Prague in the nineties..."

"I know. You loved Prague," Bridget says.

"I did. Something about that particular mistake sounds to me like English isn't his first language. Sounds like one of my students."

"I don't know, Trudy. He says he was a hobo riding the rails until he became a hermit. Though now that I say it, it sounds sketchy, doesn't it?"

"How did AF get a hermit? Was it Rufus?" Trudy asks.

"I think so. Let me call Jeebie. He'll know," she says, picking up her phone.

"Are you calling to deliver the three bottles of wine you owe me?" Jeebie says when he answers.

"Afraid not," Bridget says. "Temporarily out of stock."

"You're having the Pruneto right now, aren't you?"

"Last sip," Bridget says. "I'm putting you on speakerphone. Trudy had a thought."

Trudy explains and then asks, "How did we get Marvin? Didn't the town hire him?"

"If I remember correctly," Jeebie says, "the town doesn't pay him. But the town owns the lightning-splitter and he gets to stay there for no rent."

"Whose idea was he?"

"It was Rufus' idea," Jeebie says.

"Rufus couldn't have come up with it on his own," Trudy says.

Bridget nods as Jeebie pauses to consider this.

"That's true," Jeebie says. "Good point. What are you thinking?"

Trudy says, "Something's off about him. Can't say exactly."

"I trust your instincts, Trudy."

"Helloooo. I'm here, too," Bridget says.

"Your instincts, too, Bridget. Let me add Jenny to this call."

When Jenny answers, Jeebie says, "You're on speaker with Bridget and Trudy."

"*You're* on speaker with me and Wilky," Jenny says.

"Helloooo, Wilky! It's your godmothers Bridget and Trudy!"

"Bridget..." Jenny says.

"We're your *supercool* godparents," Bridget says.

"Bridget..." Jeebie says.

"Hi!" Wilky says.

"Has something else been stolen?" Jenny asks. "Is there anything left to steal?"

Trudy fills her in.

"So how did we get Marvin?" Jeebie asks.

"Rufus," Jenny says. "But I don't know the details. Tishy would. Hang on."

"Yuh?" is how Tishy answers her phone. After a recap, she replies, "Didn't pay much attention to Rufus when he was mayor, definitely didn't when he was a lame duck. Now that you mention it, he wouldn't tell me the details about Marvin. Hard to believe Rufus could keep his mouth shut about anything. But he did that time. Why, what's Rufus done now? I thought after sending bombs to Plopeni, he'd used up all his stupid. He's done something again, I can feel it."

After the call, Trudy takes a sip of her cocktail, thinking of the steps that led her from Prague to Arnold Falls. "I wouldn't trade any of it," she says out loud.

"I have to," Bridget says. "I promised him three bottles."

~

"E-3"

"Miss," Wilky says. "H-7."

"Miss," Tishy says.

"Who won Battleship last game?" Wilky asks.

"You, you rascal. You knew that. B-9," Tishy says.

"Miss."

"Hold on," Tishy says, as she answers the phone. "Good morning, Mayor Jagoda's office. Oh, hi, Bender!"

Tishy looks at Wilky excitedly and points to the phone, nodding her head.

"Hi, Bender!" Wilky shouts.

"Wilky says hi," Tishy says. "I don't know, something about Marvin the Hobo. Okay, I will."

"J-10," Wilky says.

"Hit!" Tishy says. "Damn!"

"In Bender's store, you would pay twenty-five cents for the swear."

"Are we making progress, do you think?"

"Mayormama and Bender?"

"Yuh," Tishy says.

"I think she like him but she's busy."

"What do you mean?" Tishy asks.

"Being Mayor. Many stolen things. Having me around. I think she don't admit she like him."

"How did you get so smart?" Tishy asks. "C-7."

"Hit!"

"Ha! I don't care if you are nine-years-old. I am going to crush you."

Wilky grins.

~

JENNY SEES A LOUNGE CHAIR, A WHITE BATHROBE DRAPED over it, and the rolling hills of Rufus' sunbathing silhouette sprawled atop. He's got headphones on, and a pair of pink protectors over his eyes. There is a squeezed lemon on the table next to him. Jenny takes out her phone and snaps a picture because, she thinks, you never know. Then she remembers she has the air horn they used for vitilla last week still in her bag and gives it one long blast.

"Jesus, Mary, and Joseph!" Rufus says as he jumps up, throwing on his bathrobe, his headphones falling onto the grass. "What the fuck?"

As he takes off the eye protectors, the strap breaks. He blinks at Jenny.

"Lemon's giving you nice highlights," she says.

"This is private property."

"Call a cop."

"You know, when I was mayor, I didn't go sneaking into people's backyards. I spent my time at City Hall."

"Yeah, playing Candy Crush."

"Angry Birds," he says. "You made me break my wife's eye protectors."

"They're yours, I know when you're lying," Jenny says.

"Am not! Why are you in my backyard?"

"Where did Marvin come from?"

"Who?"

"Marvin the Hobo," Jenny says.

"I guess from Hoboland," Rufus says.

"Rufus, I am not playing. Whose idea was getting a hobo for Arnold Falls?"

"Credit goes to yours truly."

"I didn't ask where the credit goes. I asked whose idea it was. It wasn't your idea."

"You don't know that!" Rufus says.

"I've known you since kindergarten. I know how you think. *Please* tie your bathrobe."

"What? Oh. Well, let me see if I can remember. Long time ago."

"Seven months. And I am going to kill you in seven seconds if you don't tell me where Marvin came from."

"Okay, don't have a cow. I think, uh, another mayor mentioned it to me."

"What other mayor?"

Rufus mumbles something.

"Did you say Lammy?" Jenny asks. "Who's Mayor Lammy?"

"Haralambie. Mayor Haralambie. From Plopeni."

There is a long silence. Finally, Jenny says, as evenly as she can, "After you sent all that ammonium nitrate, didn't the FBI tell you not to have any contact with anyone from Plopeni or with anyone from *anywhere* in Romania?"

"In a way," Rufus says.

"Rufus, did Mayor Haralambie suggest getting a hobo for Arnold Falls? Or did he suggest *Marvin* for Arnold Falls?"

"Number two," Rufus says. "And we're *Emollimax* now."

"So Marvin didn't come with references."

"Mayor Haralambie was his reference. What's the big deal? I said no to ArnPlop."

"Arnold Falls and Plopeni co-hosting an international ideas forum was ridiculous. They were just trying to get something from us."

"You're wrong there, Jenny. Haralambie's okay. He's the mayor!"

"Yeah, a mayor who has gotten potable water, guns, a shipment of ammonium nitrate, and wanted this town to foot the bill for ArnPlop."

"Not the whole bill."

"The FBI told you not to have anything to do with them."

"Marvin's a nice guy," Rufus says.

"Who is pretending to be someone he's not."

"How do you figure?"

"I've gotta go, Rufus," Jenny says, rubbing her temples. "Go back to sunning yourself."

"Not in the mood now," Rufus says sullenly.

As she's walking back to City Hall, Jenny calls Ash Plank.

～

"HI, OUCHIE," VERA SAYS.

"'Sup, Vera. Judge wanted to see me."

"Come in, Ouchie," Judge Harschly calls from his office. "Have a seat."

"I do something, Judge H.?"

"Nothing like that. I guess you've heard about things going missing around town?"

"Nothing to do with me, Judge, I swear."

"I know that, I know it. Somebody broke in here and stole my gavel. Now, it's one thing to take the statue of Hezekiah Hesper. No harm, no foul. But that gavel has sentimental value to me."

"Passed down the generations?" Ouchie asks.

"No, I won it at the Skowhegan State Fair, 1968. I just thought you might have heard some talk about the bric-a-brac that's gone missing. Anything at all?"

"Nothing, Judge. I could ask around."

"Would you do that? See what you pick up. Maybe *solve* a crime for a change. That was the other thing I wanted to talk to you about, Ouchie. *Don't* take this the wrong way but you're a *terrible* crook. I think you should give some serious thought to another line of work. You're just not cut out for it. How many times have you been in my court?"

"Fifteen."

"And how old are you?"

"Twenty-eight."

"There you are! That's not a winning margin. How else can I say this? You're *just not good* at criming. And the sooner you face that fact, the better off you'll be. I know it must come as a bitter disappointment to you. Look, it would be one thing if you got away with it, oh, I don't know, every third time. Lord knows I've seen bad crookery in my time, but *you*!"

"I'm not that bad, Judge H."

"You get cuffed while you're still trying to break in."

"That only happened once. Twice."

"Vera?" Judge Harschly calls out.

"Six times," Vera shouts back.

"You want to argue with Vera?" the Judge asks.

Ouchie shakes his head.

"Tell me, did you or did you not advertise an Art Deco estate sale, a week after you cleaned out Deco-Rations?"

"My timing was a little off."

"You put up *flyers*. And another thing. I hope you've learned your lesson, Ouchie. You can*not* use Uber for a getaway car."

"Okay, okay, Judge. I get your point."

"Even if your common sense is questionable, my hunch is there's a stand-up guy somewhere in there. Anything you think you might be good at? Less terrible at?"

"Maybe a life coach."

Judge Harschly peers at him over his half-moon specs. "Anything else?"

"I like sports."

"Watching or playing?"

"Mostly betting."

Judge Harschly holds up his hand. "*Did not* hear that. I withdraw the question. Let me see what I can do. And let me know if you hear anything, gavel-wise, on your end."

Chapter Twenty-Three

Darnell Pressley has just given me a tour of the show on Miss Georgia, saving the last room until Doozy and Nelle get here. They have done an extraordinary job of bringing Miss Georgia to life, of telling her story, and putting it in the context of the Great Northern Migration — so much history I was never taught in school.

Finally, Doozy and Nelle arrive and we pause in the hallway behind the curtained entrance to the last part of the exhibit.

"I'm so excited for you to see this," Darnell says to Doozy. "Are you ready?"

"As I'll ever be," Doozy says.

We enter into a large, dark, black-box room with two benches in the middle, facing a hanging projector screen. Doozy sits, we stand off to the side. After a few moments, a black-and-white home movie comes up and I realize it's Miss Georgia next to an apple tree. There's no sound to the movie, though Mildred Bailey's "It's So Peaceful in the Country" accompanies the images.

"Well, look at that. That's the orchard. Eiderdown," Doozy says. "By the big hill."

"Look how beautiful she is," Darnell says. "Look at that sweet look she gives to the person shooting the film. Unfortunately, we don't know who took it."

"I know who took it," Doozy says. "I did."

Miss Georgia mugs for the camera, making various funny faces. The camera shakes.

Doozy laughs. "She always doing that to make me laugh."

"When do you think this was taken?" Nelle asks.

"Maybe 1950," Doozy says.

"Exactly right," Darnell says. "The canister had the year on it. Must have been midsummer, right around now. Apples weren't ready."

"That was a hot summer. Most houses didn't have no air conditioning. We used to go over to the orchard in the afternoon, nap in the shade of an apple tree. Whenever I smell apple blossoms, I think of them days. Nice people who ran that place. There! You see? Mama's sitting down, leaning against the tree. Time for a...siesta she call it."

The scene fades out, a scene in color fades in.

"This is probably 1956 or seven," Darnell says.

"That's in the house. The parlor. That's Mama with a few girls."

They sing "Happy Birthday" to Tilly.

"Yeah, Tilly," Doozy says. "Didn't remember how pretty she was. And that's May next to her. Carrying the cake is whatchacallit. I forget her name now. Wasn't there long. I think they called her Bobbie, something like that. I liked being with them, too. Kidding around all the time. Bad work but they made the best of it. Same's true for Ma."

Tilly blows out the candles and the scene fades to black.

Then something astonishing happens. The projection

screen disappears into its ceiling panel and the room is completely dark until a small group of musicians appear, seated, tightly lit in the darkness, and begin to play. They're not there, of course, they're some kind of hologram, but they sure look like they're there. The intro music sways gently and, holy moly, Miss Georgia appears to step out to the microphone, in a black dress faintly shimmering with rhinestones.

I look over at Aunt Doozy, who is leaning forward, eyes wide, like she's seeing a ghost, because she is. I get goosebumps as I watch her watch her mother. I'm seeing a ghost of the little girl that Doozy was.

Miss Georgia begins to sing an Ethel Waters song, "Baby, What Else Can I Do?" and Doozy stands up.

Doozy slowly raises her hand out and says, "Ma."

It appears as if Miss Georgia is singing directly to Doozy, "If you want the moon/I'll bring the moon right down to you" and even if the lyric is hackneyed, Miss Georgia turns into a flesh-and-blood human for me at that moment, an insight into what may have motivated her to live the life she lived. Doozy seems both transported and immobilized, if that's possible, and I look over at Darnell and Nelle, whose eyes are glistening, and Miss Georgia's dress is sparkling, and the bond between mother and daughter in the ether is so loving, so fiercely loving, that it overwhelms me.

It's almost a relief when the song ends. Miss Georgia blows a quick kiss into the future and the musicians fade back into darkness and swirling dust.

Doozy sits back down on the bench. Nelle sits at her feet.

"Your Ma sang good, too," Nelle says.

Doozy nods.

"Had you ever seen that?" Nelle asks.

Doozy shakes her head. After a moment, she says, "She

used to sing that song to me. That was her way to say, say what she want to say."

We let that sink in and wait quietly until Doozy is ready to go.

She stands. A summing up? A final thought?

After the smallest of sighs, she says, "Time for lunch."

~

DARNELL, NELLE, AND I DO, IN FACT, HAVE LUNCH AT THE Shack, but Doozy won't sit with us.

"I'm working," she says, "and anyhow, I don't want to know how you did that."

"How *did* you do that?" I ask, as Doozy goes to wait on another table.

Darnell says, "It's an old technique from the 19th century called Pepper's Ghost, just augmented with new technologies."

"What's Pepper's Ghost?" I ask.

"Basically, it's a trick," Darnell explains, "but a really good one. It was created in 1860 by John Henry Pepper using a reflection of something onto an angled glass, to make it look like what we would call a hologram, although it's not. When they needed a ghost scene in the theater — think *Hamlet* — it was perfect."

"That must have cost the museum a bundle to do that!"

"It's being used more and more. Even those projected information displays in your car are descendants of Pepper's Ghost. And I have a friend who works in that field, so he did it for cost."

"You're quiet," I say to Nelle.

She nods and says, "Time travel takes it out of you."

"And?"

"And, I don't know. Why did Miss Georgia record that? Where were they? Who were the guys playing?"

I look at Nelle and we have the same realization at the same moment.

"Do you have a digital file of it, Darnell?"

"The whole Pepper's Ghost thing, what we just saw? Yeah."

I call Jenny and say, "I think we may have found some friends of yours. Check your email."

Chapter Twenty-Four

✿

Wilky texts Tishy: *Something happening!*

Tishy: What?! I can't see in, the door's almost shut.

Wilky: I know. I have my headphone on but don't listen to my book. She sit at her mayor desk. He stand behind her, leans in to the screen. His hand on her necks.

Tishy: Her necks?

Wilky: Épaules.

Tishy: Wait.

Tishy: Shoulders.

Wilky: They look very hard at the computer. Mayormama's mouth is open. I move headphone down from my ear.

Wilky: 'That must be in Gorga's house,' she say.

Tishy: They're looking at something from the show about Miss Georgia.

Wilky: They're breathing together. Same time. I have to listen, not look.

Wilky: 'Holy shit,' she say. 'Unbelivabel,' Bender say. Il s'accroupit next to her. I don't know it in English.

Tishy: Wait.

Tishy: Crouch. Is his arm around her?

Wilky: It is now. Old woman is singing.

Tishy: Old woman?

Wilky: Woman. Song is old. I just look over.

Tishy: And???

Wilky: I think she like him.

Tishy: !!

Wilky: He say, That's them! How's weerd is that. It's like they've been brawt back to life since you went to the basement.

Wilky: Like we're where we're supposed to be, Mayormama say. Getting mushie.

Tishy: About the chamber ensemble I think.

Wilky: Oh-oh! Got quiet.

Wilky: I can't look.

Wilky: Could be kissing.

Tishy texts back exploding fireworks.

Wilky: Bon. Come in. Ça suffit. It's enough now.

JENNY FEELS THE SUN WARMING HER BARE, PALE ARMS while a breeze is giving those arms a ripple of goosebumps as she walks from City Hall to the pocket park three blocks away. Hamster, the janitor at the Court House, lopes toward her.

"Morning, Hamster," Jenny says.

"'lo," he replies in his usual, taciturn way.

She has to fight the impulse to hug him. Instead, she leans against Winstian's Antiques to collect her thoughts.

Kenny Winstian comes out and says, "Morning, Mayor."

"Hi, Kenny. Gorgeous day. How's everything? When are you starting up work with Trudy?"

"Going to work with Trudy in the fall. How's everything with you, Jen?"

"Kenny, has love ever just hit you? Out of the blue?"

He sighs. "Yeah, I know the feeling. Mostly great, a little terrifying. Which way is up?"

"Exactly," Jenny says.

"I've always been fond of Bender."

"What! What made you say that?"

"Come on, Jen. You know how it is here in the Land of No Secrets."

"But *I* didn't know."

"It goes that way sometimes."

She kisses his cheek and continues her walk, trying to focus on this meeting with Rufus. It's only geography that has made Rufus part of her life. Jenny knows that. They've lived within a mile of each other forever. But in spite of his many, many shortcomings, a small part of her considers him like an annoying brother. And now that she and Ash Plank are going to pressure him to do the right thing, she feels for him: he won't do the right thing willingly, and when he finally does it, he'll never do it the right way.

They meet at Bean Here, Done That, the outdoor coffee cart set up in front of the pocket park a few blocks down High Street. When Jenny arrives, she and Ash shake hands. She orders a cappuccino.

"You want me to do the grilling?" Ash asks.

"Let me handle him."

Rufus walks up, wearing madras plaid shorts and a yellow polo shirt. "Morning," he says.

After they get their coffees, they sit at one of the small, round tables.

"Whatever this is, I don't like it," Rufus says.

Ash says, "Rufus, I was very clear — the FBI was very

clear — that any further dealings with Plopeni in general, and Mayor Haralambie in particular, were a bad idea and could put you, and Arnold Falls, in jeopardy."

"Yeah, I guess I remember something about that," Rufus says.

"Do you know what's going on at the hospital?" Jenny asks.

"With Marvin?" Rufus asks.

"No, nothing to do with Marvin," Ash says.

"You lost me," Rufus says.

Jenny explains the embezzlement at Queechy Gen.

"You're going to stay in the good graces of the FBI," Jenny says, "by helping us with our hospital problem."

"Oh, yeah? Why do you figure I'd do something like that?" Rufus says.

"Could be a conspiracy charge in there," Ash says.

"For hiring a hobo?" Rufus says.

"I know so many things about you, Rufus," Jenny says. "So many things."

"That right? It would be nice if Archie were still with us. Shame to lose him when we did."

Jenny smiles. "Rufus. Rufus Meierhoffer."

"Hit me with your best shot, Jenny Jagoda."

Jenny brings out her phone and shows Rufus the picture she took of him sunbathing. "So Instagrammable," she says.

He knows he's beat.

"What do you want me to do?"

"You play poker sometimes with Dr. Jantzen, right?" Jenny asks.

"Yeah, not all the time. But sometimes at the Friday night games."

"You and Bunny Liverwurst."

"Yeah, and some others."

Ash says, "We want you to wear a wire."

"Cut the crap. What do you want me to do?"

There's no response.

"Aw Jeez," Rufus says.

~

AFTER TWO-AND-A-HALF HOURS OF LISTENING, COURTESY
of Rufus' wire, to the Friday night poker game at Dr. Jantzen's
house, Rufus hasn't gotten a single piece of useful information
yet, though to be fair, he hasn't had a lot of opportunities.

Finally, Dr. Jantzen says, "It's 10:30, and that makes it time
to call it a night. The days are already getting shorter..."

As Dr. Jantzen blows smoke about Daylight Savings, Ash
hears chairs moving and the sounds of a party, or at least a
poker night, breaking up. Bunny Liverwurst says, "Night,
Emil," and, from what he can tell, Rufus is the last to leave.

Rufus clears his throat and says, "So, Dr. J., lot of thefts
going around, huh?"

"I don't know what you mean," Dr. Jantzen says warily.

"The Schlitz clock, for one, whole lotta Clagger, Hesper
statue. They think it might be Marvin."

"Marvin?"

"Marvin the Hobo," Rufus says. "Wondered if you heard
anything, you know, on the street, about that. I personally
don't think it's Marvin. Nice guy, references and everything.
Doesn't make sense."

"I'm afraid you're not making any sense to me, Rufus. I
have no idea what you're talking about it. A mild case of
aphasia, I should think."

"No," Rufus says. "He's fit as a fiddle."

"Ah!" Dr. Jantzen replies. "Are fiddles truly fit? Thanks for
being here. Good night."

Ash is looking at the wall next to him, deciding whether or not to bang his head against it. A moment later his phone rings. It's Rufus.

"I did good, right?"

"Rufus, you were supposed to ask Dr. Jantzen about the *hospital*. Not the Schlitz clock."

"Lotta people love that clock, chief."

"Rufus..." Ash says, as sternly as he can.

"Okay, okay, I'll go back in."

"Say you forgot something."

"What did I forget?" Rufus asks.

"Improvise."

"Yeah, okay. I can do that."

Ash hears him walk back and open the front door of the Jantzen house. Rufus says, "Oh, hello."

After a moment, Dr. Jantzen says, "Did you forget something, Rufus?"

"I...forgot...I forget what I forgot. That ever happen to you?"

"I'd really have that looked into," Dr. Jantzen says. "Good night now."

Ash buries his face in his hands. As his phone rings, he seriously considers quitting the FBI, moving to Key West, and opening a bed and breakfast.

"I'll do it again next week now that I've had some practice," Rufus says by way of apology.

"I may be retired by then," Ash says.

"You're a young man!"

"I was when the evening started."

"Don't be like that. Play your cards right, you could end up successful like Dr. Jantzen. Good job, nice house, little something on the side. He's a lousy poker player, though. Doesn't actually play his cards right. Blabbermouth. You gotta just keep at it, cause like I told you, you look the part of an FBI guy."

"Maybe," Ash says. "Not sure I'm really cut out for this."

"Look, I'll wear a wire for you next week and we'll wrap the whole thing up."

"I've got to give a report this week. There's always — what do you mean a little something on the side?"

"You never heard that expression?"

"I have," Ash says. "But who's his little something on the side?"

"No idea."

"Then how do you know he has a little something on the side?"

"It's not really on the side," Rufus clarifies. "He's a widower."

"Okay, but who are you talking about?"

"That chick who was there when I went back. I assume that's what she is. And she's not really a chick, if you know what I mean. I mean, she's a woman, just not, you know, not in her twenties, no offense to her. Don't want to be that g—"

"Rufus, are you saying there was someone else in Dr. Jantzen's house when you went back in?"

"Yeah."

"Not part of the poker game?"

"No. Never saw her before."

"Describe her."

"I don't know, maybe fifties, tight face, attitude. You think it's a clue?"

Almost too easy for what may be the last item on his list. Breaking into the Chicken Shack at one in the morning requires no skill at all. The back door gives with one extra push. It's less than a minute before the framed photo is removed from the wall. Next to the cash register, there is a pad of paper and the intruder stops to write a note: "I have John Fitzpatrick Kennedy. Do not try to find him. Sorry, Doosy."

Heading to the back door, a quick check of the refrigerator, a disappointed curse:

"*La naiba!*"

No fried chicken to go.

"DAGNABBIT, *DAGNABBIT!*" DOOZY SAYS.

"What's the matter?" Sal asks as he flips hash browns.

"They stole JFK," Doozy says, pointing to the wall where the photo had hung.

"*Cazzo!*" Sal says.

Doozy nods. She hands him the note.

"Call Chief Williams," Sal says.

"I'll call Jenny."

Chapter Twenty-Five

I t's a Saturday morning and Will should be at the farmer's market, but there's heavy rain mixed with hail, so the market is canceled and he's home doing the laundry. I've set up a little office by the laundry room, which Will says now looks like Carrie Mathison's workspace in *Homeland*, I guess because I have pinned a few (dozen) things to the wall.

Watch this.

"Will!" I call out.

"Yes, Carrie?"

See? He thinks it's funny. There's a lot to keep track of. I've already talked with Percy Tunnion of Traitor's Landing. Percy said he'll ask performers if they'll do a mini-concert at the hospital. We're going to have some kind of programming twice a week, Wednesday at noon and Saturday at 5pm. Dr. Sharma has been so great.

What I've got so far, in addition to Traitor's performers, is Nelle, Theo Nyqvist for painting, Juliet from the library to read. Depending on his schedule at Cornell, Will said he'd love to draw with the kids. Chaplin already has his therapy-turkey certification, though Dr. Sharma is going to check if there are any issues with having a turkey in the ward. And Wilky wants to be involved, which Jenny okayed, so I'm calling him a goodwill ambassador.

And speak of the devil, Jenny's calling.

"Hello, Mayormama."

"Hello, Giblet. Listen, our thief broke into the Shack last night and took the photo of JFK."

"Oh, cripes," I say.

"Yeah. Aunt Doozy is pissed off and upset. This is getting out of hand."

"You want my advice?"

"That's why I called," she says.

"I'd get a few people together, like Judge Harschly, and Ash Plank, and Chief Williams, and work this through."

"I need you there, too," Jenny says.

"I'm a civilian."

"*Because* you're a civilian. And because I need you there."

"When?"

"This morning. I know it's crappy out."

"It's okay. Where?" I ask.

"Somewhere we can have privacy."

"What about the Pipe Room at the library? Saturday morning in summer, no one's going to be at the library."

After I get a text back from Jenny confirming the meeting, I tell Will I have to go out.

"I'm going to need you to go on a mission," he says.

"I'm your man."

"Fabric softener," he says.

Even the short walk from my car into the library has left me drenched, my umbrella now inverted and useless.

"Good morning, Jeebie," Juliet says.

"It's a dark and stormy...morning," I say.

"I don't think that's an improvement."

"Not the time for quibbling," I say, as I drip copiously in the library's vestibule.

"Do you want a cup of tea? Come into the back and help yourself."

"Thanks, I will."

As I let the Earl Grey steep, Juliet hands me a macaroon on a napkin.

"Anyone else here?"

"You're the first," she says.

"We have a little crime wave," I say.

"So I heard."

"Even the little libraries were trashed, though that could be a different thing altogether."

"You can have more books any time," Juliet says.

"Thanks. How are things with Alec?" I ask. She's been dating *The New Yorker* (and *Merryvale*) writer since last fall.

"He can be a pain in the ass but nothing I can't handle. How's Will?"

"He's a prince," I say. Before I can add more, Jenny and Chief Williams arrive, followed in short order by Ash Plank and Judge Harschly, all water-logged and out of sorts.

As we head to The Pipe Room on the library's second floor, I can hear the wind whipping the branches of the old oak that spreads over the building, scraping the roof, while each step we take triggers spooky, diphthong creaks from the wood floors.

"A lot of noise going on," Judge Harschly mutters.

The room where we're headed is a recreation of the original Pipe Room, which was located in the Worsham Hotel, now long gone. The pipe collection isn't exactly a star attraction at the library and, apparently, neither was the original at the Worsham, but it is a little piece of Arnold Fallsiana. The small collection transferred from the now-demolished hotel includes a number of the corn cob pipes favored by town notables over the years as well as a dozen clay churchwarden pipes, attached to a rail along the ceiling, said to have belonged to the original settlers of the town.

Juliet opens the door and turns on the light.

"Goddammit, no!"

She's looking at the corn cob pipes, or I should say the wall where the corn cob pipes used to be.

"At least the churchwarden pipes are still there," she says. "Probably too high up to snatch. Fuck. Excuse me, Judge."

"'Fuck' seems straight to the point," Judge Harschly says.

"I'll write up a report, Juliet," Chief Williams says. "We'll talk after the meeting."

She nods and goes back downstairs. Jenny starts the meeting blowing air from her cheeks, which gets a counterpoint from a gust of wind outside. It's thunderhailing, too.

"Let's gripe it out," she says. "My gripe is that everything having to do with Arnold Falls that isn't nailed down, and even stuff that is, is getting swiped for no reason that we know of. Judge?"

"That includes my gavel. Brazen thuggery. Jenny, I also think Ouchie would make an excellent coach for the vitilla team."

"Really?" Jenny says. "People might not want someone with such a long record coaching the kids."

Judge Harschly replies, "Can't separate kids from adults with a sheet here. You know that. You'd just end up with a town full of orphans. I think Ouchie's okay."

Jenny nods. "I trust your instincts. Would you consider being a — I don't know — supervisory coach, while he proves himself?"

"Done," Judge Harschly says.

Jenny asks, "What are we going to do about this crime spree of whatever you want to call it? Memorabilia, let's say. Chief?"

"My first gripe is I'd like to get a new unmarked car. Peggy's Rugs and Plugs now reeks of perfume. Can't get rid of it."

"You have enough in your budget?" Jenny asks.

"Yeah."

"Then get a new beater."

"Good. Now about the thefts. We need a break on where all this stuff is going, where it's being held. It's too much stuff for quick fencing. I mean, who's gonna pay money for the Hesper statue?"

"Marvin the Hobo may be involved," Jenny says. "Rufus told me that Marvin was recommended by Mayor Haralambie. Some connection to our beloved sister town of Plopeni."

"The stuff could be in his basement," Ash says.

"The lightning splitter doesn't have a basement," I say.

"Ouchie told me yesterday," Judge Harschly says, "that there's talk about bushes trampled around Arnmoor."

"Everyone knows not to go near there," Chief Williams says. "It's obviously haunted and I don't even believe in that stuff."

"We could look around the Arnmoor ruins," Ash says, "but I want to know what's behind all these thefts first and I don't want to spook anyone, especially if it's Marvin. The people of Plopeni are very superstitious," Ash says.

"Maybe there's a way to use that," I say.

"How do you mean?" Jenny asks.

"Not sure."

"In any case," Ash says, "the big-ticket item is the issue at the hospital."

"What issue at the hospital?" Judge Harschly asks.

"I can't say too much," Ash says.

He's already talked a lot and I don't have time for this. "I will then. I found out that there's nothing for kids in the pediatric oncology ward. No music, no nothing. And then I found out the hospital has been declining in the past few years. It all seems to coincide with the arrival of Popsy Siddons-Swain and a million dollars that have been drained from the hospital coffers."

Judge Harschly stares at Ash Plank. "Is this true?"

Ash nods.

"Where is she?" the Judge asks.

"Left the hospital in April, hasn't been seen since," Ash says.

I see a flash of anger on Judge Harschly's face. "Abominable!" he says.

"Not seen," Ash continues, "until last night. Rufus was wearing a wire at Jantzen's Friday night poker game — did I mention that Jantzen and Popsy were involved —"

"*Involved?*" Judge Harschly asks.

"Romantically."

Judge Harschly rubs his eyes. "I play cards there every so often. I had no idea. What happened last night?"

Ash explains about Rufus wearing a wire and the woman he saw when he walked back into the house. "Can't confirm it's her, but seems likely. We're watching the place now while the forensic accounting people finish the money hunt, which should be soon, and then we'll have plenty to charge her with. We don't know yet how involved Dr. Jantzen is."

I raise my hand. "Do I get a gripe? My gripe is I want the

chance to confront Popsy. To speak for those kids. Even if it's just for a minute."

"I don't know how we'd work it, Jeebie," Ash says. "Let's see how it plays out."

"Between the items being stolen and embezzlement at the hospital," Judge Harschly says, "that's enough to keep everyone's gripe card filled. But I have to say this, Mayor. I think we have a bigger problem."

It's silent in the room and I notice the wind, the rain, and the hail have let up.

"Jenny," the judge continues. "I understand why you made the deal with Emollimax, I do. Money's always in short supply around here. But I'd give it back. Something's not right about this town at the moment."

"I signed a contract," Jenny says.

"I know you did. We can work that out."

"Though we haven't received any money yet. It's only six months. We'll be fine, Judge," Jenny says.

"We were talking about the Plopeni people being superstitious. That may be. The people around here aren't. Least of all me. But I'm telling you," Judge Harschly says quietly, "Arnold Falls is out of joint."

No sooner has he spoken those words, than the churchwarden pipes falls off their rail and crash on to the wood floor, narrowly missing Jenny. And then the lights go out.

Not a word is spoken for an uncomfortably long time. I hear Juliet running up the stairs.

"Is everyone okay?" she calls out.

As Juliet opens the door, Jenny says, "We're fine. The churchwarden pipes are smashed. I think we just had a seance."

～

After the pipe room incident on Saturday morning, to which the *Valley Observer* gave front-page coverage the following day, there was a change in the air. The town was different and everyone noticed it. By Monday, it was felt Something Needed to be Done, though no one could say with any certainty what needed to be done, or by whom.

I'm back in my Carrie quarters. First on my list is Ash Plank — Will has Ash's cell phone number (note to self: follow up on this) — so I call him. I tell him that the loss of the churchwarden pipes has caused a lot of consternation, that patience for a resolution is wearing thin, and I have an idea.

"What do you have in mind?" Ash asks.

"You said on Saturday that you didn't want to spook Marvin. But I think that's exactly what we should do."

We talk through it and then I call Bridget. "Bridget, I have an acting job for you."

"I just so happen to be at liberty. What are the terms?"

"No terms. A chance to get Martha's mobcap back, if you can get through a day without being arrested."

"You have my attention, Giblet."

Chapter Twenty-Six

I like 'Roar,'" Wilky says. "And 'This is Me.'"

"Katy Perry and Keala Settle," Bender says. "Can't argue with them."

Wilky had asked Jenny if he could spend part of the day with Bender at the record shop. Bender had jumped at the chance. Right now, Wilky is playing with Humboldt, holding a toy mouse by its tail for the cat to swat.

"You think he knows it's not a mouse? Wants to play anyway?" Wilky asks.

"I think that's right," Bender says.

The kid is so curious, Bender thinks, he wants to know everything about everything. He's a blast to hang with.

"And George Ezra," Wilky says.

"'Paradise'?"

"Yeah, that one."

"You like really upbeat songs, huh?" Bender says.

"I guess. What music do you like?" Wilky asks.

"How much time do you have?"

"I'm here all morning," Wilky says earnestly.

He's nine, Bender thinks. I keep forgetting that.

"Well, I like almost any kind of music if it's good."

"A few details, please."

"The Beatles, The Grateful Dead, Laura Nyro, The Allman Brothers, Aretha Franklin, Stephen Sondheim, Mozart, Sly and the Family Stone, Joni Mitchell, Fleet Foxes, Dr. Buzzard, Patrick Watson, Everything But the Girl, Prince, Charlie Parker...should I keep going?"

"If you want to," Wilky says. "I don't know all those names."

"I can teach you."

Wilky bobs his head up and down.

"Okay, let's listen to 'Dance to the Music,' by Sly Stone. Bender finds it on Spotify and plays it loud on the vintage Advent speakers.

As Bender watches Wilky dance around the store to the song, he has the odd sensation that his old record shop is somehow transformed, that he's in a different place. Like in the movies, when the walls of a room expand outward and the character is all of a sudden in a completely changed environment. But no, there's his beloved NCR cash register, Humboldt's toy collection is in the corner next to his water bowl, there is the usual, faintly-damp smell of old records collecting dust. It has to be Wilky dancing to Sly Stone at this moment in this place. And the woman who adopted him.

"I like that one!" Wilky says, when the song finishes. "Sly!"

Do you know "The Chicken Dance"?

"Is it by Sly?"

Gotta love this kid. "No, totally different. But it's a dance they do around here all the time, so you should know it. I'm surprised you haven't heard it yet. I'll teach it to you, it's easy. They usually do it with a lot of people in big circle, so just pretend we're in a group."

"Yes, boss."

He plays the polka and they join hands and start sidestepping. Bender says, "Now to your left" and "now to your right," and then "now you're a chicken," and he begins the three-part mime: the talking beak using your hands, flapping your elbows, shaking your tail, then four hand-claps. "Got it?" Wilky nods. "It's gonna get faster!" Bender says.

"I'm ready!"

The music speeds up and they move to the left, then switch to the right. Wilky is giggling, trying to keep up with the beak, the wings, the tail, and the four claps. As the music speeds up again, Wilky lets out a yelp. At that moment, the front door to the shop opens and Nelle walks in.

"Chicken dance!" she shouts and joins in. They finish up the dance, giving themselves a round of applause and a few clucks.

"Why a Chicken Dance on a Monday morning?" she asks.

"Why *not* a Chicken Dance, I ask you?" Bender replies.

Nelle bends down to give Wilky a hug.

"Are you in for a browse?" Bender asks.

"I need a song for the benefit Jeebie's organizing."

"At Fridsy's farm?"

"Yeah."

"Can you narrow it down at all?" Bender asks.

"I thought a song about singing because Fridsy sings to those cows and I think it's so beautiful. Something like The Carpenters' song 'Sing,' but not so cloying."

"Easy! 'Sing' by the Dresden Dolls."

"Oh, yeah. Haven't heard that in a hundred years."

"Yup. The lyrics are kind of sweet but also edgy, for sure. Here, I'll play it. Can you handle a curse word, Wilky?"

"No, I will melt," Wilky says.

After the song finishes, Nelle says, "I knew you'd come

through. I'll work with it and see how it goes. Thanks, Bender."

"I wanted to ask you something, too," Bender says. "You heard about the stash of records that Jenny found?"

"I did. Jeebie told me."

"You know the group Black Violin, right?"

"Yeah, classical mashup with hip-hop. Love them. What are you thinking?"

"Some kind of group. Porch music from my house? Not sure yet."

"I love it! Tell Jeebie. They could play as part of the hospital arts program he's working on. What do you think, Wilky?"

"I don't know about that music," he says. "How does it sound?"

Bender samples from Black Violin and Wilky's face lights up.

"What do you like more? Black Violin or the Chicken Dance?" Nelle asks.

"Both," Wilky says.

"Jenny's turning him into a politician," Nelle says.

The shop phone rings.

"I gotta run. Thanks, Bender. See you, Wilks," Nelle says, flapping her wings, before she leaves.

"LST Records," Bender says. "Hi. It's going great, right Wilky?"

Wilky gives him the thumbs up.

"Whenever you want," Bender says. "I thought I'd take him to Darlene's for lunch. Okay, we'll come to City Hall after that."

Wilky practices the Chicken Dance routine, starting with the talking beak, then flapping his elbows.

Bender says, "I'm so glad you found a home with Jenny."

Wilky shakes his tail and says, "Maybe you find a home with her, too," followed by four hand claps.

≈

"JUDGE HARSCHLY'S CHAMBERS."

"Hi, Vera, it's Tishy."

"City Hall calling? Must be bad news."

"Ungh. Not always. But in this case, yeah. Jenny talked to the head of Emollimax. Super snippy about it. And we just got an email from their attorney saying they won't agree to break the contract."

"Judge is in court right now. He's not going to be happy about that. Is it true about Jenny and Bender?"

"You and I need to catch up. We haven't had drinks in a few weeks. Friday?"

"You're on," Vera says.

"I'll fill you in then."

When Judge Harschly returns to his chambers later in the day, Vera relays the message about Emollimax and their unwillingness to cancel the contract.

"Not very sporting," he says. "Can you get Terry Gross on the line for me?"

"From NPR?" Vera asks.

"That one."

Several minutes later, Vera says, "Judge, I've got Terry Gross on line one."

Judge Harschly picks up the phone and says, "Terry! It's Lionel."

≈

"STILL NO SIGN OF MY GAVEL, I SUPPOSE?"

"We're working on it," Jenny says, sitting across from Judge Harschly in his chambers. "How are Alice and Ellie doing? I haven't see them in so long."

"They're coming to visit their old man over Labor Day. They asked if you were going to be around. And of course they want to meet Wilky, too."

"I think we'll be in town. I'd love to see them. I'll text them."

"Good. Now, who is the scoundrel from Emollimax that screamed threats at you?"

"His name is Lance Cadelle. Head of the division. He's insufferable."

"Lancelot...Cadelle," Judge Harschly says, writing it down his name on a yellow pad. "Let's give Mr. Cadelle some what-for and put an end to this nonsense. You have the number?"

"Vera has it."

"Vera!"

Vera appears at the doorway.

"Can you get Mr. Cadelle on the phone?"

"Certainly, Judge."

"I'm going to put him on speaker. You might want to sit in with us. Could be entertaining."

"You've got the interview ready?" Judge Harschly asks Jenny.

"All set."

"Fine. How's Wilky?" the Judge asks.

"The best," Jenny says. "The best thing ever."

"Glad to hear it. Dating Bender, are you?"

"Jesus!" Jenny says, laughing. "Is nothing private in this town?"

"I assume that's rhetorical."

"I've known him all my life. We were always friends but in

the way of a friend who's just *there*. And all of a sudden it's different."

Judge Harschly looks at Jenny over his half-moon glasses and nods his head. "Alice and Ellie were thrilled to hear it."

"I've got Mr. Cadelle holding for you, Judge," Vera says, taking a seat in the chair next to Jenny.

"Lancelot Cadelle? This is Judge Harschly up in Arnold Falls. You'll note I said Arnold Falls, not Emollimax."

Cadelle starts to say something.

"Don't interrupt me. That won't go well for you. I'm going to play a portion of an interview I just taped for NPR."

Jenny plays the recording.

TERRY GROSS, HOST: This is "Fresh Air." I'm Terry Gross. It's summer in the small of town of Arnold Falls in New York's Hudson Valley, where the long days are typically spent at swimming holes and barbecues. Today, though, the town is living through a cautionary tale, at the intersection of commerce and civics. Joining us today from Arnold Falls is the Honorable Lionel Harschly. Full disclosure: I've known Lionel since I moved to Philadelphia in 1975, where, at that time, he was a clerk for Judge Oliver P. Stanley. Welcome, Lionel! It's a pleasure to have you on the show. How are things in that charming town of yours?

HARSCHLY: Hello, Terry. Always good to hear your voice. The town has been better. Let me tell you a little story, if I may, about a place that changed its name and got a rash.

GROSS: And you're not just speaking metaphorically.

HARSCHLY: Indeed I am not.

Judge Harschly briefly describes the decision to temporarily become Emollimax, New York.

GROSS: And what happened next?

HARSCHLY: I tried the product. All of a sudden I have a rash. Can't say it was a result of using Emollimax, but can't say it wasn't. And when I say rash, I'm talking DEFCON two. Not just a rash. *Welts* and *carbuncles*! I have dozens of photos, lots of closeups.

GROSS: Yes, those images you sent me are inhuman.

HARSCHLY: It got worse: cysts, boils, and abscesses, *scrofulous* skin. Not to mention a deeply suspicious fireball in a tent near the burning of this ointment for allegedly salutary aromatherapy purposes. Blew the top of the tent off! Oh, and did I mention *pustules*? *Festering* pustules.

"Stop the tape there," Judge Harschly says to Jenny. "Would you care to hear the full interview, Mr. Cadelle? I believe it is scheduled to air Monday at noon."

"No, that's enough. I got the point," Lance says, still on speakerphone. "Contract's void. I'll have our attorney send a document to that effect. I don't know what to say to you people."

"How about 'goodbye'?" Judge Harschly says, and hangs up.

"I always thought you missed your calling," Vera says. "Oscar calibre."

Jenny asks, "Any of it true?"

"Not a word," the Judge answers.

"Why did Terry Gross agree to do it?" Jenny asks.

"I did her a big favor once. A long time ago. Leave it at that. She wasn't going to air it, of course, though the full interview is a hoot. All right. The docket calls. Meanwhile, take that out of your worry basket, Mayor."

Chapter Twenty-Seven

B ridget and Fayette have been in Fayette's trailer for a long time, while Giles, Ash, and I wait outside for the reveal of the wardrobe and makeup crew's work. Giles and the writer, Alec Barnsdorf, have been diligent about capturing actual moments of daily life in Arnold Falls and working them into the plotline of *Merryvale*. Verisimilitude, I guess, though I'm not sure how he could shoehorn this in.

When the trailer door finally opens, the two ladies are unrecognizable, yet I can tell the "characters" Bridget and Fayette improvised during the bank scene have fully transformed into...whatever is before us. They've got gray wigs that mix tight barrel curls with punky spikes. Their noses have been puttied to add witch's crooks, their cheeks sprout a few stray hairs. Bridget has blood-red lipstick, Fayette's is black. Their outfits mix Eastern European schmattes with goth spikes on the shoulders and arms. For a moment, no one speaks.

Fayette cackles and launches into an insane tirade: "DARK 'twere the night we two wizzle-sanctafrimpen were regurged from the fires 'neath the scabby earth, sturky nettles of mysterium and no-you-don'ts heaved o'er the sins of Gomorrah on the Hudson."

Bridget answers, "My sister jabuls in sooth. No quarrel 'ave we with ye, lest ye be hobo or hermit, which must be banished or suffer a disenpacklectomy afore the sun rises thrice."

"EEE-hee-hee-hee," they say to each other and do a little dance in front of the trailer.

Well, it wasn't quite what I had in mind, but we'll work with the crazy that we've got.

"Giblet, if we came out of the woods on a dark, summer night, it would spook you, right?" Bridget asks.

"It's spooking me now," I say, which elicits another "EEE-hee-hee-hee" from the two of them.

"Then we'll have Marvin on the run," Fayette says, "and have all the bits and bobs he's got returned to their rightful owners."

"Mobcaps included," Bridget says.

Giles has put down his camera and I say to him, "It could work, right? If he's superstitious and all."

"Definitely. No one wants a disenpacklectomy."

Ash says, "Marvin usually walks to Arnmoor a few minutes after sundown — which happens soon, 8:08 tonight."

"We should go up there and get in place," I say.

I'M HIDDEN WITH GILES AND ASH, OUR EYES TRAINED ON Bridget and Fayette, standing on the path. Their body language suddenly changes.

"Stop!" Bridget says.

"Oh! You scared the devil out of me!" Marvin says.

"Your name!" Fayette says.

"Be ye hobo or hermit?" Bridget asks.

"What the hell is this?"

"Your NAME!" Fayette thunders.

"Marvin."

Fayette and Bridget have a brief, whispered conference. I'm pretty sure I hear them saying 'rhubarb.'

"Be ye hobo or hermit? Which is it? We'll NOT ask AGAIN!"

"I was hobo, now I'm a hermit."

"'Tis fate which brought ye here to this place," Bridget says, "for a warning."

This ridiculous colloquy seems to be having the intended, unsettling effect on Marvin. "Okay, what is it?"

"Aye," Fayette continues, "my sister tells you verily. When the moon is in the Seventh House..."

"And Jupiter aligns with Mars. Then peace will guide the planets," Bridgets adds.

Please don't let them break into song.

"Tis written, ye must flee the shire," Fayette says, "cleaving the trestles til Dido returns, turning your pork-sword into ploughshares, sunching the cabblenack until the Firth of Forth besways again."

Bridget looks at Fayette, doubtless wondering, as I am, what in God's name Fayette is on about.

"What my sister says, so artfully, is clear, so it is, sir," Bridget says. "Afore the cock crows thrice, ye must vanish — away, away — and ne'er return. Else you and your nearest will suffer the most righteous flames of hell."

Marvin is now quaking from all of this nonsense. I guess he really is superstitious.

"When you say cock crows th-th-thrice, what if it crows three times on one day?"

"Never mind the FINE PRINT," Fayette shouts. "Little time, have ye! GO! Prepare ye for a journey. Get cracking."

All of a sudden a black cloud of smoke erupts behind Bridget. Marvin shrieks and runs back down the path toward his house.

We wait until he's well out of earshot and give Bridget and Fayette a well-earned round of applause.

"How did you do the smoke?" I ask.

"It's a wire-pull canister, ten bucks online. Here's the receipt," Bridget says, producing the piece of paper from somewhere. "Who's reimbursing?"

MARVIN TOOK HIS MARCHING ORDERS THIS EVENING, before the third crowing of the cock, which you'll recall, was his deadline. It's past midnight after the events have concluded, and we're out on Bender's porch, drinking everything from iced tea to Clagger. But that's not what you want to know, so let's cut to the earlier chase: Has the blue Princess phone been restored to its rightful place at Argos? Is Martha Washington's dust cover back on her head? Has Hezekiah Hesper been sold for scrap? Here's what we've pieced together about how the whole crazy night went down:

The sun has just set. Jenny and Chief Williams are parked near Marvin the Hobo's house and after fifteen minutes, Jenny notices movement at the front door. Chief Williams picks up his binoculars and watches Marvin leave and walk toward the woods that connect to the path leading to the Arnmoor remains. He's carrying his bindle and a small suitcase.

Jennys sends out a text: *Hobo hoboing.* Officer Velez, stationed near Arnmoor, texts, *Standing by.* Ash Plank, parked on Flensing Lane, around the bend from the future Van Dalen Park, texts *OK, going to the marsh area by the big rock.*

There's a sharp tap on Jenny's car window, which makes her jump. Giles Morris. She lowers the window.

"It's happening now, isn't it?" he whispers. "Sofia told me Argos is empty so something must be up."

Chief Williams said, "Just don't get in the way, Giles. We don't quite know what we're dealing with here."

"I won't. Mostly too dark to film anyway."

Jenny texts me: *Hobo night. Giles is here, so you might as well be, too. Meet us on Flensing.*

I've had more gracious invitations. But I couldn't pass up the chance to see how it would play out. Will has no interest: he's been devouring books having to do with conservation biology, getting ready for his masters program this fall, and I leave him curled up with a book called *The Man Who Planted Trees.*

I find Jenny and Chief Williams parked on the side of Flensing Lane, and get into the back seat.

"Where's Wilky?" I ask.

"He's with Bender," Jenny says.

"How's that going?" the Chief asks.

"I lucked out, Chief. Great kid." Jenny says.

"I meant with Bender," the Chief says.

"Jesus."

"Is that a spreadsheet?" I ask.

"Of course," Jenny answers. "Have to track all the goods."

After a few minutes, Velez texts: *He just left Arnmoor w/ packed handtruck, headed W on path to river.*

The path doesn't go all the way to the Hudson; the only place Marvin can emerge from the woods without being in someone's back yard is at the new park just east of the river, so we should be able to see him from our vantage point, as will Ash from his. When Marvin appears, he pauses to make sure no one is around, then continues to the park contractors' trailer and unloads the handtruck: bindle, small suitcase, Schlitz clock, and three small boxes. He hurries off back into the woods, handtruck in tow, back the way he came.

Ash texts: *Looks like Arnmoor contents to trailer in park, then maybe river pickup?*

A woman rides a bicycle to the entrance of the park, gives the kickstand the business-end of her shoe, and now I can see that it's Judge Harschly's secretary, Vera. She stands there waiting a few moments before Ouch Macgillicuddy comes running out of the park and hands something to her. Something which looks very much like a gavel. He's gone in a flash and she gets on her bike and rides away.

Ash: *Who were they? Where did the guy come from? Did they just take the gavel? Evidence in a criminal case!*

Jenny: *Tell it to the judge.*

We hear an owl hoot and I'm reminded that Bridget's crowing-of-the-cock riff has brought us to this place. I decide to send a courtesy text to her which says that she and Fayette have now spooked Marvin into action.

She texts back: *Way ahead of you.*

I do not like the sound of that.

Then she adds, *Fay and I are in costume, out of view, at Bonebox Point. If needed.*

Officer Velez: *Hobo back at Arnmoor, loading second trip. Had to chase off lookie-loos just before he got here. Word's out.*

Ash: *Rufus and some guy smoking joint at gazebo by water. Not helpful. I'm walking closer to the trailer.*

Jenny to Rufus: *You and Dub need to get the flying fuck away from there. At least stay hidden, you idiots.* She attaches the photo of Rufus sunbathing to emphasize her point.

All three of us lean forward as something moves at the contractors' trailer. The Chief looks through his binoculars.

"Stripes," he reports.

Ash: *Bear!*

Jenny texts back: *Harmless. Just let him do his thing. His name is Stripes.*

"Stripes has a paw in Marvin's bindle," the Chief says. "Now he's pulled out a paper bag. And now he's eating, looks like doughnut holes. Some noise startled him."

We can just make out Stripes, with bag, sugar-rushing into the woods as, moments later, Marvin arrives back at the trailer. He unloads the Welcome to no Falls sign, the vintage mailbox, and two cases of Clagger, before noticing that his bindle is open and his doughnut holes are as missing as the letters A, R, L, and D on the sign. He glances around unhappily and returns to the path toward Arnmoor.

"When was the no Falls sign stolen?" I ask.

"Yesterday," Jenny says.

A few minutes later, a man enters the park and heads for the trailer.

Ash: *Someone just took the mailbox. FFS. No evidence, no case.*

"Yep, there he goes. Lou Pastorella," says Chief Williams.

Lou, our postmaster, had been quite distressed about losing the small, charming Doremus mailbox, installed in front of the post office around 1895.

When Marvin returns, he's visibly winded from pushing the Hesper statue tied to his handtruck. In short order, Marvin unties the statue and lays it on the ground, leaving Hesper looking like a sad, deposed dictator.

Rufus texts Jenny that he's spotted a trawler headed upriver towards the dock.

Jenny forwards the info to the rest of us. Ash responds:

Need to get Marvin's phone and keep him quiet so he doesn't warn boat.

"Too bad Bridget isn't around," Jenny says. "For once, we could use her skills."

"She *is* around here with Fayette," I say. "She texted me." I call her.

"Hellooo, Giblet," she says.

"Not much time," I say. "We need to stop Marvin from communicating with the trawler that's coming into the dock. Where are you?"

"Bivouacked at Bonebox."

"He'll be coming from Arnmoor, should be soon."

"Leave everything to me," she says, which is about ten-percent reassuring and ninety-percent not.

Marvin returns with the fourth and apparently final haul, and which includes, per Jenny's spreadsheet, the remaining four cases of clagger, the mobcaps, and the Princess phone. And, damn it, he's got a little library with him, too. Instead of stopping at the trailer, he continues on to the dock.

"I'm going to get closer to see what goes down with Bridget," I say to Jenny and Chief Williams, and hide behind a tree until Marvin passes on the path. I tail him, keeping my distance. I see can see, to my right, Bridget and Fayette gingerly hobo-tracking, too.

After dropping off the load at the dock, he moves quickly back toward the trailer.

"YOU!"

Marvin turns to see Bridget and Fayette facing him, their arms extended, their fingers pointed at him. A can of white smoke goes off.

"*AH!*" Marvin shouts.

I note their faces are almost fully covered with veils, no doubt because they didn't have time for hair and makeup.

"Ere ye go to lands unknown, ye must have a laying-on of the hands," Bridget says.

"First, an incantation," Fayette intones.

"I'm in a bit of rush," Marvin says.

"Do not disrespect my sister!" Bridget says. She looks at Fayette. "Do the abridged one."

"Very well," Fayette says. "An owl hoots on the CUSP of a journey. The ninth house is for transit and the bird's plangent tones fermiculate into the dark of night, the smoky, black, FEARSOME nothingness, which entangles the tendrils of wormwood and horehound, a profusion of..."

"This is the abridged one?" Bridget asks.

"We'll skip ahead to the laying on of hands," Fayette says.

Bridget nods and does a jazz hands/pat down on poor Marvin, who ends up lighter by one cell phone and none the wiser. Bridget then stands directly behind him, reaches around to his face, slathers Witness Protection all over it. As he realizes what is happening, he reaches for his cellphone.

"Who took my phone?" he asks. "What the hell is going on here? Have you seen my phone?"

Marvin scans the path. "I know I had it. Do you know how to use Find my Phone?"

He looks more closely at Bridget, whose veil has slipped. "Hey, I know you!" His attention is diverted by the trawler approaching the dock.

"Should be any second now," Bridget says to Fayette.

"Any second for what?" He tries to shout to the boat but only "MMM HMMM MMM!" comes out as the Witness Protection kicks in.

Bridget and Fayette add an "EEE-hee-hee-hee" and a little dance here as three cops coming out of the grove start running toward Marvin. He takes off onto the path for Arnmoor. The cops give chase.

Meanwhile, Darlene's Doughnut Truck has driven up next to the gazebo and a line forms before they can even open the window.

While Marvin is on the run, Bridget and Fayette zip over to the pile of stolen goods for mobcaps retrieval on the dock as the captain steps off the trawler.

They're stopped by Officer Mills. "Where are you...ladies from? Arnold Falls?"

"Oh, no," Bridget says. "Lower Hacklesbury."

"Where's that?" he asks.

"A little past Merryvale," Fayette says.

"You with Hullaballoo?"

"The *circus*?! Absolutely not," Bridget says.

"Can I see some ID?"

Fayette says, "You see that boat captain there? Ask HIM for ID."

"He's harmless," Mills says. "Look, he's getting on the doughnut line. ID please."

"We don't have time for this," Bridget says and pops another can of smoke. Bridget and Fayette run onto the dock, find the mobcaps, and beat a hasty retreat back toward Bonebox Point.

I can't quite make out who is now walking toward the trailer. A young woman. Oh! It's Juliet. Doing her duty on behalf of the library, I guess, reclaiming the corncob pipes from a box into the Tupperware she's brought with her.

Ash: *What's going on? Who is that? People can't just help them-selves. The police were supposed to secure the scene.*

Chief: *Don't you have anybody?*

Ash: *One guy. He's watching the Jantzen house. This town* :(

Marvin comes running down the steps just north of Flensing Lane when he sees Officer Velez sprinting toward him from the park, so he turns tail and heads north along the river.

Jenny gets out of the car.

"Where are you going?" Chief Williams asked.

"No no-Falls sign, no good," she says, and goes to fetch it.

When she gets back to the car, I say, "No fit."

"No problem. I called Archie IV. And there he is!"

Archie IV drives up in a van and jumps out to open the rear doors. He waves over to us and, after placing the sign into the van, has a brief conversation with Jen. Archie IV makes a run for it, grabbing the two cases of clagger from behind the trailer, drops them at his van, and then speeds off to the dock, where he recovers the other four cases.

Ash: *Could everyone stop taking evidence, please? Chief, can you secure the scene?*

The Chief texts back *Busy chasing hobo*, when, in fact, I can see him in line for doughnuts.

A minute later, Ash texts again: *That guy w/ Rufus just took the Schlitz clock from pile, rode away w/ it.*

Jenny: Little fireplug guy?

Ash: Yes. On a mobility scooter.

Jenny: Dubsack.

"I should probably get the photo of JFK for Aunt Doozy," I say. "And the little library."

"Get the Princess phone, too," Jenny says.

"I have faith in you, but hurry," Jenny says, and I go out on my mission, passing Chief Williams, now at the front of the doughnut line.

"You're all tampering with evidence," he says to me. "Technically. Two chocolate frosted, please."

Officer Velez texts that she's chasing Marvin back this way. Ash emerges from his redoubt to box Marvin in from the south as three of AF's finest step out onto the path from the north. Chief Williams ambles toward the confrontation, swallowing what I'm sure was the second doughnut.

Marvin sees that the jig is up. I have to give him credit for pulling a Hail Mary, loudly asking for asylum, saying he will be dealt with harshly if he doesn't return to Plopeni with the Arnold Falls haul. This momentarily confuses the process but it's decided that an arrest has to come before anything. He's handcuffed and led into a police cruiser.

Jenny walks up beside me. I've set the little library on the ground, still holding tight to the Princess phone and a bubble-wrapped JFK.

"Looks like everything has been returned to its rightful owner," she says.

"Yup. The only thing no one wants is Hezekiah Hesper."

Chapter Twenty-Eight

elle was eager to catch up on the events of last night, so Jenny and I are meeting her at the Shack for a mid-morning breakfast. The first thing we do when we arrive is return the photo of JFK to Doozy, who is glad to have it back. With a nod from her, I restore the frame to its place of honor on the wall. Nelle is waiting for us in a booth, where we can discuss matters of state without eager ears straining our way.

I tell Nelle that at his arraignment this morning, Marvin pleaded not guilty to Grand Larceny in the Second Degree. Judge Harschly asked for his bindle as bond and he was told not to leave the county, and that the trial would begin on September 24. I thought Judge Harschly seemed rather sympathetic to Marvin, though he roundly condemned the thefts themselves, including that of the "instrument of justice," as he referred to his gavel. The trawler captain was charged separately.

"Grand Larceny in the Second Degree?" Nelle asks. "Isn't that a big charge?"

"It's for when the goods are over $50,000 in value," Jenny

explains. "And they valued the Hesper statue at $60,000, which obviously bears no relationship to reality. Jewel Guldens is defending him. I'm sure she'll ask for a lesser charge."

"Sounds like last night was carried off in true Arnold Falls style," Nelle says.

"More people were involved than should have been," I say.

"Bridget and Fayette?" Nelle asks.

"I have to hand it to them, they were effective, though a *lot* of scenery was chewed."

Aunt Doozy comes over to take our order.

"Who do I have to thank for getting the picture back, Jenny?" Doozy asks.

"Group effort, Aunt Doozy."

"Thank you to the group," Doozy says.

After we order, Nelle asks, "What's the latest on Popsy?"

"Ash Plank thought there would be a development soon," I answer. "That's all he would say."

"While the grass grows under his feet," Nelle says.

"He's okay," I say, which gets a skeptical look from her.

"I just hope the hospital can get some of that money back," she says.

"I think we will," Jenny says.

"Is there any basis for that optimism?" I ask Jenny.

"No. Not really. But I still think so."

His phone rings and Rufus sees it's Fayette calling.

"Hello, Fayette."

"You're going to LOVE this, Rufus. I want to buy Dr. Jantzen's house. He's not listing it, he's selling it through an attorney."

"Great news, Fayette. What's he asking?"

"$666K."

"Really? I don't think that's a good number. Sign of the devil. I'll check the comps, as they say in the biz, just to make sure but that house is a beauty. I'll call you later today."

After he hangs up, he gets up from the lounge chair and ties up his bathrobe. The sun's getting too hot, anyway, he thinks. He slips on his flip-flops and goes back into the house. As he throws the squeezed lemon into the kitchen wastebasket, he says aloud, "Wait a minute. *Wait* a minute! Wait just one minute! Why is Dr. Jantzen selling his house?"

He calls Jenny.

"Yes, Rufus?"

"I have good intel. What's it worth it to you?"

"Depends on what it is."

"I can't tell you what it is because then it won't be worth that any more."

"Rufus, I don't have time for this."

"It has to do with Dr. Jantzen."

"Okay, what do you want?"

"Destroy that picture you took of me sunbathing."

"All right."

"Not good enough," Rufus says. "Pinky swear."

"Rufus, I can't pinky swear with you on the phone. We have to be in the same room. Look, you have my word. I'll destroy it. On my honor."

"Okay," he says. "Dr. Jantzen is selling his house, maybe to Fayette. She just told me. He's not listing it. Private sale. Some lawyer in Albany is handling the deal on his end."

"Good work, Rufus. I've got to call Ash."

"Tell him I gave you the clue," Rufus says.

"I will," Jenny answers.

~

Bender spots Tishy from two blocks away. He can't make out what she's wearing from this distance, though it's unmistakably a Tishy original. As she gets closer, he can see it's a mottled-green, knee-length skirt with a ruffle around the neck from the same material.

"Give me a hint," Bender says as Tishy approaches.

"Vegetable," Tishy says.

"Cucumber?"

"Close. Zucchini. The eighth of August is National Sneak Some Zucchini Onto Your Neighbor's Porch Day."

"Is that —"

"*Yunh*," Tishy grunts. "It's a thing."

"Did you sneak any zucchini?"

"Don't grow it. Hate the stuff."

"You just like sneaky things," Bender says.

"Don't know what you're talking about."

"Tishy, how did Jenny and I all of a sudden end up together?"

"You're asking me?"

"Yes. I'm asking you."

"You're high. But I did hear something interesting," Tishy says.

Bender looks at the thirty-something, zucchini-clad, off-the-wall woman standing here and he has some kind of chemical flush of affection for her.

"What did you hear?" he asks.

"Percy Tunnion took the job as music teacher at the high school. He's still running Traitor's Landing, too. I heard the school wants a more performance-oriented focus. I thought maybe some connection to your chamber music/hip-hop thing."

"Great idea, Tishy, thanks. Happy Sneak Some Zucchini Onto Your Neighbor's Porch Day."

"Happy Sneak Some Zucchini Onto Your Neighbor's Porch Day to you and yours."

"I'M BRINGING YOU A DRESS," RUBY WINTER HAD SAID TO Aunt Doozy when she phoned a couple of weeks before the opening of "Georgia on My Mind."

"Naw, don't do that, I'll just wear any old thing."

"Over my dead body," Ruby says.

"You know my size?" Doozy asks.

"I was up for your birthday. You shrink since then?"

"Naw."

"Get fat?"

"Tss-tss-tss-tss."

"Then, yeah, I got you."

Ruby arrived on Tuesday before the Thursday opening and Doozy invited Nelle to join for the fitting.

Doozy wags a bony finger at Nelle. "I'm counting on you to say the truth. I haven't seen the dress and Ruby's feelings won't be hurt if you don't like it. Right, Ruby?"

"Like hell they won't."

"Pay her no mind, she's losing it," Doozy says to Nelle, taking the box into her bedroom.

After Doozy shuts the door, Ruby asks, "How's she doing?"

"She's been apprehensive about the whole exhibit, but otherwise, I think she's good," Nelle says.

Doozy opens the door to her bedroom and pokes her head out.

"How the heck you put this thing on?"

Ruby goes into the bedroom to help and after a few minutes, Doozy emerges with the dress on, minus shoes.

"Oh, Doozy! You look amazing. That is gorgeous on you. *You're* gorgeous!" Nelle says.

"Perfect fit," Ruby says.

"Yeah, okay, thank you, Ruby. Did good." Doozy gives Ruby a kiss on the cheek.

"Who's the designer?" Nelle asks.

"Badgley-Mischka," Ruby says. "Cape shoulder gown. They call the color navy, but it's a little purple, too."

Nelle nods approvingly. "You look like royalty."

"Get outta here," Doozy says.

"What shoes do you want to wear?" Ruby says.

"Hokas," Doozy says.

"*No!*" Nelle and Ruby shout.

"Tss-tss-tss-tss."

Chapter Twenty-Nine

Does the name Peggy ring a bell?

How about Rugs and Plugs? Carpet Steaming and Ear Piercing? *That* Peggy, the one who lives in Blue Birch Corners, I think, and is still very much the doyenne of carpet steaming and ear piercing in these parts. And for the past few years, she's been a *triple* threat: she also offers premium (aka the only) car service to Boston and New York airports.

Thus it fell to industrious ole Peg to ferry Dr. Jantzen and Miss Popsy to JFK tomorrow evening. I know this because the FBI, monitoring Dr. Jantzen's phone, is aware of Dr. Jantzen's reservation, for two people, on tomorrow's 11pm flight, JFK to Jakarta, and that Dr. Jantzen had booked his ride with Peggy two days ago. (Why Indonesia? Ash says they have no extradition treaty with the U.S.)

And knowing my strong feelings about what Popsy has done to the hospital in general, the pediatric oncology ward in particular, and to Makayla and Zoey and Jace most of all, Ash and Peggy have agreed that I will be the chauffeur in Peggy's wheels from Dr. Jantzen's house to the police station.

Per Ash, I am free to say whatever I like in that time, as long as the child lock is on.

Dr. Jantzen and Popsy have just now changed their plans — they must be spooked — perhaps because of the FBI-assisted arrest of Marvin the Hobo. I wouldn't want the FBI milling about if I had done what Popsy has done. In any case, I've just gotten a call from Ash that they want to be picked up *this* evening and they want to leave in half an hour, so I've put on a dark suit and am now tying up a pair of sensible black shoes. A quick look at the full-length mirror: Yes, a creditable chauffeur.

And yet all of a sudden, I've got stage freight. Not because I think anything will go wrong on the short drive, but that I will get too emotional and not say what I want to say when the moment comes. I call Nelle and explain my predicament.

"Just say what you feel," she says.

"Have you met me?"

"Okay, then advocate for Makayla and..."

"Zoey. And Jace. That's good. I think I can do that."

"I know you can," she says. "I've heard you do it."

"Thanks, Nelle."

"Serve justice, baby," she says and hangs up.

I put on the cap Will has borrowed from the firehouse and take one more glance in the mirror. Good to go.

Ash and Peggy meet me in the high school parking lot. The car is emblazoned Airport Express by Peggy of Rugs and Plugs. I get my instructions from Ash, Peggy loans me her phone so that Rugs and Plugs will show up as the caller on Dr. J's phone. Then I'm off to the Jantzen house.

I call from the curb, identifying myself as Jeffrey, and explain that Peggy was unavailable because of the change of schedule.

After a few minutes, the porch light goes on and the front door opens. I get out of the car and say "Good evening." I don't recall having to do a chauffeur voice in my voiceover work, but one just comes out, old pro that I am. I quickly take the luggage from Dr. Jantzen and keep my head down so he can't see my face clearly. I've forgotten to pop the trunk (rookie mistake!), and it's back to the driver's seat to find the trunk button. I then collect the other two suitcases.

Dr. Jantzen says, "That's all the luggage. My companion will be out shortly." He waits for her on the porch, keeping a watch on the street.

I close the trunk and wait in the driver's seat. Several minutes pass. Finally, out comes Popsy. For a moment, the two of them pause on the top step, she in a dark blue skirt and jacket with a brooch of some kind, hair swept up at the back, while he's in a tan trenchcoat, in spite of the season. They look like villains from the '50s, but I have to remind myself, they're villains in the here and now. I also have to remind myself that I'm expected to open their doors, so I jump out of the car and say, "Good evening, m'am," tipping my hat.

Once I get back in, I ask, "JFK?"

Dr. Jantzen says, "No, we're flying tomorrow night. Take us to the Pierre in Manhattan."

"Certainly, sir," I say, engaging the child lock. As I slowly drive away, Bunny Liverwurst peers out her window. I see in the rear-view mirror Dr. Jantzen turn his head for one last look at his house. The police station isn't far, so I need to speak up right away, in spite of a pounding heart.

"Makayla, Zoey, and Jace," I say. "Those are the three children in the pediatric oncology unit at the moment. Thanks to you, Popsy, there is no volunteer program to let those kids know that people care for them, people in this community care for them."

"Stop talking and drive," says Dr. Jantzen.

"No, I won't. I can understand garden-variety greed and selfishness. But to do that to children is monstrous. Steal and steal and let the hospital go to hell. Let the kids rot."

Popsy says to Jantzen, "Did you make a reservation for lunch tomorrow?"

"You have no idea what you're talking about," Dr. Jantzen says to me. "And you should have taken a left there."

"I know exactly what I'm talking about. Popsy is a grifter who stole a million dollars from the hospital. And you looked the other way."

"Stop the car," Dr. Jantzen says. "What are you doing? I said stop the car!"

"The two of you are beneath contempt."

We're in front of the police station and I bring the car to a stop, releasing the child locks. Ash and his colleague appear at the passenger doors, and Poppy and Jantzen, seemingly deflated to half their size, are cuffed and led into the station.

I sit in the car for a moment, not knowing quite how I feel about human beings. Maybe Denisovans had no chance against the worst of us homo sapiens. I doubt what I said had the slightest effect on them. No surprise. Still, I'm glad I said it. The whole experience only makes me more determined to do what little I can to bring some joy to those kids. I've never felt so sure about anything in my life.

"Have you read the *Observer* yet?"

"No, why?"

"Go get it and call me back."

"What's going on?" Will asks sleepily.

"Jenny says I have to read the *Observer*."

I do as the mayor asks and collect it from my front door.

It's not about the arrest of Dr. Jantzen and Popsy. I guess that happened too late for this morning's paper. Instead, there's an "exclusive" interview with Marvin the Hobo (I know, I snorted, too) by Ginger Abrams splashed on the front page. I sit on the bed next to Will and read him the choice bits:

"Marvin the Hobo, whose real name is Razman Vacarescu, is a resident of Plopeni, Romania, the sister city of Arnold Falls. Mr. Vacarescu, 53, studied acting at the Caragiale in Bucharest, is a member of the National Theatre company, and has appeared in several films and television series. According to Mr. Vacarescu, Plopeni's mayor, Pompiliu Haralambie, sought his help to reverse the bad fortune the town has suffered since it was settled in 1877.

Mr. Vacarescu says, "Mayor Haralambie believes if Plopeni could be more like Arnold Falls, citizens of my country could share in [the] same success as people here. The mayor told me to bring back things to give Plopeni the *farmec* of Arnold Falls." (*Farmec* is Romanian for 'charm.')

"That's loony," Will says.

Jenny calls again.

"Will says that's loony and I agree."

"She said 'that makes three of us,'" I say to Will.

Jenny asks me to go on a walk so I get dressed, leaving Will to get more sleep. We meet for coffee at Bean Here, Done That and I'm happy to see Wilky with her, running up to me. I kneel down for a most excellent hug.

Coffee in hand, we walk up High Street and then cut over to Midden Park trail. Wilky is ahead of us, exploring.

"How do you feel?" Jenny asks.

"I didn't reach heights of rhetorical glory," I say. "I was driving, I was nervous, time was short. It wasn't cathartic and I realize it was never going to be. Still, I needed to say it and it needed to be said. As for justice and restitution, it's out of our hands."

"Mayormama, look at this...I forget the word."

Spread out over a large bush is an equally large cobweb.

"Cobweb," Jenny says. "It's beautiful, isn't it?"

"It is!" he says, running ahead to find the next thing.

"When does school start?" I ask.

"Next week. Five hours a day. I'm going to be sad, I think."

"Bender?"

"What about him?"

"Don't play that game with me, young lady," I say. "How are things?"

"It's odd knowing someone for so long and then seeing them in a whole new way. Did he change or did I?"

"Maybe you met in the middle."

"Maybe. What I want to know is how come everyone in town knows about it? They all seem to have known about it before I did."

"You're the mayor. Do I have to explain how things work around here? And come to think of it, the same thing happened with Will and me. Some underground Cupid cult. Go with the flow, Mayormama."

"I'm trying, Giblet."

"What are you wearing for the opening tonight?" I ask.

"Why, are you dressing up?" Jenny asks.

"Yeah. Doozy's wearing Badgley-Mischka."

"Wilky! Come on, we've got to go."

"Where are you going?" I ask.

"Shopping," Jenny says.

PEOPLE START GATHERING ON THE LAWN OF THE MUSEUM well before the six o'clock opening. Word having gotten around that Doozy was wearing Badgley-Mischka, most people dressed for the occasion and they're now nattily sipping white wine on this tolerably humid summer evening. We almost look like a normal village.

There are a few short remarks and Doozy is introduced, looking resplendent, and she is not wearing Hokas, as Nelle told me she threatened to do. The doors of the museum are thrown open and the crowd thins outside as people begin to walk through the show.

The reception is enthusiastic: plaudits for Arnold Falls' history being openly considered, including the larger story of the Great Migration, the charisma of Miss Georgia evident even all these years later, the presence of Doozy smiling and laughing as much as I've ever seen her smile and laugh, and the story of a mother and daughter.

The only surprise of the evening is Beverly Taylor, the Collections Manager of the African American History and Culture museum, the person Bender had been in touch with, has come to the show and whenever I see her, she's hanging around Doozy.

It's an odd, selfish reaction I have to this: I don't want to share Aunt Doozy with Beverly Taylor. I don't want to share Doozy with the world.

What am I trying to protect, I wonder? This little world, this little town, as it is? Trying to stop time? The whole point of the Georgia exhibit is to share her story, and Doozy's, too. I'm too close to it all right now. Some distance will help.

Popsy and Dr. Jantzen are being held without bond, considered a flight risk since they were arrested, as you may recall, actually fleeing. The day after they were arraigned, the hospital appointed Dr. Sharma as the interim Chief Medical Officer. The good doctor called and asked me to drop by, so I do, saying hello to Makayla, Zoey and Jace, before sitting down with Dr. S.

I congratulate her on her appointment. She asks about last Wednesday and as I recount my few minutes as a chauffeur for fugitives, she nods thoughtfully.

Then she says, "Jeebie, one of my priorities is getting the entire Volunteer Services program running again. The job is yours if you want it."

"You get straight to the point, don't you?"

"Life is short."

I can't explain exactly how she says those three words, how they pain me in this place, how much sadness and resolve I hear in them. My throat closes up.

She looks at me, waiting for me to continue.

"I'm honored, Dr. Sharma."

"Call me Priya."

"Can I take a couple of days to think it over?"

"Of course."

I get a big smile from her and an even bigger one when I stop in to see Jace, who's feeling better today.

"I thought you wanted to feel useful."

"I think I went overboard. Now I'm tired. I need a vacation."

Nelle shakes her head. "Fridstöck is in four days. You better rally your ass."

Fridstöck is the name we came up with for the sanctuary event at Fridsy's farm. Fridsy herself wasn't enamored of it, saying, "It's about the animals, not me." But she agreed it was decent branding for an event. Theo had the idea of adding the (superfluous) umlaut over the O, no doubt remembering his date at Höôôs in the city and concluding it would impart some extra cool factor to the proceedings.

"And what about the performances at the hospital?"

"Dr. Sharma says the hospital is in too much turmoil right now, but she'd like them to start the second week of September. Should I take the job at the hospital? Seems like too much to commit to. I'll be just coming off the Fridsy train."

"Another round?" Sofia asks.

"Yes, please," I say.

"You mean Fridsy, who does not have a chip you can see from space? Who is actually quite delightful?" Nelle asks.

"She's fine."

"No, Jeebie, I want to hear you say what I said."

"Can't remember it all."

"Don't give him his drink, Sofia, until he says it."

Sofia says, "This round's on me if you stop acting like such an idiot."

Nelle says, "Yaaaaaasssssss!"

A little corner of Sofia's mouth turns upward, just a hint of a smile.

"Fridsy does not have a chip you can see from space," Nelle says.

"Fridsy does not have a chip you can see from space," I repeat.

"She is actually quite delightful."

"She actually *is* quite delightful."

"Cheers," Nelle says.

"Cheers. Thanks, Sofia."

"What about taking the job on an interim basis," Nelle says, "until they can find a permanent hire? Listen, you make good money doing voiceovers. You have to be practical. You can volunteer as much time as you want."

"That makes sense," I say. "I think that's what I'll do."

"And if you need to recharge, why don't you take a trip to Europe when the fundraiser is over?"

"Too crowded, it's summer."

"Go somewhere with Will," Nelle says.

"He's busy with grad school. Starts in less than a month."

"Paris and Rome," Nelle says.

"They're nice."

"No, I mean *Paris* and *Rome*."

"Why are you saying them that way?"

"I'm saying that's where you want to go."

Sofia does a silent, though highly-theatrical scream.

"Sofia, am I the cause of that?"

She starts pulling out her hair.

Nelle grins, saying, "And when you return from a trip to *Paris* and *Rome* with *Will*, you can also get to work helping me with the album."

I like the sound of all this.

Before I can respond, we get interrupted by Bridget and Trevor, coming from the back patio. By the looks on their faces, something is afoot.

"*Oh, oh, oh-oh, oh!*" Trevor says.

"We have solved the greatest mystery of them all!" Bridget says.

"Which mystery is that?" I ask.

"Mrs. Sedgewick Trumble!" Bridget says.

"Who?" Nelle asks.

Bridget and Trevor give conspiratorial looks to each other.

"Fayette!" Trevor says. "We were talking about her out there... You tell them, Bridget."

"It was last week, the night of the Marvin chase, when Fayette and I were in costume in case we were needed. Out of nowhere, Fayette started doing some shuffle-ball-changes and bits of a tap routine while we were improvising some of the hocus-pocus we could use on Marvin."

"When Bridget told me that, the penny dropped," Trevor says. "The tap-dancing. You may not recognize her name because she quit the business before she became well-known in the States, but there was a series of movies, four of them, starting in the late '70s, starring a child actress called Tazzy Potts, sort of a more contemporary Shirley Temple-type. The movies were *It's Tazzy's World*, *Tazzy Saves the Day* — I have to look up the names of the other two.

"Anyway, they were set in a girls boarding school, the movies weren't memorable, but the thing was, she was a genuine talent. She was smart and funny, she could sing, she could tap like nobody's business, she could break your heart. And for a while every young girl in the country was told they should be more like Tazzy Potts."

"So what happened to her? She just disappeared?" Nelle asks.

"That's exactly what she did. I had to google her to remind myself of the few details that are known. Tazzy's mother was her manager and blew all the money Tazzy made. Show-biz mom from hell. The mother wanted her to keep working, Tazzy wanted to have a normal life. And one day she was gone. The tabloids published every rumor imaginable, that she had died in a car accident, or defected to Russia, or went to live in a tiny corner of Switzerland with relatives. That's really all I know."

"Are you sure it's her?" I ask.

"The pieces seem to fit," Trevor says. "And when you look at pictures of her as a youngster, I'm fairly certain that that is our Fayette. Fayette de la Nouille is Tazzy Potts."

"Will you say anything to her?" I ask.

"No, absolutely not. Bridget and I agreed."

We look at Bridget.

"We did. It would be wrong to bring it up. That would be a terrible thing to do. It's not for us to spoil the new life she created for herself."

Bridget has surprised me yet again.

Nelle raises her glass. "To Fayette."

"To Fayette."

Chapter Thirty

꧁ꕥ꧂

"That is the most SCRUMPTIOUS Chianti," Fayette says.

"Yes, the Pruneto. A favorite around here. I got a case of it from Jeebie for agreeing to march in the Titleholder's Parade," Bridget says.

"I don't understand, why would he give you a case of wine for that?"

"I didn't want to be involved in another chase with Chaplin but Jeebie felt it was important for me to be seen wearing a mobcap so that...I don't even remember any more why. Somehow I might get Martha's mobcap back."

"But that was in your interest to help," Fayette says.

"Yes, but it was also in my interest to stock up on the Pruneto. I do owe him three bottles."

Trudy laughs, refilling Fayette's glass as she says, "That's pretty much Arnold Falls in a nutshell. And I mean nutshell. Best to just let things wash over you."

"I'm starting to see that. But I was disappointed that Dr. Jantzen's house fell through," Fayette says. "I guess it will be tied up in the courts for long time. And I'm sorry that the

Merryvale shoot is over this week. I'm definitely here through Fridstöck on Saturday.

"You're not leaving?!" Bridget asks.

"I'm not sure," Fayette says.

"What about renting a house?" Bridget asks.

"I'm feeling unsettled about whether to stay longer or not. We *have* had so much fun, Bridget. I haven't laughed that hard in EONS. And I've loved getting to know you, Trudy, too."

Trudy watches Fayette turn something over in her mind.

"There's...There's something I'd like you to know about me."

She takes a moment and then says, "A lifetime ago, as a child, I starred in a few movies in the U.K. I was called..."

"Tazzy Potts," Bridget says.

"You knew? All along?!" Fayette says.

"No, not all along," Bridget says. "Trevor and I were having drinks last week and I mentioned that you started tap-dancing while we were waiting on the Marvin drama to play out. Something clicked in his mind — he's a Brit, after all — and from that moment he was fairly certain that's who you were."

"You didn't say anything to me," Trudy says.

"No, sweetheart, I didn't. Once we had talked about it with Jeebie and Nelle, we decided that it would be unthinkable to risk disrupting Fayette's life by discussing it with anybody else."

"I'm so touched that you would take care of me that way," Fayette says.

"I'm glad you told us," Bridget says. "Although Trudy's a bit of a talker."

"Bridget!" Trudy and Fayette say in unison.

Trudy says, "Funny, Marvin being an actor, after all of that."

"I haven't heard any of the details," Fayette says.

"A good actor," Bridget says. "He seemed like a hobo to me. They don't make Method actors like that anymore! Maybe he should be a client. If he's not locked up."

"He'll probably be deported back to Romania," Trudy says.

"I suppose you're right," Bridget says.

"Back to Romania?" Fayette asks.

"Yes, we're sister towns with Plopeni. Apparently they've been down on their luck and they wanted to — how would you explain it, Trudy? Steal our mojo?"

"That's about it," Trudy says.

"What's his real name, do you know?" Fayette asks.

"I have no idea," Bridget says.

"There was a piece in the paper about him," Trudy says. "Why do you ask?"

"I knew a Romanian actor once, though he lived in Bucharest. No, it couldn't be."

"Couldn't be what?" Bridget asks.

"In the fourth movie, there was a Romanian actor who played Tazzy's love interest, a Russian exchange student at the boy's school. He was MY love interest, too. Oh, my God, DREAMY, he was. No, it's a crazy thought. It would be an impossible coincidence."

"That's an Arnold Falls specialty, Fayette. Let me check the recycling," Trudy says. She goes into the garage.

"You've seen him, Fayette. Can't you tell?"

"No, it was so many years ago. And not through all that BEARD!"

Trudy returns with the *Observer*. She reads, "'Marvin the Hobo, whose real name is Razman Vacarescu, is a resident of

Plopeni, Romania, the sister city of Arnold Falls. Mr. Vacarescu, 53, studied acting at the Caragiale in Bucharest, is a member of the National Theatre company, and has appeared in several films and television series.'"

"Raz," Fayette says quietly.

Trudy refills Fayette's wine glass.

"We were Tazzy and Raz. TOO cute. I was sixteen. He was eighteen or nineteen. I remember it was hard to use actual Russian actors in those days, so they picked him out from the Caragiale. The accents sound similar. He was LOVELY. After the movie, he went back to Romania. This was the early '80s and things had gotten extremely difficult in that country. A year later, I escaped London to live with my cousins in Switzerland and we lost touch. I wouldn't be Fayette de la Nouille if it weren't for him."

"What do you mean?" Trudy asks.

"He used to ADORE pasta," Fayette says smiling. "So when I picked a new name for myself, I chose de la Nouille. Fayette of the Noodle."

"He's out on bond," Trudy says. "You can see him any time."

"Take him to Argos," Bridget says. "Their penne alla vodka is out of this world. Jeebie swears by it."

Chapter Thirty-One

I t is finally Fridstöck.

We have a choice lineup of events, if I do say so, from 3-9pm. Fridsy seems buoyed by the whole thing, Minna remains watchful and serene.

The weather gods have been kind: the high today is going to be seventy-eight, there's the gentlest of breezes, and the skies are clear. Wasn't Freyr the weather God in Norse mythology? Sending up a humble request for whichever concerned deities to ix-nay on the underhail-thay. (Wilky and I have been doing so much communicating lately in pig Latin that I'm starting to dream in it, too). It bodes well for a big turnout, as does free admission, though people will be encouraged to stop by one of the two tables where they can pledge support for the sanctuary.

I thought I would be busy the whole day, but the event has gone off without much supervision needed. There are lots of parents with young kids on hand when Hullaballoo starts the entertainment off with a nifty circus routine. At four o'clock, Judge Harschly, Ouchie, and Wilky organize vitilla lessons and games. And then music from five to six-thirty, courtesy of Queechy Caliente, the Traitor's Landing house band, and Nelle. It all seems to run like clockwork, a rarity of hen's teeth proportions.

Fridsy had wanted to keep the remarks brief with a few acknowledgments and she's good to her word, with a modest plea for community support for the fledgling sanctuary. One thing not on the schedule was the drop-in from Governor Klingman, who talked about caring for those who need us. She didn't mention that she's running for reelection in November, but we got the point. The clambake followed.

Some of the highlights of the day included Bridget's turn at bat in vitilla (seems pickpocketing and Denisovan lineage make for extraordinary hand-eye coordination); Chaplin traversing the party, looking for chances to photobomb; and the newest members to the sanctuary, elderly, brother-and-sister goats named Tuba and Tuna, who started off in no mood for a party, only to end up dancing on the tabletops, in a manner of speaking.

I haven't even gotten to the hot-air balloons after dinner. The balloon company gave us a break on the pricing and we charged people for the twelve places in the two balloons. Then an anonymous benefactor stepped forward and covered the cost for a third balloon so that the kids in the oncology unit could ride. (No, it was not Aunt Doozy, but I'm sworn to secrecy.)

We're at the far end of Fridsy's farm, a group of lucky flyers. Will and I take our places in the balloon, excitedly, clumsily, with Bridget, Trudy, Fayette, and Trevor. The second balloon has Doozy, Nelle, Jenny, Tishy, Wilky, and Sadie. I never thought Doozy would go through with it, but there she is, wearing her Red Sox cap, ready for adventure. Seeing the third balloon does my heart good, with Makayla, Zoey, and Jace, along with three of the unit's nurses.

We're the first to take off, and it's a thrill rising over Fridsy's farm. I can see the hundred or so guests, looking up and waving, I can see the cows, though I'm not sure from here which is Minna. What I can see, most importantly, is a sanctuary.

We glide toward the center of town in that warm, supple light, the golden hour, with Will holding my hand. People I cherish floating near me, below me, by my side. We're right over the center of town and low enough that I can see Bender on his widow walk jumping up and down waving, Jenny and Wilky waving back.

The balloon is traveling leisurely, yet time flies by. Enough time, though, to think about all the small decisions that have brought me here, into this balloon, on an early August evening, and not a thousand other places. I don't believe in fate, I don't think I was destined to be right here, right now. Yet, somehow, here I am, looking down at this enchanted valley, never feeling more a part of the community fabric than I do aloft, enveloped, loved. I squeeze Will's hand.

We float over the town, right above Van Dalen Park, where poor Hezekiah Hesper is still laying by the contractor's trailer, and over the pond, where I hope the northern cricket frogs are doing whatever makes them happy.

Epilogue

There's a text from Bridget saying that Fayette had dinner with Marvin the Hobo and a rekindled romance might be in the offing. Bridget adds that a new case of the Pruneto arrived and that I will get three bottles on my return, though, she writes, strictly while-supplies-last. I smile, without stopping to reply.

Even if the Parisians are away in August, the weather is mild and Paris is as bewitching as ever. We have two days left here, then three in Rome.

We've just taken a walk through Jardin du Luxembourg, where Will was almost overcome by the beauty of the vista at the Medici Fountain. And now we've scored croissants from Boulangerie Marie-Jeanne, non-vegan though they may be, that are as delicious as anything I've ever had.

Will wants to go to the Botanical Gardens next. And one buttery kiss on St. Germain later, we're on our way.

Acknowledgments

I'm so lucky to have friends who read early versions of *Hot Air*, and offered excellent advice: Ed Cahill, Bill Foley, Nealla Gordon, Robin Howe, Deborah Olin, Whit Repp, Bill Rosenfield, and Debora Weston.

Thanks as well to Andrea Robinson for editorial guidance, to Mark Leslie for his expertise on all things publishing industry, and to Daniel Dietrich, Head of Innovations at Magic Holo, for help with the Pepper's Ghost effect. Any inaccuracies or embellishments about the process are mine.

I'm grateful to Jason Anscomb for the cheery cover design.

As always, thank you to Rainer Facklam for being there.

And finally, to the much-missed Gary Gunas, for his early and enthusiastic support of *Arnold Falls*, which gave me the courage to keep going. *Hot Air* came too late, but I hope you would have liked it, too.

About the Author

Charlie Suisman published Manhattan User's Guide, the longest-running city newsletter, from 1992-2020. Hot Air is his second novel.

Join him at charliesuisman.com

Lightning Source UK Ltd.
Milton Keynes UK
UKHW011051040522
402471UK00002B/524